"You have a purpose!" the captain cried out, moving closer. "If you knew of the coming days of power, you wouldn't hesitate. With all the power of the Party behind us, we will be as *gods*."

"The Party?" I snarled. "The Party killed us. The Party sent us to the chopping block."

He smiled grimly and continued to move slowly closer. "Mistakes were made, Strait. They're willing to admit that now. But things have changed. They need us again."

"Not me," I said. "Not for them."

Our eyes locked and we fell silent. An electricity crackled between us, and our souls met on a narrow bridge, knowing only one could pass. His hand blurred to the holster and his pistol flashed up. I crouched and fired from the hip.

The whoosh of the gyra muffled the crack of his automatic, and a bullet whispered past my ear.

JAKE STRAIT
BOGEYMAN

AVENGING ANGEL

FRANK RICH

A GOLD EAGLE BOOK FROM
WORLDWIDE®

TORONTO • NEW YORK • LONDON
AMSTERDAM • PARIS • SYDNEY • HAMBURG
STOCKHOLM • ATHENS • TOKYO • MILAN
MADRID • WARSAW • BUDAPEST • AUCKLAND

First edition May 1993

ISBN 0-373-63607-5

AVENGING ANGEL

AVENGING ANGEL

1

"I've seen God and I tell you he's crazy!" the mad prophet cried.

"Maybe he was just drunk," I said, stepping into the dim room. The old man sat deep in an ancient armchair, fat and as drunk as Bacchus. Spent bottles and hypos surrounded his low throne—the minions of a mad king. I pointed my 20 mm gyra-pistol at his head, knowing I should shoot him right then. The old man looked infirm enough, but I knew Graham's kind: evil and full of tricks.

"No! He is completely insane!" Graham shrieked, his hands fluttering over his head like bats. "Heaven is in ruins. None could stand before his terrible power. The heads of those who tried are impaled on the Pearly Gates...St. Thomas and Francis, the valiant St. Christopher who tried to warn man."

"What about St. Peter?" I asked.

"He's God's number-one enforcer. He guards the gate, allowing no mortal souls in or out."

"Are you telling me the Lord is reneging on his biblical contract?"

"He never signed the damn thing! You fools don't realize that ours is a passionate god, not some kind and bland computer full of logic circuits. He is as frail with emotion as those created in his image, and now he's completely *wigged.*"

"Jesus Christ," I said.

"*He's* missing, perhaps the prisoner of his own father."

I stared at the madman. "Where do you get your information, anyway?"

"Firsthand! I've traveled the cosmos! I've slipped beneath Heaven's gates. I've ranged the seven hells, my soul clutched tightly. I've spoken with the Devil!"

"How is Nick?"

"He surrendered his dark throne to mortal souls blacker than his own! Now he wanders the most desolate plains of hell, shamed and broken, weeping tears of the hottest flame."

I watched as Graham chased a handful of pills with a good two-inch pull from a bottle of gin. Tears welled from the red pits of his eyes.

"I have to stay awake these last moments," he sobbed. "I have to face the great unknown like a true prophet."

I nodded and removed a folded document from my coat pocket. Graham's beady eyes clawed at it.

"What's that?" he asked.

"Your execution warrant."

"You're going to read it?"

"No, I'm going to leave it with your body so everyone knows the score." I dropped it in his lap.

He fingered the document with a morbid reverence, testing the texture of the paper with his fingers. "So you're a bogeyman."

"Yes."

"How much is my demise worth to you?"

"Four hundred credits. Enough to pay the food and liquor bills for the month."

"That's not much."

"Not for a mass murderer it isn't."

"Murderer!" Fire jumped in his eyes. "I didn't murder my faithful. I dispatched them on the greatest mission mankind has ever undertaken."

"The way I heard it, you lined them up in your Church of the True Path in ten neat rows of ten, then put a bullet in the back of each head. You must have had to pause every twelve bodies or so to slap in a fresh magazine." Rage began squeezing the trigger. "One hundred men, women and children."

"Trained pioneers, all of them! Handpicked and instructed by myself." The old man wiped away tears with the back of his hand. "I didn't murder my dear children. I freed their souls. To find a new Heaven."

"What?"

"Hell is in turmoil, Heaven won't take us. Mankind has to provide for its own salvation now. We have to find a refuge before Jehovah makes his move. Even now he's organizing his dark angels to attack earth and destroy all our souls. We were a mistake, and now he wants to get rid of us. My one hundred went out to search the cosmos for a new afterlife sanctuary for mankind. They must have found one or they wouldn't have sent you."

"What makes you think they sent me?"

"How did you find me?"

"An anonymous call."

"Isn't that unusual?"

"Happens all the time. Criminals are always finking on each other. Keeps the competition down."

"No one alive knew I was here. I was very careful about that. Only the one hundred knew."

I checked my chrono. I'd spent ten minutes listening to the ravings of a lunatic I was supposed to kill. "Have you any final words of repentance?"

He laughed. "Do you really think repenting will change anything?"

"Not if God is as wiggy as you say he is."

Graham gazed at the hand scratching his immense belly. "Do you realize how little technology has advanced in the last thirty years, since the end of the twentieth century? Mankind is spiritually and genetically bankrupt, as obsolete as the dodo bird. We won't last much longer."

"Maybe we're just in a slump."

A dry laugh creaked out of his mouth, and sneaky eyes slunk up to mine. "Don't you wonder why I've told you all this?"

"Because you're drunk or crazy or both."

"No. I've told you so you'll be prepared. Because you're going with me." He opened his shirt, and around his fish-white belly was strapped a fat black cylinder the size of a fist. His hand came away with a grenade pin. "I don't want to go alone. You can keep me company. There's room in the new afterlife for ruthless young men. You can be my enforcer. I'm saving your soul, bogeyman. Eight seconds to paradise!"

"You dirty bastard!"

"Seven seconds, bogeyman!"

I pulled the trigger, and Graham's laughing head expanded into a bloodred halo. I leaped upon his flapping body and tugged at the thermite grenade, but the nylon strap held it fast. Graham's nerve-animated body rolled out of the chair, his immense weight pinning me to the floor.

Six seconds.

For a breathless instant I struggled beneath his smothering bulk, the live grenade digging into my ribs.

Five.

With desperate strength I heaved, and the trembling mass of flesh rolled off me like a monstrous bag of Jell-O. I sprang to my feet.

Four.

I lunged down the hallway, arms pumping furiously, boots booming on the hardwood floor like cannon shots. The corridor looked a million meters long.

Three.

I collided with a rain-soaked breeze pouring through the open window at the end of the hall, the very window I'd crawled through like a thief ten minutes earlier.

Two.

I leaned into my headlong stride, my entire being focused on the window, my mind, spirit and body aligned for one powerful purpose. The window became Heaven, hope, my sole salvation.

One.

With still two meters to go, I left earth, launching myself at the window like an awkward spear.

The blast grabbed me by the nape of the neck and threw me into the night like a drunk. I met the alley floor with a bonejarring crunch and slid on my belly into a row of garbage cans.

I awoke facing the sky, my eye sockets full of water. Fat drops of radioactive rain fell in vain on the flames devouring Graham's hideaway. A churning column of smoke reached into the night sky and with it went any chance of collecting my bounty. After long moments of despair, I crawled to my feet, pawing the filth from my clothes.

Except for ringing ears, jangled nerves and a big bruise that started at the bottom of my feet and ended at the top of my head, I felt grand. My fleshly shell was marred, but inside, my soul was safe. I found my pistol in the garbage, none the worse. I crept out of the alley, angling across the street.

A small group of children stood in front of Graham's funeral pyre. I checked the geiger on my chrono. With the reading above two hundred rads, they shouldn't have been outside. Over the crash of the downpour and the crackling of the fire rose a song chanted in the voice of innocence long forsaken.

> Bogeyman, bogeyman go away,
> Come again some other day,
> You killed my pa
> Cuz he broke the law,
> Killed my mother
> And my brother,
> You won't kill me,
> I'll be free,
> I'll take my life
> With a butcher knife,
> Bogeyman, bogeyman go away,
> Come again some other day.

Before I could reach my car, one of the children spotted me and screamed.

"Bogeyman!" A half-dozen fire-lit faces turned on me and for a second they stood frozen with a collective breath-stealing terror only children knew. "Bogeyman," one whispered and they scattered like leaves in the wind.

I crawled inside the Cadillac's weathered hulk and started the engine. No matter how I dressed, no matter how hard I tried to hide it, the children always knew.

2

The red sun squatted low on the horizon, swollen and corpulent. The big bay window of my third-story office also offered an excellent view of Hayward, the sleaziest street of a sleazy city. I stuck my hands in my pockets, pockets as poor as a Sunday-morning wino's, and contemplated what Graham had said three weeks earlier.

Sluggish streams of industrial workers filed past on the sidewalks below, their faces hammered slack by hours of monotonous labor. Proper citizens with real jobs getting off another endless shift, dragging their tired feet to Hayward's many bars, brothels and drug dens, hoping to loosen the rude harnesses life tightened daily. The indigent street life moved among them like jackals, going about their business with an arrogant ease that spoke of no higher authority. Pimps stood in doorways like rogue fashion plates, brooding and watchful; hustlers shuffled about, probing for human frailty; gaudy whores challenged passersby like listless sentries; junkies moved to that hectic junky beat, arm eager for the needle.

Maybe Graham was right, maybe God was crazy. It would explain a lot.

I drew my hand from my pocket and formed a fleshy pistol. Sighting down the forefinger, I let the thumb-hammer fall. Below, in my mind's eye, a pimp sprawled into the gutter, his heart ruptured. Another invisible bullet sped downward, and a pusher collapsed on the corner. A chubby hornbug was about to get his karmic reward when my office door opened and the first clients I'd seen in a month stepped in.

The pair teetered in the doorway as if my office were a yawning black abyss they had a bad feeling about falling into.

I followed their worried stares to my hand. Collapsing the pistol into a fist, I walked to my desk and sat down.

"Please have a seat," I said, gesturing to a worn plaid sofa near the door. The couple exchanged reassuring glances, clasped hands and crept to the sofa. They left the door open a crack as if they wanted a clear means of escape if things got too scary. After another exchange of glances, they very cautiously lowered their posteriors to the sofa. They sat with a straight-backed tension that suggested they were fully prepared to spring the required two meters to freedom if the need arose.

I looked them over with a professional eye. They were as out of place in the neighborhood as a bottle of Dom Perignon in the hands of a local wino. The man wore a silver executive-style jumper as if it were a suit of armor, and I could have sold his chrome-tipped wing tips to any tasteful pimp for at least two hundred creds. Over his suit hung a rumpled gray overcoat with the collar turned up. He probably imagined it helped him blend in with the neighborhood. The rumples looked somehow artificial, as though he'd had the butler put them in with a special tool. He wore his hair in the manner of the rich, long and wavy. He was smart enough not to wear jewelry.

The woman was hooched up in a loose-fitting drab gray pantsuit with flared collar and oversize cuffs. Black canvas jungle boots and crossed bandoliers complete with plastic bullets finished the costume. They probably sold it in a boutique on the Hill as the "streetwise proletariat look." Her orange hair towered into a monstrous beehive, serving to narrow her wide Nordic face. A jeweled headband and emerald choker clashed badly with the rest of her outfit, but they did serve to say that although she dressed like the lower classes, she was definitely *not* lower class. She had a plastic, contrived sort of beauty and looked too young to be the man's wife—not that that meant anything. There was also an air about her that said she wasn't getting enough sex at home but was too tasteful to look for it elsewhere, the unhappy union of frustration and resignation prominent in her eyes and mouth.

They held hands tightly and touched at the shoulders. Back at the mansion they probably fought like paranoid junkies, but there was nothing like a potentially hostile environment to make a couple intimate. He looked defensive and vaguely defiant, and she looked as though she wouldn't pass up a good opportunity to scream.

"Boo!" I said.

"Eek!" she said.

No one seemed sure what was supposed to happen next, so the man, a little wide-eyed, stood up and spoke.

"I am Dashmeil Chamberlain." The introduction packed the somber weight of someone accustomed to respect and maybe even fear. He paused for a moment as if waiting for some sign of recognition, a bow or something. When he didn't get one, he frowned and glared at me.

"And this—" he gestured economically at the woman "—is Barbara Chamberlain, my wife."

"Matching last names and all," I said. "That's super."

They both gave me pained looks. It wasn't a wise thing to say to those who might be willing to break my streak of insolvency, but I couldn't help myself. I hadn't had a client for so long I'd forgotten all my social graces.

"Just a little joke. How can I help you, Mr. and Mrs. Chamberlain?"

His first look told me he doubted very much if I could be of any help whatsoever. His next expression arrived after a resigned sigh, a look that said he might be persuaded to let even humble me have a crack at his problems.

He reached inside his coat, and I reached inside mine. He froze with his hand buried in an inner pocket, and his eye began to twitch. His wife sucked in a double lungful of air and looked ready to scream.

It wasn't that I thought Dashmeil was going to pull out anything more lethal than a pair of gold-rimmed reading glasses, but in my line of work you could never be too careful. Besides, it made me appear hard-boiled.

"Documents," Dashmeil wheezed. "Just some documents." His face squinched up, and a big, ugly pulsating vein surfaced on his forehead. His hand came out of his jacket timidly, and he laid a handful of papers on the desk. I brought out my own hand with a pack of vitacigs instead of a gun. I popped out a vitacig, and they stared at it as if they'd never seen one before. I lit the cig and left it dangling from the corner of my mouth. Leaning back slightly in the chair, my eyes hooded, I inhaled a day's supply of vitamins and gave them my cold, confident look.

"Are you all right?" Barbara asked.

I sat forward slightly. "Of course I'm all right. Why do you ask?"

"You looked as if you were in pain for a moment."

"Are those for me?" I asked, pointing a finger at the documents. Chamberlain nodded and pushed the papers across the desk. I noticed his nails were manicured and his hands were pink and soft looking.

I picked up the papers. As I flipped through them, Dash gave me a running narrative.

"The first document is a certified copy of an open warrant for the execution-without-trial of one Rolland Dillon Crawley as issued by the judicial branch of the City's Security and Protection Force."

I nodded and turned to the next page.

"Page two is a detailed list of all the crimes that Mr. Crawley has been convicted of in absentia," Dash continued.

It was.

"The third and fourth pages," he said, keeping up nicely, "state all available information concerning Mr. Crawley, including physical description, past whereabouts, psychological profile and photograph."

On a whim I went back to the first page to see if he'd start the narrative over again, like those voice machines built into museum displays. Dash gave me a quizzical look but didn't breathe a word. The guy was sharp.

"The final page," he said, jumping the gun, "is a true and legal document—a contract, if you like—stating that upon providing legal proof to any branch of the Party Bank of the demise of Mr. Crawley at your or your hirelings' hands, you will receive the sum of five thousand credits, payable to your account." He finished with a nod of self-congratulation for a job done properly and efficiently. His wife beamed with pride, and he tried not to look too vain about it.

I scrutinized the last document closely. Runaway inflation or no, five thousand creds was a tall stack of plastic. And if appearances meant anything, the Chamberlains were good for it.

"Is this all?" I asked.

They searched each other's faces for an answer but couldn't find one. Barbara said, "Should there be more?"

"How about a retainer?"

Dash gave me a tight little smile and spread his hands in front of him as if I were belaboring the obvious. The gesture bothered me. "We don't know you from Adam, Mr. Strait. You could just take our money and...?" He let the statement hang as a question, as if only I could know what fiendish things I was capable of doing once I got my hands on their check.

"I see," I said. "Well, I'm going to have to scan you."

"Is that really necessary?" Dash asked, his tone implying that it really wasn't.

I spread my hands and gave him back his tight little smile. "Trust works both ways, Mr. Chamberlain. I don't know you, either. You just might be here under false pretenses." I smiled wider and pushed a small desk-model handscanner toward him. He recoiled as if I'd shoved a vicious lizard in his face. "C'mon," I chided, "you must do this at least five times a day."

He craned his neck back and radiated indignity in waves. I basked in it. With a choking sound he swept his right hand under the scanner head. The scanner beeped, reading the tiny microchip embedded in his hand. It translated the codes into words and numbers and displayed the information on the miniature screen facing me.

"It's just a first-level scan, correct?" Dash asked.

"That's right," I lied. "That's all I'm allowed by the laws of the glorious World Party. Dashmeil Horace Chamberlain, identity number 857672332." The screen told me a lot more than that, but that was my little secret. Unauthorized possession of a third-level scanner was a big no-no.

"That is correct," Dash snapped. I stored the information and looked over at Mrs. Chamberlain.

"Me too?" she squeaked.

I nodded somberly. "We can't just do this halfway, now can we?"

"This is an outrage!" Dash exclaimed, the veins in his neck bulging unattractively.

"No, it's just the way we do business around here, Mr. Chamberlain. At least when we don't get a retainer."

They eventually calmed down, and after a consenting nod from Dash, Barbara skittered her hand under the scanner head.

"Barbara Mildred Chamberlain," I read. I sat back and let them suffer beneath the weight of my cruel grin. I knew their secrets. "It seems to check out," I said in a sinister, triumphant manner, as if now that I knew their full identities I could fully convert them into slaves of the dark forces.

They started to get up, but I sat them back down with a wave of my hand. "I have a few pertinent questions to ask," I said. "First, how am I supposed to contact you?"

"Why would you want to contact us?" Dash asked uneasily.

"Oh, I don't know. Matters concerning the case, or my payment. Maybe Barbara has a sister and we could double-date, a movie or something. You know." I shrugged.

"All we know about Crawley is to be found on pages three and four of the document. Payment will be handled by the Party Bank."

"Who put you in contact with me?"

"Our lawyer, Mr. Mallard," Dash said.

I nodded curtly as if high-powered shysters were always unloading cases on me.

"I believe he got your name out of the directory," Dash said, smiling as if he'd just earned a point. I let it go.

"Why didn't Mr. Mallard call me first?"

"He tried to, but your answering service said they wouldn't take any more of your calls until you paid your bill." Dash smiled triumphantly. "Three weeks in arrears, they said."

I was beginning to feel unworthy of the gold-lettered sign on my door. "Why didn't your lawyer deliver these papers? Or the chauffeur? This isn't a safe neighborhood."

"Because Dashmeil likes doing things himself," Barbara chirped. Dash nodded as if it was an obvious truth.

"One last question. What exactly is your interest in bringing Mr. Crawley to justice?"

"Your sign," Dash said, "states that you are a righter of wrongs, an avenger of injustices. Rolland Crawley wronged us."

"He assaulted our daughter!" Barbara clarified dramatically. She looked ready for a good crying jag. "He's an inhuman beast who preys on little girls."

"How do you know it was Crawley who did it?" I asked.

"We have our contacts in the City, Mr. Strait," Dash assured.

"What kind of contacts?"

"Reputable contacts."

"How reputable?"

"Reputable enough to get the SPF to issue a death warrant, quite obviously," he said.

"All right," I said. "No promises, but I'll see what I can do." I considered adding "If I can find the time," but I didn't think they'd buy it. I reached across the desk and shook hands with Dash. His hand was pliant, and he gave me the politician one-shake.

Babs stood and smiled shyly, fully recovered from the previous moment's trauma. "It's been a pleasure meeting you, Mr. Strait. Most people think bogeymen are such monsters, but you seem almost human."

A grimace came to my lips and I packaged it as a smile. "Why, thank you, ma'am."

She beamed graciously and mewed a little goodbye sound on the way to the door.

After they left, I went to the window and watched them exit the building. Some nameless instinct made them look up, and I waved, feeling foolish. Mike Hammer would never have done that, I reflected, sighing at yet another image failure.

Barbara waved back. Dash started to raise his hand but jerked it down at the last moment, apparently thinking it wasn't appropriate to wave in bad neighborhoods. They stiff-legged it to a double-parked luxury cruiser that had undoubtably waited the entire visit.

I went back to the desk and stared at the twin depressions in the sofa where they'd sat. For all their apparent wealth, the Chamberlains weren't much different from the majority of my clientele as far as their motives went. When I was graced with their presence, those who came to my office usually had the same story: they'd given up on the City's Security and Protection Force ever doling them out any justice, so they turned to private contractors like myself to avenge their grief. If the offended party could provide the judicial branch of the SPF with enough evidence, a warrant would be issued. The plaintiffs then had every legal right to hire a licensed private enforcer like myself to bring their criminal to justice, whether that meant apprehension or execution.

It wasn't that there weren't enough SPF troopers on the City payroll. It was just that most of them were deployed in the suburbs or guarding perimeters like the Hill to keep the riffraff from getting at the truly upstanding citizens. There were large parts of the City that didn't enjoy the presence of an institutionalized law-enforcement body, except for the odd politically motivated air strike or commando raid. It was a fact of life that most of the City was plainly lawless, and it took proud heroes like myself to extract any semblance of justice. At least that's what I liked to tell myself when I got drunk.

I wondered how many other private enforcers the Chamberlains had told their well-rehearsed story to. It would explain their reluctance to leave a retainer. Most wealthy clients liked to give me one so I'd feel indebted and servile. Then they felt they had the right to call me up in the black of night and demand why I wasn't out there in the belly of the City, racing down back alleys, tracking down their convict like a rabid ferret.

I read the five pages three times, then lit a vitacig and leaned back in my chair, letting the raw data soak in. By the looks of things Mr. Crawley was a small-time hustler with a taste for random violence. He pushed whack, crack and squeeze as his main job, with a little pimping and gunrunning on the side. On his days off he apparently liked to indulge in a little rape and murder to pass those lazy afternoons. The psychiatrist who did his profile had him figured as a homicidal psychotic driven by an impulsive need to hurt people. A wholly unsavory character, he had never been confined, but that was the way things were in the City.

Incredibly enough, Crawley's rap sheet was completely absent of political wants, which was strange because nearly all career criminals ended up stepping on the Party's sensitive toes sooner or later. Crawley must have either made a project out of staying out of the Party's way or he was just the kind of guy who had no interest in politics, a rare breed in these times. Crawley's exact whereabouts were a mystery, though he was known to haunt Barridales, a once-quaint slum currently famous for its squeeze production and gangs for hire.

The SPF reward incentive code was a lousy D-3, denoting Crawley's lack of political offenses. Maybe if he went out and distributed a stack of anti-Party leaflets he'd jump up a letter or two. If I wanted to work just the SPF reward angle, the big money was in the political offenders. I knew of a couple of private *pistoleros* who made a good living just terminating a code A or a couple of Bs a month. I didn't do political contracts, preferring client work. I wasn't real hot about the Party line myself and I'd feel a little hypocritical gunning down some guy because he organized demonstrations or ran an underground newspaper. Some would call me a romantic.

"Pretty open and shut," I said to the walls. "I'll just follow a trail of clues to his secret hideaway and deal out some much-deserved justice. Show the SPF my good deed, take the confirmation to the bank, then it's back to regular meals and clean laundry."

I went to the window and looked out at the crawling humanity. Down there, somewhere, waited a man I had to kill.

I LOCKED UP MY OFFICE, trying to ignore the hand-lettered sign painted on the door. Jake Strait, Private Enforcer, it stated in bold, uncompromising letters. Below in smaller script it read Wrongs Righted, Injustices Avenged. There was a time when I'd believed in what the sign said. Now the lofty ideals that inspired the words seemed remote, vaguely resented strangers, the punch line of sick joke. I put my back to it and went down to the street.

The sun had long since collpased, yet the thick residue of its heat still hung in the air. A torpid breeze pushed up the street, shoving ahead of it the smell of freshly roasted dog from Hayward's scattered army of kabob shops. My stomach declared its poverty, and I stared across the street at St. Christopher's Lounge like a forlorn lover. A fifteen-meter-high likeness of the good saint straddled the entrance of its namesake, hoisting high a frothing stein, his cherubic face managing to appear wholly angelic and horribly drunk at the same time. The wino saint. Whenever solvency and despair bumped into each other, I was known to invest entire afternoons and evenings inside, swilling beer and joking with the whores. I missed that more than eating.

I walked to my car, cutting through the streams of factory workers. They slid me tired, spiteful eyes, unhappy with their lot. The voices of whores rang out, harassing their ragged ranks like jackels nipping at a herd of tired water buffalo. It was always good to see the whores early on, when their makeup was fresh and they carried themselves like starlets on the lam. Later in the night, after their fourth or fifth trick, they wouldn't look so pretty.

I strolled past porn shops and pawnshops, bars and brothels, liquor stores and drug dens, used-car lots and run-down motels. Hayward was a specialized community, the dirty conscience of a perverted city. At the same time it was one of the few pipelines that brought credit into the surrounding slums, whatever the means. My Cadillac sat in front of a City landmark, Speaker's Corner. The wobbly platform that rose out of the weed-infested lot served as the unofficial platform for all the loons and goons of Hayward, and there were a few.

Presently the lot swarmed with a congregation of hooting winos, which meant Moses Perry was preaching. Perry was a whiskey evangelist, a special breed of religious wino. He was also a friend of mine. I waved at him as I got behind the wheel, but he was too wrapped up in his sermon to notice. After a coughing fit, the Caddy groaned to life and I steered into traffic.

I couldn't see the river for all the porn palaces and liquor emporiums, but I could smell it. The river ran parallel to Hayward and they shared similarities. Both were polluted by poison, one by human waste, the other by wasted humans. At the intersection where Hayward met Twelfth, I turned away from the river and headed home.

3

I awoke to voices. I shook off the lingering images of dreams about angels attacking the City and stuck my head out the bedroom window. Four stories below, knots of excited youths milled in the early-morning sun. Pipes, Molotov cocktails and other archaic weapons were in evidence, but no guns, suggesting only one thing. I spotted one of the neighbor's kids and shouted down to him. "A little early for a riot, isn't it, Vlad?"

He shielded his eyes from the sun and looked up. "Justice doesn't wait for the setting of the sun, comrade."

"What's on the agenda this morning?"

"We're going to stage an aggressive redistributive protest against the capitalist moneylenders," he said with a slight Russian brogue. Youths around him nodded vigorously, approving of Vlad's eloquent appraisal.

"You're going to loot some pawnshops," I translated.

He screwed his face up. "The unsophisticated might color it so. Do you want to come along? Should be a good one."

I thought for a moment. "Wouldn't you rather loot a food store?"

He conferred briefly with his companions. After some concerted head-shaking he said, "No, we did that last week. It's time to bring the moneylenders in line with the needs of the people." He waved goodbye as they marched righteously off.

I stuck my head farther out the window and surveyed my neighborhood. If I had to describe Rood Avenue in one word, I'd say tired. The limestone and brick towers dated from the 1960s, long before the Party came to power. The buildings must have been dignified and lovely then. By the eighties they must have been considered a little seedy but fine for lower-middle-class families. In the turbulent nineties, campy would have de-

scribed the area. By the turn of the century, Rood was assimilated by slums growing at a cancerous rate, fed by the surge of
dirt-poor refugees from Eastern Europe. That was twenty years
ago. The times had rubbed Rood's face in the grime, and
though it was a slow march to complete decrepitation, it wasn't
dallying on the way.

At least the rent was free. Four years before, the more excit-
able residents of Colfax, the borough that contained Rood,
declared the area a rent-free zone and threatened to kill any
landlord on sight. SPF troopers moved in, the barricades went
up, and riots flared. It didn't take long for the Party to realize
it was easier to slag off a couple dozen slumlords than to risk
the riots spreading to the rest of the slums. Now the borough
was completely rent free and a SPF no-go area. It made for a
brooding, lawless atmosphere I found comfortable, not to
mention affordable.

Bare cupboards could offer no breakfast, so I had a big glass
of boiling water perfumed by a bag of tea that had played the
game too many times before. It didn't really alter the flavor of
the water but it did make for a nice ritual, and one couldn't ignore the psychological comfort of rituals.

I drove to the borough of Barridales. I wasn't such an opti-
mist that I'd expect to spot Crawley lurking outside a pool hall
or topless bar, but I was of the opinion that to properly hunt an
animal you must first study its environment.

Barridales began as a wealthy neighborhood about seventy
years ago, and some of the old mansions still stood. They were
crowded by unwealthy people now, but if you looked real hard
you could still see some of their former elegance. Barridales was
also known as Barricades for all the bouts of social unrest that
kept the warm summer nights jumping. I cruised down
Broughton, the main drag, steering around burned-out cars and
the shabby skeletons of barricades, ghosts of riots past. When
things got too wild, SPF rotors and jets would shriek in for
"suppressive air strikes." Sometimes they dropped tear gas,
sometimes harder stuff. The random five-meter-wide craters
that pockmarked the area were evidence of the harder stuff.

I pulled over in front of a neighborhood store I would have
mistaken for a fortified bunker if it weren't for the Shahid's

Foodshop and Free Fungum signs in the barred window. I went inside.

The shelves were full, but full of the same things. Soy milk, soy bread, soy burger, algae cake, algae bread, algae breakfast cereal and so on, all in plain black-and-white packaging. It was typical of any Party-supplied food store.

"Can I help you find something?" a bearded Middle Eastern gentleman asked from behind the counter.

"Maybe you can. I'm looking for someone." I dropped Crawley's picture on the counter.

He didn't look at the picture. Instead, he showed me an empty hand, a hand that seemed to want something put in it. I pretended not to see it.

"I'm from Greenpeace," I said in a low voice.

He fixed me with distrustful eyes, then picked up the picture. "What do the Greens want with this man?"

"He's an agent of the Landlord Security Alliance."

The infamous name shot fear and loathing into his eyes. "He's with LiSA? I thought you Greens wiped out their last death squad years ago."

"A few of the ringleaders got away. They've reorganized and plan to restart their sinister operation." I gave him a solemn look. "They want to start charging *rent* again."

He gasped and stared harder at the picture, his jaw working furiously. He moved the picture forward and back, squinted at it, viewed it from different angles. I knew he wanted to help, desperately so, but desire wasn't enough. After a moment he handed back the picture and shook his head, tears of frustration in his eyes.

I shrugged consolingly and went outside. I sat on the Caddy's hood and surveyed the street. Members of the local militia had taken up ragged post on a street corner, unshaven youths with hangovers and assault rifles. Several of the more enterprising were trying to set up a makeshift roadblock, while the rest passed a bottle around and cast suspicious looks in my direction. Across the street was a building that might have once been a synagogue. According to the sign, it currently served as the Gay Militant Action Committee headquarters, though the leather boys sitting on the steps outside didn't seem particularly militant or even active.

Wolf whistles and shouts exploded from the direction of the militiamen as a fallen angel marched through their ranks, hunched against the weight of their howls and obscene demands.

She dressed in a uniform typical of a streetwalker: yellow spandex blouse, red plastic microskirt, fishnet stockings and too much rouge and eyeliner. She teetered down the sidewalk on absurd six-inch heels that didn't conceal her dwarfish stature, looking as if she might tip over at any moment.

"Need a ride, angel?" I asked.

She teetered to a halt in front of me, took an impatient breath, checked the stiffness of her bleach blond mane, looked to the sky and rattled off her prices in a nasal and bored voice. "Straight up, thirty cees per fifteen, round the world, forty-five cees, anything kinky is double, no ropes, bruises or friends, tip is fifteen percent, though you'll probably want to give me more. Okay?"

I stared and said nothing.

She dropped her hands to impatient hips. "Well?"

I pointed a finger at her and hopped off the hood. "I like your style, baby. I'm going to make you a star."

She rolled her eyes with a tired disbelief. "I already got a pimp and there ain't no movie-producer discount, cheapskate. Do you want any action or not?"

"What if I told you I was a hit man for Greenpeace?"

"I'd say that you get a salary just like everybody else."

I handed her Crawley's photo. "Does he look familiar?"

"After a while they all do." She laughed and passed the photo back. "Sorry I can't help you, palooka."

"How about a loan, then?"

"The nerve," she said, and stilted off.

I spent the rest of the morning showing Crawley's picture to other denizens of the street without result. It turned out Barridales wasn't exactly a center of amiability. They didn't like outsiders asking questions about their own, no matter how discreetly worded. A lot of grease money might have overridden that, but I didn't have enough credit to buy a beer, never

mind bribe some junky. It wasn't long before I came to the realization that my chances of finding Crawley using my present
methods were about as good as getting a loan from a whore.

I drove to east Barridales and parked next to People's Park.
I got out and went for a walk, hoping to run into some way-
ward inspiration. The park had seen better days. The iron fence
that separated it from the apathetic slums tumbled and curled
crazily. The ancient gate house wore so much graffiti it took on
a psychedelic demeanor, which was fitting because as I walked
through the gate I felt I was entering a topsy-turvy world. The
path I followed was slowly being assimilated from below, tiny
yellow-green pods poking their heads from the gray tar, defiant and triumphant. The wide expanses of sun-scorched grass
resembled pictures of the African savanna, their stalks high
enough to hide the packs of wild dogs known to frequent the
park. The hedges and bushes had gone completely feral, twist-
ing their spindly arms to the blue summer sky. Even the con-
servative oaks had a wild cast to them. I liked the way the park
looked, untamed and junglelike. It suited the rest of the City.

The heavy clomping of boots on asphalt jerked my thoughts
back five years to my military days. A platoon of skinheads
thundered down the path toward me, their formation tight and
disciplined. A muscular platoon leader jogged outside, calling
cadence. They all sported matching black shirts, shorts and
shaved heads. Stenciled on the front of each shirt was a symbol, three lightning bolts surrounded by a ring of fire. The in-
signia was alien to me, but new splinter groups were constantly
breaking off from the major clans. It was just a gang of your
local neo-Nazis out for a little morning exercise before a busy
day of raiding leftist rallies and stomping minorities.

When they got close, I stepped off the path and watched
them go by. Their heads gleamed with sweat, and they practiced their scowls on me. I stared impassively back; an irra-
tional pride wouldn't allow me to avert my eyes. Some faces
became rabid and threw begging looks to the platoon leader. He
didn't seem to notice.

They thundered into the distance, and I stared after them, my
stomach twitching with a sinister exhilaration. I knew some of
the skins wanted to bring me down, and had the platoon leader

consented they would have ratpacked me in true skinhead fashion. I walked back to the Caddy locked in thought, disturbed that the only kicks I enjoyed anymore were those teetering on the edge of death.

The hour of 2:00 p.m. found me in my office, staring at the wallpaper, thoroughly stumped. Dash's data sheets covered the desk, and I was about to glean them again for some overlooked clue when the office door opened and Mrs. Woo, the cleaning lady, came in to do the weekly tidying up.

"When are you going to pay your bill?" she said as way of greeting. It was a little game we played.

"And hello to you, too, Mrs. Woo," I shouted over the roar of the vacuum cleaner she adroitly maneuvered around the carpet. "How are the little ones?"

"They're hungry because someone won't pay his bills."

"Well, don't you worry one little bit, ma'am. I'm working on a big case that will be solved very, very soon."

"Why don't you get an honest job that pays money?" she suggested, attacking the sofa with the vacuum nozzle. "Like Mr. Rex, the talent agent downstairs. He always pays on time."

"Mr. Rex is a pimp, Mrs. Woo. Don't let the expensive suits and capped teeth fool you." I leaned back in my chair. "Oh yeah, I'm stumped now, but I'll soon overcome that."

The vacuum died with a wail, and she began hopping around the room with a duster. "Yeah, yeah. Last week you said you couldn't pay your bill because you couldn't take any more cases until you found yourself emotionally." Sarcasm wrinkled her face, but she never spared a glance from her work. Amazingly efficient, I thought, no movement wasted. I could learn from her.

"That was last week. This week I'm trying to find someone else. I know his name and neighborhood but not his exact whereabouts."

"Why don't you look him up in the phone book?" she said while replacing the liner of my waste bin. "That's what I would do."

I smiled politely, amused by her charming naiveté. "I wish it were that easy." My smile expanded into a chuckle.

"If you don't pay your bill by Friday I won't clean anymore." She gathered up her equipment and left. I stared after her fondly.

The phone book squatted maliciously on the corner of the desk. I whacked it with a pencil and laughed at the poor sweet naive woman.

I found a Rolland D. Crawley in the white pages, residing at Apt. 45, 1230 Close Court Ave., Barridales. I dialed the listed number.

"Hello?" a voice said.

"Hello there, is this Mr. Crawley?"

"Yes."

"Would you like to buy some life insurance, Mr. Crawley?"

"Oh, no thanks, I'm covered."

"Sorry to have bothered you." I hung up.

The nervy bastard, I thought angrily. With his rap sheet he should have been on the run, dodging from one safehouse to another like a hunted rabbit. Instead, he was in the white pages, wedged cozily between the probably law-abiding Susanne C. Crawford and the Craxton Valley Flower Shop. Another sure sign of mankind's headlong plunge from grace with God.

4

I sat in my car across the street from the Close Court Apartments for four hours before I saw anyone resembling the picture of Crawley. The setting sun didn't offer much light, and I didn't recognize him until he was thirty meters from the lobby door. I trained light-intensifying binos on him and smiled to myself. His hair and beard were longer, and he'd put on about fifteen soft pounds, but it was definitely the archfiend in question. He waddled down the sidewalk toward the apartment tower, an overloaded bag of groceries in each arm. He'd apparently stepped out on my way over, either to stock up for the month or to plan a little shindig at the apartment.

The simpler the plan, the less can go wrong. I learned that during my stint in the Rangers and it had been reaffirmed many times since. With this nut of wisdom firmly in mind, I got out of my car and stretched, trying not to look like a professional killer. I wore wraparound shades, black slacks and a dark gray canvas jacket to cover the bulky Myers 20 mm gyrapistol, the professional's weapon of choice for a close-in job. The explosive gyrajets packed more punch than a .12-gauge slug but wouldn't go through walls and rile up the neighbors. I also had a .32 snubnose Colt revolver clipped to the back of my belt and a switchblade in my pocket in case things got really rough. I honestly didn't think I'd need all of them, but they made me feel more dangerous.

I pulled a grocery bag from the back seat and strolled across the street, timing it so I arrived at the lobby door right behind Crawley. He put his bags down gently, fished out his keycard and unlocked the door.

I looked down at his grocery bags, stuffed with a myriad of delightful snacks. The bag I carried was similar to Crawley's except all the cans and boxes in mine were empty, resurrected from the bin behind my office building. I carried it for one simple reason: people don't think you're dangerous if you're carrying groceries. On-duty muggers and rapists don't carry bags of groceries. Even a squeeze-crazed psychopath could look docile with a bag of snacks cradled in his arms. It was one of those useful, little-known quirks of human nature.

He opened the door and I held it while he picked up his bags. He gave me a suspicious glance, and I smiled and stepped in behind him.

I followed him to the elevator. He pushed the Up button and we waited sharing the uncomfortable silence of strangers. The floor indicator above the doors wasn't working, but we pointed our heads at it anyway. I caught him sliding me sideways glances but I ignored him.

The elevator chimed and the doors slithered open. Two Rastas smoking spliffs got off the elevator, and Crawley said hello as though he knew them. We got into the empty car.

Crawley pushed the fourth-floor button, and I reached over and jabbed at it, too.

He reacted with a nervous twitch, as though he'd expected me to strike him. He looked at me directly, eyes narrowed. "I didn't know we had any new tenants on the fourth floor."

"Naw, I'm just visiting. My girl lives up there."

"Oh!" His face relaxed and the tension seeped out of it. "You must be Joan's new beau."

I nodded. "That's right."

I regarded Crawley, upset that his outward appearance didn't reflect his rap sheet. But then, they rarely did. Experience had taught me that those who didn't look the part always seemed to make up for it with gory deeds. Most serial killers tended to resemble cat-loving, elementary-school teachers.

"Say," he said brightly, "I'm having a cozy little poetry party over at my flat tonight. I'm making an absolutely delicious chez suzanne with a delightful little carbaigne sauce. Since you're a friend of Joan's, you're more than welcome to come over." He savored a little grin. "They always wind up being wild affairs."

Oh, I'll bet they do, judging by your rap sheet, I thought. "Uh-huh," I said.

Crawley frowned and turned his eyes to the door. He didn't seem overawed with my conversational skills, but I wasn't going to start bawling about it. The last time I'd got chummy with someone I was about to kill he tried to take me into the afterlife with him. The elevator dinged, the doors slid open, and Crawley stormed out.

The hallway was dim and deserted. I meandered behind Crawley, pretending to dig for my keycard, giving him enough time to open his door. He picked up his bags as I came abreast of him.

"Here, let me help you," I said, shoving him into his apartment with my free hand. He squealed with surprise and fell on his groceries. I stepped inside, drew my pistol and heeled the door shut behind me.

"Hey!" he said, rolling onto his back, alarm plastered across his features.

"Rolland Crawley?" I asked earnestly.

"Yes? I mean no! No-o-o!"

"Oops! Too late!" I squeezed the trigger twice. The gyrajets whooshed out of the pistol and exploded in Crawley's chest, excavating fist-size craters. Crawley sprawled spread-eagled on the spilled bags as though he was trying to protect them. I put down my bag.

I bolted the door to prevent any unpleasant surprises and cleared the apartment room by room. It was a cozy two-bedroom affair, unremarkable in every aspect except that all the walls in the room were covered with poetry written in every imaginable hue of felt pen. I'd never claimed any station as critic of things poetic, but most of what I read seemed overly dramatic to the point of foolishness.

Returning to the living room, I holstered the gyrapistol and searched Crawley from head to toe. I found a set of keycards, a pack of a popular brand of joints, a chrome lighter inscribed with his initials on both sides, a pencil and a wallet. In the wallet were rolling papers, a packet of paisley-pattern condoms, a half-dozen business cards and one of those wallet-size calendars banks give out. Nothing illegal or out of the ordinary.

Much to my dismay, there wasn't a fraction of a cred on Crawley's entire body, which meant Crawley shopped entirely by handscan. Like the Party commercials said, only fools carried plastic, and Crawley was obviously nobody's fool. I put the wallet in my pocket.

In a fit of community service, I called the three-digit reclamation number. The cheery voice on the other end sounded disappointed that there was only one reclaimable. I told her she could reclaim me any Friday night. She laughed politely and asked for my name and account number so she could credit me with the reward. Generally I didn't bother, but these weren't proud times. The reclamation agency paid one credit for every ten pounds, which meant I'd be getting about twenty creds out of Crawley.

I put the phone down and looked at the body again. Remember what he's done, I told myself, the children he's murdered, the lives he's destroyed. You've no reason to feel pity or horror or anything.

A spreading diameter of blood was making an island of him and his groceries, and I decided I'd stalled long enough. I placed a copy of Crawley's death warrant over his face so he'd stop staring at me and took a miniature battery-powered saw out of my coat pocket. To claim my proper reward, I had to take in his scanhand as proof of having done my job. It was one of the less glamorous aspects of my job.

On the way out of Crawley's apartment, I nearly collided with a very attractive young woman wearing huge sunglasses and a paisley-print head wrap. She seemed very surprised to see me coming out of Crawley's flat and looked as if she was going to say as much when she noticed the small black plastic bag in my left hand. Horror dawned on her face like an ugly sun.

Her pretty mouth gaped open with abject revulsion, and her reflective sunglasses threw back a distorted image that had me looking like some kind of twisted fiend. I mumbled a pardon and could feel her eyes on my back all the way to the stairwell. I shoved open the door and lurched down the steps, feeling for all the world like the hunchback of Notre Dame.

Embarrassment and shame had changed to righteous anger by the time I reached the Caddy. Where did she get off looking at me like that? As if I was some kind of twisted creature when the real monster was bleeding in his groceries minus his scan-hand. Why did I feel so dirty? I was the legal entity—I was do-ing society a favor. I was a modern-day paladin, a white-hat, one of the good guys. Instead of skulking out of there, I should have marched out waving a goddamn banner, shouting the news of my good deed. She was probably a criminal herself, wanted by the SPF. So why did I still feel so dirty?

5

Halfway home the fuel warning light began blinking at me menacingly, which seemed a shame since I didn't have any creds and my reclamation reward wouldn't go through until the next day. I began fretting whether I was going to make it home or not.

I decided that since it was the drive to Barridales that had used up what little alcohol I had, it was only fair that Crawley pay for it. I pulled off the side of the road and reached into my glove box for some electrical tape.

Minutes later I rolled into an alcohol station powered by sheer momentum. The engine had died of thirst. I got out and pushed the big beast the remaining five meters to the pump. My Caddy was an '05 model, the last big ones ever made. It drank more alcohol going around the block than I did on a three-day bender, and that was saying something.

The alcohol station was a big affair with twenty nozzles and a bulletproof booth for the attendant, undoubtably built during the corporate era. The Party owned it now; the Party owned all the major industries since they'd crushed the war-weak corporations twelve years ago. I operated the nozzle with my left hand, filled the tank, then walked over to the pay booth.

"Pump six," I said.

"I know that," a heavyset woman snapped from behind the transparent shield. "Creds, card or scan?" she growled as if gnawing on broken glass.

"Scan," I said with a boyish smile. "You know, it takes a lot more muscles to frown than it does to smile."

She looked at me as if I were a crippled rat heading for the pantry. I winked at her with practiced charm. She stabbed a button on her console, and I slid a hand under the protruding head of the scanner.

I was counting on two things. One, Crawley had enough credit in his account to pay for the alcohol, and two, my sparkling conversation would distract the attendant from noticing the unusual pallor of the scanhand.

"Say, are you busy tonight?" I asked hopefully, sliding her my best leer.

"I don't like men," she said.

"Sure you don't." I dropped a lazy eyelid at her.

"Which account?" she grated, her jowls shaking.

"Either one, sugar. You're fantasizing about me, aren't you?"

"Party Bank, then," she shrieked, her voice high with frustration and anger. I felt certain she wanted to hurt me.

"Naw, the other one, honey jowls."

"Second Federal!" she screeched. "You want Second Federal, then!"

"Yes!" I shouted ecstatically into the speaker grille. "And you! I want you, too!"

She stabbed at buttons with ferocious vitality, ripped off a receipt, threw it into the pass tray and slammed the tray forward. "Here's your receipt, you...*male!*" she cried, her sweating face craned close to the shield, her bulging eyes daring me to utter one more insolent word.

I retrieved the receipt from the tray with exaggerated lethargy and gazed at it for a long moment. My mission was accomplished. My car was full of fuel, and there were impatient customers behind me. But I couldn't just leave. It seemed absolutely necessary to play the scenario out to its natural end. I felt locked into the thing, and all the precious momentum couldn't be wasted. I considered and discarded a half-dozen conclusions before I hit on one that felt right.

I twisted my face into a full-scale leer and leaned forward until mere inches separated our faces. "How about a little smooch then, baby?" I whispered heavily, and planted a big wet kiss on the glass.

I fled before her howl and hunchbacked it to the car. I revved the engine and screeched out of the lot, laughing maniacally out the window.

I put five kilometers of asphalt behind me before I felt safe enough to pull over. I wheeled into an automated snack bar and scanhanded three soy-beef sandwiches, a carton of soy milk, a large bag of potato-flavored algae chips and a chocolate-flavored kelp cake for dessert. I parked behind the snack bar, ogling the snacks in the passenger seat. Before I began my first meal in three days, I pulled up my right sleeve and unwrapped the tape securing Crawley's hand to my wrist. I put the hand back in its bag, and the feast began.

The milk had never been near a cow, the chips contained no potatoes, the cake no chocolate, the sandwiches no beef. I wasn't even sure how much soy the sandwiches contained, what with all those reclamation rumors limping around. My mouth and stomach weren't concerned. I knew I shouldn't eat so much after a week of abstention but I plainly couldn't help myself. I ate until my shrunken stomach was full, then ate some more to please my mouth. I'd feel sick and maybe puke later, but I was a big believer in living for the moment.

By the time I started on the cake, my mind turned to a question lurking rudely in the back of my mind. Why did a small-time, albeit industrious, hood like Crawley have two bank accounts? And why Second Federal? Second Fed was an executive's bank, one of the few that had survived the nationalizations when the Party made the big grab. I'd pulled the taped-hand stunt before in equally desperate times, but I'd never come across two accounts. Usually they didn't have an account at all. The vast majority of banks belonged to the Party, and most career criminals didn't tend to put a lot of faith in the Party.

Between swigs of milk and mouthfuls of cake I decided I'd have to get to the bottom of the riddle. It had been so long since I'd had a case that my professional curiosity was eager to brawl with any mystery that ambled by.

I drove to an isolated Party Bank autoteller, cleared the handscan and closed the account, withdrawing 46.10 creds. I put the thin plastic squares into my empty wallet and drove uptown.

Finding the Party Bank machine had been easy. The Party Bank was the financial organ of the Party, the agglomeration of all the banks that the Party had nationalized, and they were everywhere. It took me two hours to find a Second Fed machine. It was set into the base of a shopping tower in the City's commercial district where you usually found the sidewalks rife with men and women in one-piece executive suits tight-assing it around like robots. But the sun had set two hours before, and now the streets were nearly deserted, with only a few lights burning in the long skyscrapers. I parked across the street. There wasn't anyone near the machine so I didn't bother with the tape. I left the engine running and walked across the street.

After I passed the scan, the machine politely asked for a six-digit code number. I pushed the Cancel button and walked back to the car.

I sat in the Caddy and glared at the arrogant appliance. There wasn't a lot of traffic. Late-working execs tight-assed by at about five-minute intervals. I figured I could roll down a window and empty a 30-round magazine of gyrajets into the evil machine and be home in bed before the authorities arrived.

A less dramatic idea shouldered its way in. I turned on the interior light, pulled Crawley's wallet from my jacket pocket and emptied its contents onto my lap. Crawley struck me as the kind of person insecure enough to write down his access number in case he forgot. Poets and numbers weren't natural friends.

The bank card was the obvious suspect, but its surface was free of any writing. I checked the business cards. Three of the cards had a name and phone number written on the back. A Joseph, a B.C. and a Fred II. Something pricked my subconscious, and I stared at the last one. Fred II. Fred the Second. The Second Fred. Second Fed. I chuckled, nodding to the hand sitting on the passenger seat. The cryptic devil.

The phone number was one digit too many, so I dropped the first digit. The machine rejected me. I tried again, this time leaving off the last digit. The screen read, "Thank you, Mr. Crawley," and I was in. First I checked the balance. Then I opened a new account using my own scanhand, wrote down the code number, transferred Crawley's credit to the new account, withdrew the maximum allowed amount, closed the old account and shuffled back to the Caddy.

I drove ten blocks and parked in front of an all-night supermarket. I sat behind the wheel for five minutes doing deep-breathing exercises. This is really happening, I told myself again and again, but I couldn't shake the dreamlike feeling.

Unless I was locked into some serious hallucinations, the wallet in my pocket was home to one thousand creds plus the 46.10 from the earlier withdrawal. In the electronic belly of the infallible Second Federal Bank were 253,756 credits that belonged to yours truly.

I went in the supermarket and bought enough food to last an extended winter, then rushed home to fill the fridge and cupboards to maximum capacity. I fried up a thick texturized-protein steak, microwaved potato-flavored paste into pliable submission, tossed a kelp salad and sat down to a late-night dinner invigorated by a bottle of cold ripple. After gorging myself, I retired to the living room with a six-pack of vitabeer and a mindful of trepidation.

I didn't feel guilty about taking the creds. Since Crawley was dead and the data sheet spoke of no known relatives, the money didn't belong to anybody, and one couldn't rightfully be accused of stealing something that didn't belong to anybody. It was merely a windfall of my job, a karmic reward for my good ways and clean living. And if I didn't take it, the bank eventually would, and the good Lord knew they had enough.

With that safely rationalized, I turned my high-powered logic to what really bothered me. I was torn between living quietly on my newfound wealth for as long as I could stretch it, or blowing it all in a year-long spree of booze, high living and adventure.

The idea about applying for a moving permit and fleeing the City wasn't exactly an ignored wallflower, either. I felt exposed in the City, a marked man. Crawley didn't get that kind of credit through wise investment, and whoever he took it from would want it back. I thought that my trail was covered, but with the handscan system you could never tell, and there could be a big electronic finger pointing right at me.

I decided to sleep on it. I finished the six-pack, double-checked the apartment's security system and passed out on my bed.

6

I awoke with the terrible knowledge that the events of the previous night were all a dream. I fell out of the sheets in a panic and grabbed my wallet from the top of the dresser. I emptied its contents onto the bed and jumped into the pile of plastic. I closed my eyes and laughed. It had been too long between bouts of solvency.

I took a quick shower, got dressed and had a soy-steak sandwich and a glass of soy milk for breakfast. Instead of switching back to the lighter 9 mm Browning I usually carried when not working a contract, I stuck to the bulkier gyrapistol. My newfound wealth brought with it the bastard child of insecurity. I could sense the black ravens of paranoia circling above me, haunting my every move.

It was a twenty-minute drive to the City's SPF headquarters, and I drove with the windows down. At nine in the morning it was already muggy enough to drive the bag ladies into the shade. It got hotter every year, the ever-thickening layer of global smog sealing in the sun's heat like a gray blanket. I could almost hear the ice caps melting. Doom, I thought, doom.

The bag with Crawley's hand sat on the passenger seat, thawing out after a night spent in the freezer. I almost hated turning the guy in. He wasn't much for conversation, but he was generous to a fault. But then, five thousand creds was five thousand creds, and it would give me something to point at if someone noticed a sudden change in my spending habits.

SPF HQ was on the other side of the river, so close to the old Travis Penal Institution that it sat in the prison's shadow until noon. The prison was nearly a hundred years old and resembled the kind of medieval castle an evil warlock would be comfortable in. During the corporate years it was said to have been a mercenary training center. When the Party first took power, they put it to use as a reeducation camp. I wasn't sure what was going on inside those stone walls at the moment, and I really didn't care to know.

I wheeled into the parking lot and parked in the space reserved for the chief of militia control. I took the bagged hand, and the warrant, and left my gun under the seat.

Though it was six stories high and painted bright white, the SPF HQ building still managed to look squat and ominous. It was all concrete and steel, with narrow windows and good fields of fire, ready to withstand a determined siege. All SPF stations gave that impression. I muscled open the heavy bullet-proof door and walked to the security station just inside.

One of the two guards behind the counter scowled at my private-enforcer license with exaggerated disgust. "What's your business here?"

"You must be new. My wife works here and she forgot her lunch so I thought I'd drop it by." I shook the hand bag under his nose. He recoiled, making the connection between my license and the bag.

"You're abominable."

"Spell that," I demanded. I must have stumped him because he came around the desk and gave me a rough frisk. They didn't like smart guys at SPF headquarters. He seemed disappointed he didn't find anything illegal, so he made me walk through the weapon detector twice. I'd visited SPF headquarters maybe fifty times in the past five years and they still had the same act playing.

I knew my way to warrant collection by heart. It was a long walk down a quarter kilometer of hallway, and I passed a lot of people on the way. The SPF troopers who noticed the bag labored mightily to show me their contempt, while the civilians and secretaries viewed me with a sort of revulsed awe. I'd dated a SPF secretary once. I'd had her believing I was a bank security guard until she rifled through some of my personal things.

She found some old contracts and figured the rest out for herself. She never told me exactly why she left, but we both knew the story. I could still recall her last words before she lifted her bags and marched out the door: "How can anyone be so vile and base?"

All I could do was smile and shrug as if to say, "It ain't no great effort, baby." I still missed the way she had of making soy steak taste like the real thing.

I reveled in the hard stares and repugnant looks, swinging my bag like a schoolboy. I could have hid it inside my jacket, but that wouldn't have been nearly as entertaining. It was like being the village gravedigger. I was nearly seduced by the desire to hunch a shoulder, squint an eye, drag a leg and start raving about the bells.

But that wouldn't look good. I had to win their approval and respect through dedication to duty and a professional attitude. With this in mind, I strode professionally into the warrant collection office and slapped the bag on the unmanned counter.

"Let's have some service here," I demanded. "A professional needs some goddamn service!"

A bloodless, skeletal-thin man with close-cropped graying hair appeared from an open door behind the counter. "Oh, it's you, Strait. I was afraid it was someone important."

"Respect, damn it!" I snarled. "Respect and approval is what I crave. Nothing less will do."

Assistant Inspector Degas clasped bony hands and closed his eyes. "Please Lord, drop a ten-thousand-pound shit-hammer on this man. I pledge ten thousand Ave Marias if you kill him now. Haven't we suffered enough?"

"You savage bastard!" I accused. "The mighty avenger Jake Strait brings yet another sinister archfiend to justice, and this is what I get? I demand the full accolades I so richly deserve!"

Degas shook his head sadly, lifting the bag from the counter. He removed the hand from the bag with a pair of tongs and laid it under an industrial-size scanner. "Who's your five-fingered friend?"

"Rolland D. Crawley. Murderer. Rapist. Pimp. Pusher. Purveyor of bad poetry."

"Do tell." Degas sat behind a keyboard and monitor cabled to the scanner. His fingers danced over the keyboard with practiced ease, his eyes focused on the screen.

"It's true," I said. "It took all my considerable skill and daring to overcome his huge arsenal and vicious nature."

Degas stopped keying the board and squinted at the monitor, frowning, no doubt awed at how dangerous Crawley's record revealed him to be. I yawned and tried to appear modest.

"You're right about the poetry part, bad or otherwise," Degas said, then looked up. "I didn't think you did political contracts."

I couldn't immediately comprehend what Degas was saying. It was as if he'd suddenly started jabbering at me in some strange tongue. "I don't do political kills," I said. "You know that. This guy is a violent criminal. He has a rap sheet a kilometer long."

"As far as our information goes, the only violence Crawley committed was symbolic." His eyes returned to the monitor. "He has two wants on him, both political. He penned some poems of questionable political content for an underground newspaper, and he was photographed taking part in an illegal demonstration protesting the conversion of a library into a reclamation depot. It was an apprehension warrant, not an execution. You sure you didn't get your contracts mixed up?"

I stood dumfounded. I wanted Degas to tell me it was just a big joke, but I knew he wasn't the kind to screw around. I'd never even seen him crack a smile. His dead gray eyes looked up from the monitor, and he said, "He must have tried to attack you during apprehension."

"Yeah, that's right," I said, but my words held no conviction. They just slipped out on their own. An instinctual sense of self-preservation took over while my brain scrambled to get back on line. "He pulled a knife. I had no choice."

"Bullshit!" Inspector Blake stormed into the room so fast he had to put one hand on his hat so it wouldn't fly off. He leaned over Degas's shoulder and stared into the face of the monitor. "You murdered some goddamn poet on an apprehension warrant! You stupid asshole!"

I'd met Inspector Blake a few times before. I despised him from the start and liked him less every time he opened his mouth.

"I guess all those years in sap school weren't wasted, were they?" he continued. Sharklike, he smelled blood and was intent on getting as much of my ass as he could. He gestured extravagantly to the hand resting under the scanner. "Well, at least you apprehended part of him."

I clawed Crawley's warrant out of my breast pocket and slammed it down on the counter. "I have a death warrant right here, Blake."

The inspector snatched the warrant off the counter. He glanced at it without really looking and said, "Don't bring your forgeries in here, Strait."

"That's a certified copy!" I hollered.

"This is certified shit." He crumpled the paper into a ball, and it disappeared into a pocket of his raincoat. He turned to Degas. "What does a Class D-3 apprehension warrant pay? It's been so long since anyone brought one of those in I can hardly remember. Twenty credits, isn't it? Give the hero twenty credits, Degas."

Without looking up, Degas opened the cash drawer and counted out twenty credits. He laid them on the counter.

"Go on, handchopper," the inspector said. "Take your 'fooking' pennies and get your stinking ass out of here."

I hated the inspector. I hated his face. I hated the dirty snap-brim fedora and black rubber raincoat he always wore. I hated the way he mispronounced his obscenities. I hated his soul. We would never be chums.

"Up yours, Inspector," I said, too wound up to be original. I picked up the creds and threw them at him. "Go buy yourself a new hat, screw."

His voice caught up with me at the door. "We might just pull your license for this, Strait! If we don't press murder charges!"

I slammed the door as I went out, but that didn't seem enough. The hallway felt as hot as an oven and too narrow for my hulking shape, each step an off-balance, self-conscious lurch as sweat trickled down my back.

It was even hotter outside, but instead of walking straight to my car I detoured through the staff parking area. A huge black late-model, all-terrain pickup with whip antennae and a row of lights on the chrome roll bar squatted in the space reserved for

Inspector Blake. Figures, I thought, taking my keys out of my pocket. Casually I walked down one length of the truck then the other, whistling as I went to cover the high-pitched squeal of scraping paint. I ambled over to the Caddy, my heart many times lighter, hoping Blake would realize who did it.

I drove to the nearest branch of the Party Bank, located in the bowels of a sprawling bubble mall, a dinosaur from the corporate heyday, crammed full of people from the burbs and security cops.

I got good eye contact with a pretty brunette teller while waiting in her line and realized it had been nearly three months since I'd had a date. When it was my turn, she brought out a beautiful smile shackled to an appraising stare.

"Hello, Teresa," I said, reading her name tag. "Haven't we met?"

"No, I don't think so," she said.

"Well, it's time we did." I held out both my hands. "I'm Jake."

She held out her hands, and I checked for a ring. There wasn't one. I hung on to her left hand and turned it over.

"Lord God!"

"What? What's wrong?" she said, staring at her palm.

"Why, that's the deepest love line I've ever seen. Are you a romantic, Teresa?"

"Well," she said, calming down. "I do like candlelight dinners and walks in the rain."

I sighed as if the great search were finally over. "You know when you're walking in the park in the autumn," I murmured, "and the leaves are all down, and it just stopped raining, and you can smell the leaves, the grass, the rain?"

"Yes," she whispered. "I know."

"Then a lonely bird starts to sing, and you cast your eyes to the misty skies and you feel as if at that unique moment, all the eyes of all the angels in Heaven are upon you and you fall in love with the whole world. Have you ever felt that way, Teresa?"

"No," she murmured. "But I want to."

I loaded my eyes with a thousand promises and whispered, "You shall, Teresa, you shall," then handed her the contract. After a dizzy minute we parted eyes and she took a look at it.

Her smile collapsed like a dynamited bridge. "I'll have to get my supervisor to look at this," she gasped, and fled. She came back a moment later, hiding behind a thin, mustached man in a somber blue suit. He smiled perfunctorily and passed the contract back to me.

"I'm afraid we can't help you, sir," he said.

"What? I know it's not stamped, but you can call SPF HQ to get a confirmation of the kill." The last word made Teresa flinch, and I could sense heads jerking behind me.

"There is no need to call, Mr. Strait. That document—" he nodded toward the paper "—is a fake. Not a very good one."

I'd heard that twice since breakfast and I didn't like it any better this time. I wanted to say something, maybe make an ugly scene, but the events of the day had left me defeated and tired. I glanced at Teresa peeking over the supervisor's shoulder, and her eyes told me she would never walk in the park with me, never ever.

Taking the contract, I turned around. The people in line stared at me. I knew what they thought of my kind. Only now, with Crawley's innocent blood on my hands, they were right. My shining armor of self-righteousness had collapsed around my feet, and my conscience lay bare before their daggerlike stares. What the hell, I thought, and did my drag-leg, hunchback routine all the way to the door.

I drove with a rude fury. I'd been played for a stooge, and somebody somewhere was enjoying a good long laugh at my expense. It burned me up. I didn't mind getting beaten, shot at or rejected; that was all in the nature of the game. But when somebody played me for the fool, used me like a back-street whore fed on sweet promises of country cottages and white-picket fences, I had to make somebody pay.

7

But first I'd get drunk. I picked up a quart of vodka and a gallon of orange-flavored drink on the way to the office.

By five in the afternoon the vodka was gone and the orange drink didn't taste good by itself. By five-fifteen I got tired of my own company. I was talking to myself and I hated listening to drunks. I was thinking too much about my lost self-image, and more than anything else I wanted to forget.

I walked across the street to the St. Christopher's Lounge. The bartender there was a friend of mine, and if it wasn't too busy he'd sometimes listen to my drunken gibberish. His name was Amal. He had one ear.

Like most Hayward bars, the St. Chris was frequented by prostitutes of both genders. They fit right in with the decor. If you walked into the place when it was dead empty, you could still tell it was a whore bar. It just had that feel about it.

I sat where I always sat, at the end of the bar farthest from the door. I ordered a screwdriver from Amal and checked the odds. At 5:20 p.m. the whores outnumbered the fish three to one. I knew some of the girls and waved at them. I wasn't feeling too sociable, and they must have picked up on that because they didn't come over to talk to me. Or maybe they thought I was still broke.

A sullen-looking pimp was getting quietly loaded two stools down. Quarterly earnings were probably down. A loud fat man sitting at the closest table was telling stories about his college combatball days to two whores who smiled and nodded but really didn't give a damn. He was drunk and his actions stank of the burbs. His wife was probably spending the weekend visiting the folks so he decided he was going to hit the town and pick up a couple of loose City girls. Hell, they were all sluts anyway, he figured. He was the type who'd get mad when he found out all they wanted was his money. He'd pay them, but he wouldn't tell his buddies back in the burbs that. Hell *no,* those sluts paid *him.* I turned my back so I wouldn't have to look at him but I could still hear his voice. I thought about picking a fight, but one of the whores would probably stick me.

Amal came back with my drink but wouldn't surrender it until I showed him some money. He was wise to my tricks. I gave him a fifty and left the change on the bar. I put half the drink down in a single swallow. I didn't know how to drink mixed drinks, and that was why I usually drank beer. I couldn't evoke enough self-discipline to make myself sip.

But tonight I didn't care. I was going to wrestle with that wily demon alcohol; we were going to grapple like the sworn enemies and best chums we were. I wanted to get so incredibly legless that my mind would go blank and my only worry would be getting Amal to understand my next order.

I looked at my reflection in the mirror behind the bar. It was one of those smoked types, the kind that always makes you appear mysterious and handsome. I heard the voice of doom in my head. The man you see in the mirror, ladies and gentlemen, is a murderer. And he's going to pay for it. Even in the dim lighting I could see certain doom gathering darkly inside my eyes, the sure knowledge that I would wake up with nothing gained but a grotesque hangover, a gutful of self-pity and perhaps a darker understanding of myself. But then, I thought, raising my glass and saluting my reflection, sometimes that was all one could ask for. I spent another couple of minutes staring at myself out of habit, then dropped my eyes to my drink.

Someone slipped onto the bar stool next to me, and I checked my watch. Six minutes since I'd sat down. Not bad, but with as many sharks and few game fish in the water it was nothing to get vain about. I slid my eyes sideways to see what breed of mutant my good looks had reeled in.

I could always spot a hooker from first glance, no matter how she dressed or acted. They all had that unmistakable aura of accessibility about them, even the classy, expensive ones who would never see the inside of a dive like the St. Chris.

She didn't look like a whore. Or maybe I just didn't want to believe someone so beautiful was available to any loser who cashed a paycheck. She had the femme fatale look down to a habit: full, pouting lips painted a glossy black, petite, slightly upturned nose, high cheekbones and long almond-shaped eyes, a face right off the cover of a fashion magazine. Her hair, cut in a short bob and dyed a lustrous blue black, lived in dramatic contrast with her alabaster white skin. A black cotton gown clung to the curves of a model-thin body whose tone hinted at an athlete crouching inside. She possessed the perfection of beauty you couldn't take in all at once; you had to gape for a while to realize its depth, then everything came together and there she was.

"Would you like a drink?" I asked.

"Yes, thank you. Whatever you're having is fine." Her voice was sandpaper rough yet unmistakably cultured. She put on a pouting smile that carried to her raven eyes, and I sat mesmerized for a horizonless moment before I could bring myself to order the drinks. I knew I was gaping like a yokel on his first sojourn to a topless bar, but since the day of my birth my poor head was slave to the black passions that ruled my fool heart.

When the drinks arrived I said, "You shouldn't hang around in a place like this. Somebody might take you for a whore."

Her smile uncurled a little, and I waited for her to tell me she was just an art student hopping dives for kicks, but she didn't. She didn't say anything, which was answer enough.

"Oh," I said, the knowledge murdering my heart in cold blood. "You don't resemble one."

"I'm new."

I wanted to tell her she didn't belong there, not in the St. Chris, not on Hayward, not in the City. I wanted to kill her pimp and set her up in a nice safe cottage in the burbs. I wanted to shield her from all of life's ugliness.

"Aw, it's probably not as bad as my job," I said. Crawley's face reared up in my mind, and I tried to drown him. I showed Amal my empty glass and he brought me a replacement. I swallowed half of it to show my appreciation.

"You drink very fast," she said.

"I'm in a hurry," I said.

"Where are you going?"

"Unconsciousness."

She nodded. "Are you drinking to forget or to punish yourself?"

I gave her a long look then finished the rest of my drink. "Since when are whores so philosophical?"

She turned to the mirror and we stared at our reflections.

"My name is Britt," she said.

"I'm Strait."

"Is that a declaration of your sexuality or your name?"

"Both."

"What do you do, Mr. Strait?"

"I get by."

"What do you do for a living, I mean?"

I looked at her. "Why all the questions? You taking a survey for your pimp?"

She smiled darkly into the mirror. "I'm sorry. You just interest me."

"Do you really want to know?" I turned to the mirror and stared into those inkwells.

"Yes."

"Okay." I regarded my drink. "I'm an insurance salesman. Best damn policy peddler in my office. Wanna buy one?"

She laughed and reached for her drink. She took the glass in both hands, wrapped full, bee-stung lips around the pair of straws, tilted her head forward and looked dead at me from under long, black eyelashes. Classy moves, I thought. She wasn't from the City.

I excused myself and stumbled to the men's room. After relieving myself I washed my hands and looked in the mirror above the sink. It amazed how much the smoked mirror behind the bar had been deceiving me. The vodka had suckerpunched my looks. My eyes were puffy and my face stretched toward the floor. My hair was going in no particular direction, and the scar on my cheek stood out on my flushed skin like a line of chalk. I had drunk myself ugly. I felt unworthy of the girl at the bar. Someone should have jerked me off my stool and given me a good shaking, demanding just what the hell did I think I was I doing with a woman like that. What did she see in me?

"Jesus Christ," I said to my reflection. "She's a prostitute, you simple knave, all she wants is your money." I tried to bring anger down on her mercenary greed but I couldn't swing the emotion. If anything, I was disappointed at her for associating with someone like the bum in the mirror. I splashed cold water on my face and ran a comb through my hair. It didn't seem to help.

When I came back out she was gone. A dizzy panic got a stranglehold and squeezed the breath out of me. Damn, I thought, crawling onto my stool, I should have been more charming.

Hope told me she was freshening up in the ladies' room. Fifteen minutes and two screwdrivers told me she wasn't. The ice in her drink had melted, and Amal was giving it vulturelike glances. It was three-quarters full, which proved she hadn't just been hustling a free drink. I tried hard, but couldn't squeeze a whole lot of consolation out of that.

I practiced staying upright all the way to the jukebox and filled its belly with change. I had a strong taste for angst and anguish at the best of times, so I punched in ancient punk and new deathblues. I warded off a descending male hooker with a hard look, retook my stool and ordered another drink. While Amal subtracted from my stake on the bar, I hooked his sympathetic ear with my earnest sorrow.

"I tell you, Amal," I said, trying to feel like Bogart. "I'm really low."

Amal nodded sympathetically.

"I'm a murderer, a stooge, and now my woman has left me heartbroken and ruined."

"Your woman?" Amal echoed, raising an eyebrow.

"Yeah, the one that was just sitting here," I said.

Amal rolled his eyes.

"Okay, so she's a working girl," I said. "Everyone needs a profession."

"Yeah. I've never seen her here before. Must be new."

"That's *right,*" I said. "I really thought I could *change* her."

Amal laughed cynically and left to attend fresh customers. The after-work crowd was starting to show up, rowdy gangs of T-shirted workers. The women swooped down on them from their bar-stool perches like hawks, hitting them up before they got both feet in the door. Four heroes of the assembly line laid noisy siege to the bar, confusing Amal by yelling out all their orders at once. They shouted and laughed and slapped each other on the back. They'd been working on some assembly line all week, and now that they had their hard-earned paychecks they meant to cut real loose. Four prostitutes moved up behind them, laying their own siege, causing the factory guys to elbow each other and giggle, as if it were their looks instead of their fat wallets that attracted them.

The sullen pimp finished his bourbon and left to look for a quieter place to wrestle his demons and I did a little spin on my stool, putting my back to the bar. I was beginning to feel a little loose myself. My brain had checked out and the extremities of my body were starting to tingle. I'd plunged headlong off the cliff of reality, and though I would hit ground sooner or later, for now I was flying.

A not unattractive redhead swung over to the jukebox. After looking over the play list she fed in some creds and punched in some songs. Instead of swinging back to her seat, she hung out by the juke, perhaps waiting for one of her numbers to come on. She casually faced in my direction as if she was checking her hair in the mirror. Her eyes flickered to mine on the way back to her purse. She dug out a book of matches and a pack of joints. She took her time about lighting one, making a show about how sensual lighting a joint could be. She inhaled deeply, blew out a veil of smoke, then dropped smoldering green eyes on me. They did sprints up and down my length then settled on my eyes. She smiled a sly little smirk as if we were sharing a secret joke. It must be my good looks, I thought.

It was obvious she was selling something, but I admired her presentation. She held the joint next to her head, and her rounded hips swayed almost imperceptibly to the beat. Someone seemed to be messing with the thermostat, and I thought about taking my jacket off. Suddenly her eyes plunged to her full breasts, where she delicately brushed ash off her green velvet dress. Then she looked up slowly, her eyes rising like twin suns, brighter and greener than when they'd left. She tilted her head the tiniest bit to the right and gave me a long, slow wink. The wall between my desires and virtues crumbled like the shabby facade it was, and I smiled helplessly back. She took her cue and began swinging slowly toward me.

"Here comes your woman," Amal said from behind me.

"I'll say," I said, watching her.

"No, I mean your woman. The one that left you heartbroken and low."

I looked back and followed his nod to the door. Britt cut through the crowd like a perfect knife. Three-quarters of the men in the place watched her moves with hungry eyes, and the other quarter was gay. With a soaring heart I realized she was walking my way. I glanced at the approaching redhead and I looked at Britt. I determined they would arrive at precisely the same time.

They became aware of each other and neither seemed willing to give up. Working-girl pride. Just when I thought they would leap upon each other like alley cats, Britt shot the redhead a look. The look only lasted an instant, but the magnitude of violence it implied was incredible. If I added that look to my repertoire, I wouldn't have to worry about clients stiffing me. The redhead's resolve vaporized, and she veered off to the ladies' room.

Britt slid onto her stool and smiled at me as if she had never left. In the light of her beautiful smile, the look she'd given the redhead seemed an impossibility, a false memory.

"I'm sorry for leaving, Mr. Strait," she said.

"Call me Jake."

"Jake. I had to make a call."

"Of course," I said as if there could be no other explanation.

She smiled and I stared. My brain seized up, and I couldn't think of anything to say that wouldn't sound contrived or secondhand. I felt a strong need to charm her but I felt more numb than clever. Her overpowering presence magnified the monstrous silence, and I was starting to smother when Amal handed her the phone.

She frowned, said yes into it three times, then handed it back. She traded her frown in for a demure smile and sipped her drink.

It was probably her pimp calling to give the new girl a little pep talk, the odd pointer. Maybe he'd come in and coach her with subtle hand signals from across the bar, or even stand behind her and feed her good lines.

She didn't volunteer an explanation and I didn't ask. We faced each other, and the weight was settling on my neck again when my old chum trouble muscled in.

"Hey, hey!" One of the loose factory boys tapped Britt on the shoulder from behind, and Britt smiled as if she'd been expecting it all day. "Yo, baby," he continued in his eloquent style. "You're wasting your time talking to pretty boy there. Come sit with us, one hundred percent beef over here." He laughed at his little joke and looked back at his friends to make sure they got it, too. They yucked it up to show that they did.

"No, thanks," Britt said, and her lips curled up, igniting her eyes. She wiggled on her stool, a slow, happy movement. "I prefer the company of a man to that of boys."

The factory boy narrowed his eyes at the back of her head and looked confused. He wasn't accustomed to bar girls talking to him that way. He was the type who figured that when he had a fat wad of creds in his pocket, every girl in town was in love with him. "Hey," he growled. "What's that supposed to mean?"

"What does it sound like, boy?" Her breathing picked up, her nostrils flared, and her full lips parted a little to take in more air. She leaned forward until her eyes were so close I thought I was going to drown in their black depths. She's hypnotizing me, I thought.

The goon glanced back at his three friends who'd taken up position behind him, eager to show their assembly-line camaraderie. He clamped a hand on Britt's shoulder and said, "Listen, you whore—"

Technically his terminology was correct, but the word stabbed my belly like a cold blade.

"Take your hand off her or I'll shove it up your ass," I snarled, proving I was no stranger to eloquence myself. I could sense the goon glaring at me, but that didn't matter. I couldn't tear my eyes away from Britt's; they were all I could understand. Britt smiled wider, gave me a nod and I felt as if I was taking a cue. I slipped off the stool and looked into the face of the enemy.

He was a burly six-foot-three, an inch taller than me. He shoved out his chest and threw his arms out a couple of times to make sure I noticed that he was bigger. He looked confident because he saw a pretty face and to him that equated weakness.

"You have exactly three seconds to get out of my sight, pretty boy," he said in his best low growl. "Or I'll kick your ass from one end of this dive to the other."

I wanted to laugh, to tell him to think of something clever and original instead of that redneck rehash. I wanted to tell him to keep talking and glaring because I wanted to hate him with all my heart, because I knew that two things determined who won a fight: muscle and hate. *Muscle* meaning strength, reflexes and experience; *hate* meaning just who wanted to hurt the other bastard worse. Whoever wanted to win the most usually did, and since it looked as if they might ratpack me, I wanted to be consumed by hate when words turned to violence.

"Well?" he said, alarmed I hadn't disappeared yet.

"I'm waiting for you to start counting."

He stabbed a finger at my chest. "You just made the biggest mistake of your life."

"How would you know?" I said suspiciously. "You been following me around?"

"You're dead," he growled, but didn't immediately follow through with his threat. Instead, he rolled his big shoulders like the champ loosening up before a match, swung his eyes back to his friends, then jerked his head back around to slap a fresh glare on me.

"Looks don't kill," I said. "That's just an old saying."

His buddies whispered encouragements to him, and I could hear Amal saying he didn't want any trouble, but they all sounded a million miles away. The familiar rush of exhilara-

tion was hitting me in waves, each more powerful than the last.
My emotions pyramided, my body became taut, and a light-
headedness washed over me. The rush peaked and I washed up
on a beach of serene and ruthless hate. When the violence began I wouldn't have to think about it—my mind would be a
spectator.

I dropped a quick glance to Britt. She still sat between us, her
eyes focused on my face, her expression bestial. I sensed she
was feeding off my raw hate and refining it into pure pleasure.
I gestured with my chin, and she slipped from between me and
my opponent, baring her teeth like a wolf.

The goon looked sorry to see her go. He was picking up on
my heat, and his tough-guy image was fraying at the edges. He
was obviously accustomed to winning fights with hard looks
and well-delivered one-liners.

Suddenly he lost it. I saw the meanness in his eyes break and
terror crawl in its place. Sweat beaded on his forehead, and I
could smell fear oozing out his pores. His friends tried to in-
flate him with low shouts, but his raft had already sunk.

"Hell, let's get back to the girls," he said in a shaky voice.
"I ain't got the time to stomp no wimp." He smiled to his
friends over his shoulder to see if he'd saved face, then put his
back to me.

A good man would have let him go. I couldn't. I couldn't
come down, not then, not like that. There was so much adrenaline in my system that if I didn't feed the beast in my belly I'd
have the shakes for the rest of a long night. Besides, he'd called
me a wimp.

"I'm afraid you're too late," I said to his back, my voice
alien and hoarse.

He turned around and there was a fateful horror in his eyes.
"What'd you say?"

"I said 'Here comes the train.'" I drove my left fist into his
solar plexus and he doubled over, his head sinking to chest
level. I shot my right hand skyward, the heel of my palm con-
necting with his chin on the way up. His head flew back until
his nose pointed at the ceiling, exposing his neck. I drove extended fingers into his Adam's apple, and his windpipe col-

lapsed like balsa wood. Two of his buddies caught him on the way to the floor.

I became vaguely aware that Amal was shouting and women were screaming, but they were doing it more out of tradition than alarm. Violence in its many forms was the daily fare on Hayward.

One of the fallen hero's pals seemed unimpressed with my fine display of fighting talent. He rushed me, fists hefted high on either side of his head, chin down, elbows tucked. He'd probably boxed in college and maybe still sparred at a gym on weekends. He rummaged out a decent left-jab-right-hook combination that probably worked fine on rummies and drunk sailors.

I ducked the left and deflected the right. He must have been used to at least one of the punches landing because he didn't pull his guard back up, pointing at me with his chin instead. I knew a sweet deal when I saw one. I dropped my right fist somewhere near my boots and brought up the kind of donnybrook they used to write ballads about. He lifted a full four inches off the floor, then gravity got a firm hold and jerked him back down with a vengeance, smacking him on the hard tile like a sack of wet cement dropped from a third-story window.

With two down there was a lull in the action. I shot Britt a look, and it struck me that I wanted to impress her. She looked impressed, or maybe just primal. Her face was twisted with malevolent euphoria and I half expected to see drool trickling down her chin, but I knew she was too classy a girl for that. Her eyes glowed, backlit by inner pagan fires, and they egged me on—*press the attack, there can be no quarter!* A brutal, coarse energy flowed between us, and we were made intimate by it. She was vampire and cheerleader at once, and I moved forward, as much to satisfy her terrible hunger as my own savage lust for violent justice.

One of the two remaining stood frozen against the bar, his face locked up with abject horror. What the hell made a man look like that? I wondered. The other was kneeling on the floor, cradling the head of the original goon in his lap. He looked up at me as if I was a rampant Hun and said, "Haven't you done enough?"

He probably felt safe playing the role of the medic. I wanted to yell at him, I wanted to tell him that it was they who had started it. They were the evil bastards and I was just an innocent joe dispensing justice as I went along. Instead, I leaned back a little and aimed a kick at his chin. He tried to duck it and got it in the nose instead. Blood sprayed from his nostrils, and he flipped over onto his back and twitched. That'd teach him that in war, medics got shot, too.

The last of the foursome realized he was most probably next in line and decided he wasn't up to it. He started backpedaling for the door, running into tables and patrons as he went. He faced me the whole way, as if he thought that if he turned his back on me for a bare second I'd leap across the room and sink fangs into his neck.

"Get him! He's getting away!" Britt screamed, her voice high and urgent.

"No," I said. "Let him go and tell the others so they know of my valorous deeds—" I paused to catch my breath. "—and fear my just wrath."

"Huh?" she said hoarsely, as out of breath as I.

"I don't think it would look good if I chased him down Hayward. I think I'd come off as some kind of monster."

Britt stared at me blankly, then nodded, a shadow of disappointment in her eyes.

The entire fight had lasted less than ten seconds, which was about average if someone knew what they were doing. I'd ridden a mean wave to victory but now the wave had crested and I was coming down fast.

Amal looked at me as if I were a traitor, and the Sex Pistols wailed from the jukebox. I held my hand out to Britt and she took it, looking drained and content, like a lioness after a big feed. "We better go," I said. Britt worked up a grin and nodded.

People got out of our way as if we were contaminated, and we made it to the door without my having to face down any young mavericks out to win a reputation. The second we stepped outside, Britt threw her arms around me and kissed me on the mouth, and it felt as natural as hell. The brawl had done more to bring us together than a month's worth of small talk and candlelight dinners could have. During those hot ten seconds we had shared a passion most lovers would never know.

She pulled away from me without letting go and looked into my eyes. "You were so great in there. Where did you learn to fight like that? It was so incredibly brutal!" She rolled her eyes back like a feeding shark and the look endeared her to me.

I shrugged. "I got lucky."

"Lucky? No, that wasn't luck. That was *fantastic*." She eyed me shrewdly. "Are you sure you're an insurance salesman?"

"Sure I'm sure. You wanna go to my place and look at some policies?"

She threw her head back and laughed. "Are you asking me to go home with you and look at insurance policies when we've just met?"

"I'm sorry. I'm paid on commission and I get carried away sometimes."

She laughed again. "It's all right. I accept your apology and your offer." She kissed me again.

"Britt, does this mean we're going steady?" I deadpanned, then put a blush on. Like my father, I could blush at will, part of the Strait arsenal of charm.

"Well." She gave me an odd, searching look. "At least for tonight. Listen, though, I have to make a phone call. Wait here and I'll be right back."

"I'll go with you," I said quickly. The idea of her walking away terrified something deep inside me.

"I'll only be a minute. Wait right here." She pushed off, and I was left with a double armful of nothing and a bellyful of want. I watched her walk a block then turn a corner, feeling as if I might die.

I slunk to a sunken doorway to wait. It smelled of vomit and urine. I checked my pistol then put it back in the shoulder rig. I took a switchblade from my back pocket. I rolled it in my hand, considering the possibilities. If she came back with her pimp, I'd have to knife him. I'd come up from behind and use the sentry-removal technique: left arm around his neck, right hand driving the blade between the fifth and sixth ribs, with a little twist to make sure the heart stopped pumping. There didn't seem to be any way around it; my emotions were over-powering my sense. I did some stretches to loosen up my body and clear my head, but the adrenaline was retreating and the alcohol was shambling back, shameless and unafraid.

I checked my chrono. Ten minutes on the gallows. Street life crept by, the sun was dying, and the animals crawled out of their holes, hungry for kicks. Hornbugs, devils disguised as middle-aged businessmen, slid sinister looks to the young boys who sold their youth for hard cash. Bums stumbled by, incomprehensible hopelessness blurring their eyes, and clubbers, slaves to dance and bizarre fashion, paraded past like strange peacocks. As usual, Heaven was in full retreat.

I did some more stretches and checked my chrono again. Fifteen minutes. My heart became so heavy it sank down to my stomach and began to feed.

Three teddy boys wearing pin-striped suits and pompadours stopped in front of the doorway and demanded spare change. I showed them the knife, and they shrugged and moved on. Screaming broke out from across the street, where two drag queens pounced on a burb who had probably said the wrong thing. They scratched and kicked, and he covered his face and tried to escape, futilely crying out for the spifs. The queens harried him for half a block then let him stagger away, his face and neck bleeding from a dozen scratches, a hard lesson learned.

I decided I'd just learned a lesson about waiting around for strange whores when Britt came strolling down the sidewalk from the opposite direction she'd left. She walked alone, which meant I wouldn't have to answer to the Hayward Pimp Association after all. I lurked in the dim doorway and watched, admiring her form the way a naturalist would a tigress. She stopped at the spot we'd parted and pivoted, casting black eyes in each direction. The panic on her face made me feel flattered and uneasy at once. I snuck up behind her and grabbed her by the waist.

"Gimme all your love!" I demanded.

She whirled, and I saw that lethal face again. "Don't you *ever* do that to me!"

"Afraid I got tired of waiting?"

She gave me a long, penetrating stare. "Yes, I was." Her eyes dropped to my chest, and she adjusted my lapels. "Let's go see those policies."

8

I managed to drive home without killing myself or anyone else.
I always drove well, even when loaded. What I lost in reflexes
I gained in an instinctual feel for the road, a sort of psychic ra-
dar. What didn't help my driving was the fact I kept blacking
out. Chunks of time vanished without a trace as I slipped in and
out of the stream of consciousness. I'd emerge from the black
waters and find myself laughing insanely at a joke I couldn't
remember and driving down a street I didn't recognize. But it
seemed okay because I was blacking out other things, too. I was
forgetting I was a murderer and the woman next to me was a
whore, and in my black little world that seemed important.

I broke surface and found myself standing in my kitchen,
unable to recall how I'd got there or what I'd done with the
Caddy. I was mixing drinks, margaritas by the looks of them.
Two bottles of tequila sat in front of me, one empty and the
other not much better off. The stove top was the site of a beer-
can massacre, and kitchen utensils and uncoordinated ingredients sprawled on the countertops. I must have tried impress-
ing her with my excellent culinary skills, I surmised. The
kitchen floor tipped this way and that and it seemed funny it
should, so I laughed. A sweeter laughter answered from the
direction of the living room, so I laughed some more.

I blacked out again. Nothing really noticeable, more like a
long blink. I surfaced leaning against the counter, breathing like
a winded moose, rolling with invisible waves of nausea. I noticed my arms were bare, which meant I was no longer wearing
my jacket, and by further supposition I assumed my shoulder
holster and gyrapistol were exposed. It was good to know all the
drinking hadn't dulled my deductive powers, not by a hair. I
looked down at the 20 mm hanging from my side, big as day-

light. I didn't think it would do much to substantiate my insur-
ance-salesman story, but I bet it did a lot toward adding to my
mystery and glamour.

The drinks looked more or less finished, so I got a hand
wrapped around each and prepared myself for the trek to the
living room. The floor rolled sickeningly, and I wasn't sure I
was up to the journey. Another laugh floated in from the living room, and I got motivated. I shoved off from the counter
like a one-legged sailor negotiating a deck during a hurricane
and nearly slipped on the wet tile. I steadied myself in the middle of the floor then launched myself at the doorway. I missed
by a foot, laid a shoulder into the doorjamb, executed a ca-
reening half spin into the living room and managed to spill only
half the drinks.

"Some bartender you are," Britt mocked from the sofa. I
stood up straight and weaved with dignity toward the coffee
table. Beer cans and empty glasses crowded its top, a damning
congregation of mute witnesses. Have I drunk that much? I
asked myself, and couldn't say whether I had or hadn't.

"Are you sure you're an insurance salesman?" she asked.
Her lipstick was smeared and her top was unbuttoned to the
waist, exposing a black lace bra. Was that my work? I wondered, pining for moments forever lost.

"Of course," I answered. "I mean, why not?" I wanted to
sit on the sofa beside her, but if I sat down I knew I wouldn't
be getting back up, not tonight.

"Where'd an insurance salesman learn to fight like that?"
she slurred.

"You've obviously never been to an insurance convention,"
I said. "You need those skills just to get a drink at the beer
counter."

"You wear a big gun."

"I'm a firm believer in the hard sell."

"Really? What kind of insurance do you sell?"

"All kinds. We're nationwide." The story snaked along on
its own. Lies come easy to a natural liar.

"Life insurance?"

"Sure."

"So you pay people when someone gets killed." She smiled a funny half smile, *funny* as in *weird*.

"Yes, basically."

The funny half smile matured into a funny full smile. "Are you sure it isn't the other way around?"

I frowned. My head felt thick and I couldn't get a firm grip on her meaning, so I turned away from the labor. I supposed it was time to discuss prices, but I felt that would detract from the romance of the moment.

"You're wondering how much," she said, and romance fell flat on its face. An ugly silence hung around for a while.

"Yeah, it always comes down to that," I said. "But we have to make a living."

"Yes," she said, and stood, stretching like a lazy cat. She finished with a sigh, came around the table and stopped in front of me. She took the forgotten drinks out of my hands and let them fall to the floor. Entwining her arms around my neck, she pulled her body tight against mine and said, "You'll pay me, but not with your money."

"With what, then?" I asked, afraid for my soul.

"We'll talk about that in the morning." She took me by the hand and led me to the bedroom.

It took me about ten seconds to get undressed, and I did so with all the grace of an elephant trying to shake off a collapsed tent.

Britt took her time. She was the kind of girl who could look languid falling down a flight of stairs. Every movement, every turn of the hand, every roll of hip was a luxurious tease, fluid with an understated sensuality that didn't come off as burlesque. It was nothing anyone could learn; you either had it or you never would. She had it and she wasn't unaware of the fact.

I sat on the bed and tried to act as if I'd seen it all before, but we both knew better. When she finally ran out of clothes, I ran out of breath. She stood there for a moment, hands on firm hips, promise in her posture. Long muscles rippled, toned and hard, and there was a ruthless desire in her eyes that didn't lean anywhere near tenderness.

"You're going to hurt me," I whispered in a voice heavy with doom. She acted as if she didn't hear me and flicked off the lights. She stood in perfect skin, her form defined by the deluge of moonlight pouring in from the window, and I nearly drowned in the intensity of that mean moment.

She pounced. Caught by surprise, I was pinned in three seconds flat, the victim of an obvious professional. She sat on my chest, put her fingers in my hair and sank her teeth into the flesh of my shoulder.

"Vampire!" I yiped. "I knew it!"

Her head came back up, and the blood on her teeth and lips appeared black in the moonlight. That's *my* blood, I thought, and a malaise spread through my heart.

"So," I said. "You want to play rough." I grabbed her by the shoulders and rolled left, and the power struggle began.

There is an animal in all of us. A vicious, ruthless beast crouching in the cage of our hearts. Most keep it locked away, embarrassed by its grotesque face, shamed by its ugly methods.

Britt's beast didn't live in a cage. It lived behind a thin curtain, a fabric so sheer that if you looked hard enough you could see it pacing restlessly back and forth. I'd seen the beast poke its head out when she warned off the redhead and during the fight. Now, in bed, the beast ripped the curtain down. It was at the controls; the beast had become Britt and Britt was the beast.

There wasn't a moment of tenderness or an instant of love—those weren't the emotions that fueled the fire. It was a brutal, muscular contest, an act of black passion that lay somewhere between war and orgy. I was stronger, but Britt was quicker and gifted with a powerful sense of leverage, a wolflike feel for weakness. We grappled and sweated and scratched and bit, and crawled to the highest peak of pleasure and plunged into the deepest pit of pain, and the two mixed and fused until I couldn't tell one from the other. I ebbed above and below waves of alcoholic stupor and at one exhausted moment nearly submitted to her terrible will. But the idea of giving in to her terrified something at the very core of my soul. When I looked into those burning black eyes, I instinctively understood that giving in would entail something more than just having to say uncle.

I realized just how little I knew about her. For all I knew, she was a psychopath with a thing for castration; the City was full of them. I felt like the male black widow spider in the grips of its mate, and it was with a fearful desperation I struggled for dominance.

I don't know who won—maybe no one was supposed to. But hours into the black act, I slipped under for good.

9

I awoke to a pounding at the apartment door. I crawled out of bed, my brain in traction. My equilibrium had deserted me, and I staggered to the door like a cripple who'd lost his crutches.

I opened the door. It was Crawley, his naked body bloated and lily-white. Two gaping holes left his chest deflated, and his scanhand was missing. Of course it's missing, an inner voice shrieked, I took it from him!

"I need a hand! Can you give me a hand?" he screeched in my face. "Don't you get it? I need a fucking hand!" He shoved his way past me and shambled into the kitchen. From the door I watched him pulling utensils and ingredients from the cupboards.

"Guests will be here any minute and I haven't even started on the carbaigne sauce!" he wailed, his bare feet slapping on the tiles. "I'll be the laughingstock of the entire poetry circuit!"

Blood began dripping from the stump, forming a puddle on the kitchen floor. That'll be hell to clean up, a delirious inner voice pointed out. The trickle became a stream, and the stream a torrent. The rush of thick, hot blood hit me with the intensity of a fire hose, pinning me against the wall. Crawley rolled his eyes back and screamed. Out of respect for the dead I joined him.

My own voice woke me. I wiped frantically at the sickeningly warm blood on my chest until I realized it was only sweat. I breathed with hoarse gasps, my throat raw with screams.

"Bad dreams, dear?" The words came from a dark corner near the window and were made ugly by sarcasm. My internal clock told me it was well past noon, but the bedroom was as black as a tomb. The heavy curtains were drawn, and light squeezed in through the tiniest of pinholes. The burning red eye of a cigarette floated at hip level in the corner from which the voice had come, and I could make out the faint outline of a body.

I felt as though I'd spent the night in the dryer with a rabid alley cat. Bruises and scratches up and down my body competed for sympathy. I propped myself up on one elbow and rubbed my temples with thumb and index finger.

"Oh, poor baby," said a voice as cold as a pimp's heart. "You don't feel well?"

I stared at her silhouette. In the hand that wasn't holding the cigarette, she gripped a dim shape that looked big and familiar. "Pretty grouchy before your first cup of kelpee, I see," I said, my tongue tasting like something I wouldn't put in my mouth.

"Go to hell," she snarled.

I stared at her form, and a minute dragged its feet to the chopping block. "Be honest with me now, Britt," I said. "You're really the Devil, aren't you?"

A lethal shape rose in front of her and was caught and defined by the needles of light from the window. Oh, I thought. The big familiar thing is my gyrapistol. Its snout pointed at my head.

"Afraid I wasn't going to tip?" I asked.

"I'm not a whore."

"I know that."

"And you're not an insurance salesman."

"I know that, too."

"You're a murdering thief," she spit out.

"Am not, you big liar."

"Tell Rolland Crawley that," she growled.

"Bring him here and I will."

"It's a little late for that. I saw you walk out of his apartment with his hand in a bag!" she shouted indictingly.

Oh-ho, I thought. So she was the one in the lovely head wrap and shades. I had the same trouble with memories as I did with women: getting them was easy, convincing them to hang around was the trick I couldn't figure. "It wasn't a hand," I said. "It was a bag of synthetic carrots I borrowed from Rolly. I was making stew for the big shindig."

"I found him inside on the floor," she screeched, hysteric with incredulity at my dashing defense. "Dead and missing a hand!"

I bet she thought she had an answer for everything. She was edging me in points, and that was a damn shame since she had the gun. "Dead and handless? Really? I thought he looked a little down."

She made a low guttural sound. "This is all a big joke to you, isn't it?"

"Is that a trick question?"

She yelled at me for a moment, then calmed down enough to demand, "Where's my money?"

"I thought you said you weren't a whore," I protested.

"I'm not! I want my quarter of a million creds."

"Jesus! Isn't that a little steep for one night?"

"I want the money you stole."

"You don't have an extraordinarily high opinion of me, do you?" I said. "What money was I supposed to have stolen?"

"The goddamn money you took from Rolland Crawley's bank account!" She showed her exasperation by shoving the snout of the pistol at me. "The quarter million!"

"Oh, *that* money." I folded my arms and set my jaw, the very embodiment of proud defiance. "I won't tell you. And you can't tickle it out of me, though you can try if you want."

"You'll tell me or I'll shoot you."

"It's in the living room closet."

She gestured with the pistol. "Let's go."

"Let me ask you a question first," I said.

"What?"

"Do you know how to use that thing?"

"I know how to pull a trigger."

"How do you know there's a round chambered?"

"Oh, I don't know, you just strike me as the kind of macho jerk who would carry it around with a round chambered."

She had me figured. "One more question," I said.

"Is it important?"

"I think it is," I said somberly.

"Go ahead."

"Does this mean we're not going steady anymore?" I asked. She screamed and I felt I could take that either way. "Because I'd hate to blow what could be a beautiful relationship over a silly little misunderstanding like this."

She didn't say a word, but I could sense her trembling. I could almost hear the hiss of burning fuse.

"Heck, we'll talk about all that later," I said, getting out of bed. "Let's get you your money, what do you say?"

She wouldn't let me put my pants on, so I went into the living room in the buff.

"It's in the vault," I said. The "vault" was a closet with a heavy steel door.

"Open it," she said flatly.

"It has a combination lock. It's 36-6-11. Start left, pass the second number twice."

"Open it," she repeated. She probably thought it was booby-trapped, that I was trying to pull a fast one. I was shocked at how transparent I obviously was.

"I can't see without the lights," I said. She turned them on, and I took a good look at her. She was fully dressed, and her lipstick and makeup were perfect. I liked a woman who made an effort to look good all the time, but unfortunately the pistol clashed badly with the outfit, spoiling the overall effect. I thought about telling her, but she didn't seem the type to take criticism gracefully. As I moved to the closet, I asked, "How'd you find me, anyway?"

"The reclamation crew asked for you when they came to drag Rolland away. I looked you up in the book."

"Of course."

"I followed you from your office to that bar," she said. "Since you're an idiot, it was easy."

"So everything that happened last night was just a big act," I said.

She stone faced it, but I thought I saw something in her eyes that told me I was wrong. Maybe if I bought her flowers and groveled, she'd take me back.

"Get on with it," she ordered.

I crouched in front of the dial. "So what's your connection with Crawley?"

She didn't say anything.

"Lovers?"

She laughed harshly. "Not hardly."

"You gave him the money, didn't you?"

"Yes, I did," she said. "It doesn't matter if I tell you. Once I get the money, you won't be telling anyone anything."

I didn't like the sound of that. It made me feel temporary. "Who'd you steal the money from?" I asked.

"What makes you think I stole it?"

"Because you don't make that kind of plastic turning tricks on Hayward. Not even with your act."

Under her makeup she might have blushed. "I told you, I'm not a whore. I liberated it from my reactionary parents."

"Oh, I see. And Crawley was the treasurer for the impending revolution."

"Stop screwing around with the dial and open the door," she said.

I stopped screwing around with the dial and opened the door. Inside was a file cabinet, the twin of the one in my office. "It's in there," I said, pointing at the cabinet.

She moved closer but stayed out of arm's reach.

"How do you open it?"

"With a key."

"Where's the key?"

"In my pants." We went back to the bedroom and got the key. She still wouldn't let me put my pants on.

Back in the living room, I said, "I'll open it."

"No," she said, taking the key. "I'll do it." She probably thought I had a gun in there. I did. And that wasn't all. I acted disappointed, mimicking her perpetual pout.

She made me lie on my belly with my hands on my head. She was no fool. She kept distrustful eyes on me as she inserted the key and turned.

The spray of tear gas hit her in the face, knocking her out of the closet. I leaped up from the floor like a coiled spring and backhanded the pistol out of her hand. It ricocheted off the wall and scuttled under the furniture.

Even with a lungful of tear gas she was fast. She swung out a professional roundhouse kick from nowhere that caught me flush on the cheek. The world went fuzzy, but I shook out of it in time to hop away from a vicious front kick aimed at my exposed testicles. She moved into the attack, wiping her teary eyes with one hand. In the other hand she held a six-inch blade.

"Hey," I said. "Why don't you throw that thing down before you put somebody's eye out."

She grunted and lunged at my throat with the knife. I leaned left, and the point of the blade shot over my shoulder. I aimed the heel of my hand at the bridge of her nose. She ducked it handily and opened up my right thigh up with a low horizontal slash. Warm blood trickled down my leg. I took two steps back and we squared off.

"Next time I'll cut your dick off!" she promised.

"You're not a very nice girl, are you?" I shouted, my direst fears realized—a date with a homicidal castrater!

She screamed and jumped forward, sweeping the blade up in an arc designed to open me up from groin to sternum like a gutted fish. I leaned back, and the tip of the knife tickled my chest hairs. When her knife hand apexed at eye level, I got a wrist lock on it and squeezed. She grunted with pain and tried to drive a knee into my beleaguered groin. I twisted sideways, and the knee numbed my hip. I completed the turn and with one fluid motion twisted her arm behind her back. The knife thunked on the carpet, and she howled, more in anger than pain.

I put my lips next to her ear and whispered breathlessly, "I never knew a first date could be so much fun!"

She screamed again and brought a spiked heel down on my instep. I yelped with pain but held on to her wrist. She did it again. I yelped again. She brought her foot up for another go, and I released my grip and shoved her to the carpet. She went down, executed a somersault with the agility of a gymnast and sprang to her feet, ready for round two. I picked the knife up and got into my knife-fighting stance: left foot forward, slight crouch, weight balanced on the balls of my feet, right hand holding the knife back near my thigh, left hand forward, ready to create an opening for the blade.

She sized me up, then broke for the door. I didn't try to stop her. I reckoned we both needed our space right then. After she worked the bolts she jerked the door open and spun around.

"You idiot!" she screamed. "They'll kill you and your kind, too! Not just us!"

I stared at her, uncertain of our mutual feelings or even if our relationship was a viable one. "Well, don't go away mad," I said. "How about dinner tonight? Do you like Chinese? My treat."

She screamed and was gone.

After a moment I hobbled to the door and looked outside in case she'd had second thoughts and was pouting down the hall. She wasn't. I slammed the door and cried, "Love is dead!"

I retrieved my traitorous pistol from beneath the coffee table and opened a window to expel the odor of tear gas. I went to the bedroom and took my wallet from my pants.

It was about a thousand credits lighter than it had been last night. At least she didn't go away empty-handed. I sat on the edge of the bed and held my head in my hands. What was I doing taking home strange killers? What the hell was I thinking of? Hadn't my mother warned me about girls who wore black lipstick? Had I used a condom? What the hell was wrong with me?

My offended instep began to throb and swell nicely, so I stuck it in a bucket of ice water while I ate a breakfast of rehydrated egg substitute and chunks of protein shaped like sausages. I put the dishes back in the sink and forced myself to drink eight glasses of water to combat alcohol dehydration. It didn't do much for my headache so I chewed up four aspirin, took a long shower and wrote the day off as an unsalvagable loss.

I spent the day in bed with my foot elevated on cushions from the couch. I read from the seemingly endless passages of Cervantes's *The Adventures of Don Quixote,* ate kelp chips, drank vitabeer and contemplated the current state of romance in the world. Looking from the window of Cervantes's old classic, it could be readily seen that romantic love had taken on a decidedly evil slant since Don Quixote's day. Instead of some divine and wondrous ocean lovers were only too happy to drown in, romantic love had become a huge vat of radioactive waste, mutating anyone who came near it. I felt it an obvious truth that over years of exposure, modern love had made an emotional mutant out of me. My romantic motives ranged from sinister to sterile and all vile things between.

My feelings for Britt represented a perfectly black example of that. I tried to look at the situation rationally, but a brutal gang of masked emotions muscled their way in and strong-armed my powers of reasoning. I knew instinctively it wasn't one of those sickly infatuations that would eventually wither away. The brute was loose in my heart and was out to fix me, but good. If I was to be rid of the beast, I'd have to sneak up behind the big bastard and go at him with a butcher knife. At the moment I didn't have the emotional fortitude or desire to do the job.

It wasn't just her diabolical beauty, though that had a lot to do with it. It was her toughness, her independence. She was the kind of girl who wouldn't let a heel like me walk all over her, at least not without pulling a knife. It struck me that she could have handled those four barroom bravos by herself. She was evil, primal, a beast. She embodied cold violence, and framed in the fires of a cold and violent world. She was beautiful. I felt I was still on the side of the angels, but I found myself hopelessly in love with the Devil's daughter.

It was too bad she wanted to rob, castrate and kill me. It didn't seem a promising start to a relationship. Around midnight I swooned myself to sleep.

10

Sunday was carnival day on Hayward. Traffic was closed off for ten blocks, and stalls and temporary shops sprouted overnight like toadstools on the street and sidewalks. Everything was for sale: knickknacks, sex, electronics, weapons, drugs, people, produce from the City's thousands of backyard and roof gardens, even some real meat if you had that kind of money, though anybody who bought meat was taking their chances. Usually if you thought you were buying beef or veal you were really getting Labrador or goat or even dressed-up soy.

Suburbanites came to gawk at the lowlife and buy things you couldn't get legally in the burbs. Every now and then I would even spot someone from the Hill, dressed down and looking for kicks. It was a special day for the Hayward denizens, too. The pimps wore their sharpest outfits, the punks put their hair up, and the ridiculously overproportioned transvestites strutted in self-conscious parody. It reminded me of a circus I'd went to as a kid; it had the same kind of flash and flurry, except on Hayward the ringmasters were pimps, the clowns dressed in drag, and all the animals had only two legs.

I looked down on the street through the blinds of my office window. I'd been scanning the crowd all morning, hoping to see Britt lurking around. I was enamored with the idea she would take another try at me. With that possibility in mind, I wore an extra pistol and my best cologne.

An old woman with a produce stand was doing lively trade under the three o'clock shadow of the wino saint. I thought about strolling down and buying some fresh vegetables. It was an expensive idea, but my wallet was fat with a fresh advance from Second Fed, and it had come to the point that I'd forgotten what a real carrot or potato tasted like.

I went to the coatrack and selected a black leather motorcycle jacket with spikes on the lapels and epaulets. It went well with my black T-shirt, mean jeans and jump boots. I checked my hair in the mirror. It was doing the carefree spiky thing, which was fine for Hayward on Sunday. I locked up the office and moved down to the street.

It was a warm summer afternoon, but you could feel that junky autumn lurking around the corner. I bought two carrots and an apple at the produce stand for fifty creds each. She gave me a discount because I was a local. I bought a quart bottle of warm homemade beer from another stall, then sauntered around, checking out the action. I eventually retired to the steps of what used to be a church but now was Pinky's Porno Emporium. I shared the steps with a gang of neopunks. They were young and drunk, flaunting pierced noses, tall mohawks and bad attitudes. I ate my apple and drank my yeasty beer, watching the crowd go by, thinking about my next move.

I wanted to get out of the City. There was a lot of negative energy floating around, and sooner or later it would be knocking at my door. The problem with running away was that there wasn't anywhere to go. Even if I somehow got my hands on a relocation permit from the Party, I couldn't go anywhere except another city. The suburbs had laws to keep people like me out, the farmlands were garrisoned fortresses, and what was left of the countryside was supposed to be still living in anarchy, unrecovered since the corporate collapse. Not to mention being contaminated with nuclear and chemical waste.

One of the punks, a cute girl of about eighteen with matching blue eyes and hair, sent over what one of us imagined to be a seductive look. I met it head-on and she smiled. I smiled back and was beginning to feel flattered when her eyes dropped purposefully to my bottle. I went back to watching the crowd.

Eventually the punks moved on to wherever punks went on warm Sunday afternoons. I wanted to go with them, forget everything and just worry about getting drunk and finding a girl to spend the long night with. A simple, irresponsible life, uncomplicated with moral dilemmas and ugly emotions, each passing day a bridge ashed behind me. A half-dozen chetniks claimed the steps, bare chested and sweating in their fake-fur trousers. They talked about the girls going by in gutter Russian and passed a bottle of whoosh around, taking sniffs and laughing, marching their youth to impatient graves.

Since I couldn't run from my troubles, I'd have to confront and destroy them. That was one of those essential lessons I picked up since I'd become a bogeyman, one of the reasons I was still alive in a perilous profession. If I waited until my troubles caught up with me, they would. I had to root them out and squash them before the worm turned and they came to squash me. That meant I'd have to get down to some serious detecting.

I got up and slipped into the crowd, letting the human current carry me down the sidewalk, eating my carrots as I went. They tasted like dirt.

A fistfight raged in front of the St. Chris. Two shaggy-haired winos, one young, one old, hammered away at each other, heads down, swinging blindly. Some of the crowd around them shouted encouragements, though they probably didn't know either one. The young one got a handful of gray hair and started arcing crude uppercuts into the old guy's face. The funny thing was they were probably drinking buddies at other times.

A middle-aged burb woman bulging out of a grotesque flower-print dress turned to me and said, "Why don't you do something? If that was you out there, wouldn't you want someone to do something?"

"Depends if I was winning or not," I said, and she shot me a look that matched her dress. She looked at the fight with utter distaste, yet didn't seem able to turn away. I looked at the faces of the other spectators. The burbs stared with a fearful fascination, relieved that they weren't involved, afraid that somehow they might be. The City people were either dead eyed with apathy or rabid with excitement.

The old wino was on the ground, and the young wino kicked him in the head until he got tired. A tall pimp came out of the crowd with a big chrome revolver and broke it up like a sheriff in an old Western. He was just trying to be symbolic, though.

The fight was already over. The victor waved his hands over his head and whooped it up through bloody lips. The crowd turned their backs on him and moved on, looking for new excitement. He was interesting when he was kicking someone's head in, but now he was just another bleeding wino. I looked up at the wino saint. From street level his cherubic smile looked sinister.

I walked inside the St. Chris, where it was cool and quiet. The big ceiling fans rotated lazily over mostly empty tables, churning cigarette smoke to haze, and a solemnness hung in the air. A handful of patrons shared the emptiness, mostly off-duty streetwalkers smoking joints and full-time rummies getting an early start on the evening. If you wanted fun and excitement you went outside. You came in here to contemplate, consider your losses and brood.

The same redhead sat at one end of the bar. When she looked over and saw who it was, she made a point of looking the other way.

I took a stool at the other end of the bar. Amal idled at the redhead's end and tried hard to pretend I wasn't there. I suspected my popularity wasn't at an all-time high. After a lot of innocent smiles and heavy gesturing on my part, he walked over as if he'd strapped on fifty-pound weights instead of sandals that morning.

"You shouldn't come around here, Jake. There are people who want to hurt you."

"You don't know the half of it," I said. "I came in here for information, not trouble."

He looked at me as if I was setting him up for a particularly cruel prank.

"You remember the girl I was with Friday?" I asked.

"Your woman."

I grimaced. "Yeah, that one. Remember when she got that call?"

He nodded.

"If you never saw her before that night, how did you know it was for her?"

He rolled his eyes back as though he was trying to see into his brain and said, "I asked him to describe her."

"Did he ask for her by name first?"

"Yeah, he did."

I breathed a sigh of thanks to a usually hostile god. "And what was that name?"

He told me. I dropped twenty creds on the bar and walked over to the redhead. She heard me coming but wouldn't look my way until I stood beside her. When she did look, she squinched her nose up as if I'd been paddling around in the sewer all morning.

"Buy you a drink?" I asked.

"No, thanks, I ain't thirsty."

"How about a pack of joints, then?"

She shot her chin toward a pack on the bar. "I got plenty."

I stared at her and she blew smoke in my face.

"Maybe you'll answer a question for me, then," I said. She didn't say no so I asked. "I was with a girl the other night. Do you remember her?"

"Do I? How could I forget? She gave me the creeps." She squinched up her nose and slid me a look. "No offense if she's yours."

"None taken and she's not. Have you seen her anywhere before or since Friday?"

"No, never."

"Are you sure? A lot of girls come and go."

"I'm sure. I'd remember that one." She squinched up her nose again.

"Keep doing that and it'll stay that way," I warned.

"Huh?"

"Nothing. Thanks." I made to leave, but she caught my arm and presented me with a smile that would appear a lush oasis to a lonely drunk.

"Say," she said. "I'll take that drink now."

I smiled, bought her a double and went back to my office.

Sitting down at the desk, I pulled the handscanner in front of me. After it warmed up, I went to the name file and retrieved the Chamberlains's scan data.

I hadn't paid too much attention to the data during the scans. I was taking too much pleasure in toying around with Dash. I pulled a notepad close to the scanner and picked up a pen. I noted first that the Chamberlains lived at 1206 Stag Hill, Hillsdale. The Hill. I'd guessed that much. The second thing I noted was their classified credit rating. That meant one or both of them worked in the upper echelon of the Party. The last item I noted paired up with a hunch of mine and made me lean back in my chair and release a long low whistle. The Chamberlains had one daughter, adopted. By her birth date she was twenty years old. Her name was Britt Bernice Chamberlain. The caller at the St. Chris had asked for a Ms. Chamberlain. It was either a king-hell coincidence or I'd discovered a big goddamn clue. A whole new outlook on the tangle walked in, stared me in the face and dared me to do something about it.

11

I drove to City University. C.U. sprawled throughout the borough of Riverside, ten klicks down the river from my office. It was the part of town that had poetry bars with tags like L'Expression de Vie! and posters announcing the Impending Marxist Victory. In the lot where I parked, a dozen young underfed students with fervent eyes and rampant acne listened to a similar type in a red beret declaiming and gesturing wildly from a tiny podium. He barked nervously into a microphone that fed back every time he tried to raise his voice, and the banner draped across the front of the podium said he was addressing the evils of Creeping Neocapitalism In Our City. Though the lad's rap was impassioned and trembling with conviction, my friend Moses Perry would have harangued him into the asphalt. When I got out of the Caddy, the audience, without doubt all buddies of the speaker, fixed me with ravenous eyes. Had I come to join their cause? Would I be fervent and self-righteous with them?

I smiled and headed for the art building. I wanted to hang around and crack a few nuts of wisdom with them but I was there on business.

The receptionist's desk for the art department's offices lay abandoned, so I moved directly to the hall beyond. I walked past a bank of doors until I came to one labeled Dr. Joseph Drake, Professor Of Art Studies. I barged in without knocking. An anemic-looking man with a receding hairline, scraggly mustache and thick glasses hunched over a small steel tray, rolling a joint.

"I told you I wasn't to be disturbed while I'm on my afternoon break, Ms. Rossalini," he said without looking up.

I sat on a folding chair in front of his desk, and eventually he looked up. His face broke into a grin, and he stood up halfway, stretching a hand over the desk. "Hey, killer, how's death?"

I shook his hand and said, "Not bad, Joe, how's the hairline?"

"Like your intelligence, Jake, receding every day." He whinnied and sat back down.

Joe and I had served together in the army, back when there was an army. I was a wild-eyed young Ranger, and he was a manic-depressive draftee serving as a chopper pilot. The Party drafted him during his graduate studies, ran him through flight school, then shipped him to a Ranger fire base in the Colorado Rockies. The World Party had clawed to the top only six years before but was still consolidating its power base, especially in areas where a world government was still being violently resisted, like in the area that had once been called the Western U.S. Joe had piloted many of the missions I'd participated in, including the last one, and we'd become instant friends when we'd discovered we were both from the City.

We'd drink in the base club together, a perfect pair: he bought the beers with his warrant officer pay and I'd drink them. He'd whine manically and I'd pretend to listen. He'd get his frustrations out and I'd get drunk. Perfect.

"I need a favor, Joe," I said, pulling up my chair.

"I bet you do." He leaned back on the spring of his swivel chair and pushed his glasses up the bridge of his nose. "What is it this time? Need your living room painted?"

"Nope. It's a lot easier than that."

"Oh, really?" His freshly rolled cigarette disappeared into his mouth then came back out coated with saliva. He lit it. The earthy smell of hashish snaked from its tip.

"Sure. You get invited to a lot of art parties on the Hill, don't you?"

"You know I do. The beef eaters like to have a few scholarly *artiste* types on hand to lend a quiet humility to the affair. We nod our heads and make vague remarks about the 'emotional quotient' of some horrible junk that some exec's wife spent two hours' work and a lifetime of feelings on. Then we take our fee and go home.''

"Sounds like a fun evening," I observed.

"It's a load of shit. But the food is real and it's a free drunk, so what the hell."

"How do you get on the Hill? Past the security, I mean."

"Certified invitation and a handscan at the gate to make sure you're the same person the invite says you are."

"When's the next party?" I asked.

"Well, let's see." He put an index finger to the bridge of his glasses. His thinking position. "The Petersons are showing their retarded son's impressionist works on Tuesday."

"He's really retarded?"

"No, he just paints like he is."

"I want to go," I said.

Joe eyed me suspiciously. "Since when do you have an interest in the Hill art scene?"

"I don't. It's business. I need to see someone on the Hill and I can't think of any other way to get past all the armed patrols, mine fields and electrified fences."

"Why don't you ask this person to send you a visitor's permit?" Joe asked.

"I want it to be a surprise visit."

"Oh," he said, and got back into his thinking position. After two minutes of that I was ready for some heavy wisdom to come down. "I could probably call the Petersons and tell them you're a visiting impressionist expert. From France. That'd do it."

"Great."

He gave me that suspicious look again. "You're not going to cause any trouble, are you?"

"Shucks, no," I said. "I'll even bone up on my high school French. You'll see."

"Okay, I'll trust you." He smiled shrewdly from behind a veil of exhaled smoke. "It's going to cost you, though."

I was expecting it. Ever since Joe had developed the habit of smoking a half gram of hash a day he was always short of cash. "How much?"

"Three hundred."

"Jesus. Okay."

Joe looked surprised. I knew he'd expected me to haggle with him but I wasn't in the mood.

"Business that good, Jake?" he asked.

"A cred here, a cred there. Plus all the aluminum cans I save up."

"You know," Joe said, his eyes getting distant, "sometimes I wish I was still in the action. The gunplay, the glamour, the girls."

"Yeah," I said dryly, "especially the girls. What time does this shindig go down?"

"The showing starts at nine. But we want to get there early to load up on drinks before we have to look at that shit. Be here at seven and we'll take my ride."

"Great. I'll bring the creds." We stood up and shook hands again.

"Yeah, just like old times," Joe said, his eyes getting misty again. "Me transporting you into the shit."

"I hope it works out better than last time," I said.

His dreamy smile mutated into a grimace. "Couldn't be much worse."

I walked out to my car. The rally was still going strong, but my mind was elsewhere. I started my car and pointed it home.

The last time Joe had transported me into the "shit," he'd dropped me off in the middle of what the history books called the Houston Insurrection. It was supposed to have been a quick in-and-out raid on the rebel command-and-control area. We'd execute the rebel leadership, then be airlifted out before the troops could react. Their command structure was scattered over a square mile of downtown Houston, so the entire Second Ranger Battalion was mobilized.

It was obvious from the moment we touched down that the mission had been compromised: they were waiting for us. The rebel militia wasn't a highly trained unit but they were fanatics: they knew the pogrom that would follow if they lost. The Party would execute anyone even slightly involved, so the rebels literally had nothing to lose.

We accomplished the mission, but with incredible casualty rates. During two days of the most vicious street fighting since

Stalingrad in 1942 or the Denver Rebellion in 2011, we successfully liquidated the rebel leadership and a fair percentage of the militia. What was left of the battalion assembled on a high school football field and radioed for extraction. We were sitting at about fifty percent casualties, dead, missing or wounded. Whole platoons had disappeared, all of Bravo Company had vanished, surrounded and wiped out in a bus depot.

I remembered lying in the darkness, surrounded by the smell of cordite and grass, thinking about all the friends I'd lost. Word came around that since the mission had taken so long to accomplish, transportation was currently unavailable. For three hours we lay exposed in the field, getting hammered by rebel mortar and rocket fire, waiting for helicopters that never arrived. The battalion commander finally decided to disobey orders and shift to a more defendable position until we got positive word on the time of extraction.

We took our wounded and fought our way into the adjoining high school complex. Most of us made it. We stacked desks and crates of textbooks in the windows and waited for the blessed angel of extraction. The rebels knew what we were waiting for and came at us in desperate swarms. We beat back wave after wave through the infinite night and into the next day. The bodies stacked up and our munitions dwindled. We called in a resupply drop, and they promised we'd get it. We didn't. The rebels did. Instead of landing on the roof of the high school, the parachuted crates of weapons, ammunition and explosives drifted into the hands of the rebels surrounding us. With these new resources they redoubled the attack.

When the bloodred sun crept behind the burning skyline, we were down to fifty men from the original eight hundred. The acting battalion commander, by then a first lieutenant, declared that extraction was a wet dream, shot the radio that told us to be patient and wait and decided we'd stage a breakout. We picked the weakest point in the closing ring and poured every bullet and grenade we had into it. We punched a hole just large enough to squeeze through, broke into our predesignated three-man escape-and-evasion teams and headed for the suburbs.

We ran like hunted jackals, chased by blood-hungry rebels. I was teamed with a big blond sergeant named Booker and a PFC with a belly wound named Garcia. Garcia had family in Houston and wanted to hole up with them. Sergeant Booker nixed the idea because he was a California surf boy and we weren't going to stop until we got to Venice Beach. Picking up weapons as we went, we fought a brutal running battle through the burning streets of Houston, killing anyone who got in our way.

Sergeant Booker caught a bullet with his head as we sprinted across a K mart parking lot. Garcia and I left him dead and twitching on the asphalt and dodged from building to building until dawn. We holed up in a bombed-out and looted hardware store and waited out the day. Party jets and helicopters pounded the city as streams of refugees choked the streets, heading for the countryside. I redressed Garcia's wound with cotton and tape I found in the store, but it wouldn't stop bleeding.

When night fell, I crept out. With an empty rifle I commandeered a pickup truck stacked with stereos and televisions from drunk looters. I drove back and loaded Garcia into the passenger seat. We drove through the dying city into the suburbs. Two hours later we ran into an advancing column of Party tanks who directed us to a Party fire base near the town of Waller, thirty miles northwest of Houston.

Garcia died on the way. He just ran out of blood. I spent three months in an army hospital at Fort Hood, Texas. They told me that as far as they knew I was the only Ranger who made it out. They never explained what happened exactly. Top secret.

During my stay the Party disbanded all four branches of the military and replaced it with the SPF. When I got out, more or less healed, they gave me sergeant stripes, a Purple Heart and an early discharge. I was happy to go.

12

I stopped at a Party food store on the way home, picked up a box of vitabeer, then walked next door to the Istanbul Kabob Shop and, after standing in line for twenty minutes, bought two kabobs. Turkish kabob shops had a reputation for using a fair percentage of real meat so they enjoyed enormous popularity. They also had the reputation of running dog- and cat-kidnapping rings, which answered the question as to where they got their meat. There were also stories of basement rat farms, but I tried not to think about that.

I swung by the Happy Hillbilly Pawnshop and picked up my TV, VCP and music system. Not happy with the twenty-five percent pawn fee, the happy hillbilly behind the counter tried to tack on a twenty-five percent "protection fee" to compensate for the extra security hired to protect the shop from a recent rash of lootings. I beat him on the quick draw, so I was excluded from the fee.

I parked in front of my apartment building and decided I'd take the brew and kabobs up first. Since I hadn't run in a week, guilt demanded I bypass the elevator and jog the stairs.

As I cleared the third landing, an explosion boomed down the stairwell. The acoustics of the stairwell weren't good enough to do a decent mariachi band justice, but they were good enough for me to be certain the explosion came from the fourth floor. In fact, the explosion had a distinctly personal sound to it. I set the vitabeer and kabobs down on the steps, drew my pistol and listened. The door of the fourth-floor landing banged open, followed by a jumble of footsteps on the concrete. Because of the switchback midway up the final flight, I couldn't see the landing, so I crouched low and waited.

Initially all I could hear was heavy breathing. Then whispers began floating down in short bursts, like the rustling of tines in a gusty wind. I couldn't quite make out what was being said.

I began moving up the steps, one at a time, pausing and listening between each. I reached the switchback and peered up the stairs.

They crouched on the landing deck with their backs to me. They were taking turns peeking through the cracked door that connected to the hallway. There were two of them.

"I don't know what the fuck happened," a Rastafarian with long dreadlocks spilling down the back of a faded field jacket said in an exasperated whisper. "Toby was jimmying the door and it exploded—*he* just exploded. Got his blood all over my jacket."

"Somebody must have heard it, they had to of," worried a tong with a crew cut. He wore a black nylon jacket with a stylized red tiger on the back. He sounded panicky and held a revolver up beside his head. "Someone'll call the spifs."

"Not in this part of the City they won't. Even if someone did call, they wouldn't come. This is a motherfuckin' no-go area." The Rasta sounded as if he was half trying to convince himself, but everything he said was true. "We just got to sit tight. When he comes out of the elevator, we'll get the keys to the door and vault and get the plastic. Ain't nothin' but a thing."

"Toby's dead, isn't he?" the tong asked.

"He sure as hell ain't takin' no nap, Georgie."

"When he sees Toby lying there he's going to get suspicious," the tong worried. He didn't sound motivated for the task at hand. Seeing a friend explode seemed to have snapped his nerve.

"Damn it, Georgie," the Rasta snapped, "the girl said I was the leader of this here team and we ain't gonna go till we get the stash. He won't have time to be suspicious anyway. The second that evil bastard steps off the elevator I'm gonna let him meet up with my little honey here." He hefted something I couldn't see.

I was willing to bet creds to croissants that the evil bastard in question was me and the little honey he was holding out of view wasn't his pet gerbil. It seemed certain they wanted to do me grave harm.

I crept around the switchback and pointed my pistol up at them. All my instincts begged me to shoot them in the back, but I was fearful of the amount of drinking that plan of action would entail.

"Hey, guys," I said. "Looking for me?"

The jumpy tong spun around first, his almond eyes bright with an awakened sense of mortality. His hands jerked over his head, the revolver in his hand forgotten.

I was willing to take prisoners, but the Rasta had other ideas. He shoved his pal Georgie down the stairs and hauled up a big archaic-looking, double-barreled .12-gauge shotgun. The sentimental guy was using his pal Georgie as a distraction so as to give himself enough time to let me have it with the lovely old antique.

Georgie hurtled toward me, arms flailing, blocking my shot. We seemed destined to collide unless I did something clever. I did the obvious instead, shooting Georgie twice in the chest. The impact of the gyrajets suspended his body for a split second between me and the Rasta.

A deafening double boom, and the nostalgic smell of cordite crammed every inch of the stairwell. Georgie was propelled down the stairs like the Superman of old, trailing a cape of blood and gore. I ducked the body but got caught in the ensuing downpour. I wiped the blood out of my eyes and aimed.

The landing was empty. I pumped up the stairs, nearly slipping on the messy steps. The door was swinging shut, and I fired three jets at it to make me feel good. The fractured door collapsed under the impact of my shoulder, and I did a roll into the hall, wondering how fast the Rasta could load his shotgun on the run.

He was halfway down the hall to the elevator, moving at a dead run, cursing and dropping shells as he went. It was too far for a good shot, so I rolled to my feet and sprinted after him, firing as I went.

I made the midway point and I still hadn't hit him. He was leaning with his back against the elevator doors, the call button lit. He clawed at the shotgun and jabbered insanely at me, his words jumbling together in his excitement.

Logic told me one or a combination of three things was about to happen. One, the elevator would arrive and he'd make good his escape. Two, he would load his gun and I would die because in the narrow hallway there was no way I could beat the spread of pellets. Or three, my favorite, I would get lucky and hit him with a wild shot. As it turned out, everything happened at once.

The elevator chimed and the doors slid open. The Rasta closed the shotgun with a triumphant *clack* as he backed into the elevator, shouting happy gibberish at me, bringing up the dual barrels of the shotgun. I dived onto my belly and bet all my chips on an all-or-nothing snap shot. I squeezed the trigger and my muscles reflexively tensed to receive the hail of shotgun pellets.

Half the Rasta's neck disappeared in a spray of blood and arteries, and his hands flew into the hair. The shotgun went off into the elevator ceiling, sending pellets whining up the shaft and bringing down a rain of ceiling tile. He stood for a moment, his arms held above him in the stance of somebody who had just scored a touchdown. I shot him again because it seemed like the right thing to do. His right rib cage exploded open, exposing lung and bone. He did a little twirl like a drunk ballerina and tumbled to the floor.

The elevator doors tried to slide shut, as if to signify the show was over, but one of the Rasta's legs was sticking out into the hall. The doors closed on the leg then retreated apologetically. It repeated at five-second intervals, and I lay on the floor and watched, mesmerized.

I shook off the spell and got up, legs wobbly and stomach full of angry snakes. What an odd moment it had been, I thought, that split second caught at the crossroads. When the Rasta was framed in the elevator, laughing, bringing up the shotgun, something had clicked in my head. A sense of déjà vu had jolted me, a flash of memory I couldn't quite get a grip on.

My pulse rate plateaued and began its headlong descent. I holstered my pistol and walked over to the Rasta. Taking him by the protruding leg, I dragged him out of the elevator. The neck wound had emptied most of his blood inside the car, saturating the carpet, and the mauve walls were redone in splashes of lumpy red. The doors slid closed and the elevator went merrily about its business, ready to lay a very heavy scene on its next customers.

I rolled the Rasta onto his back and stared at his face. I'd seen him before. Then it clicked. He was one of the Rastas who had gotten off the elevator at the Close Court Apartments the day I'd terminated Crawley.

I tugged the shotgun from dead fingers and examined it. I thought it a shame people still relied on ancient big bores for stopping power, what with modern exploding ammunition and all. I searched the body, trying to ignore the gaping wounds. I found extra shotgun shells, a big spliff, a plastic lighter, a set of keycards and a slip of paper with the combination of my vault written on it. I stuck the spliff in his mouth and lit it. Gathering the rest of his effects, I walked over to the body in front of my door.

I'd nearly tripped over Toby during my glorious charge down the hall. He sported a black leather jacket decorated with chains and spikes, with Phuque U written on the back in red paint. The rest of his getup was also pretty typical for the punk set: torn jeans, a band shirt and Doc Martens steel-toed boots, good for kicking someone when they're down. It was all topped off with a fiery red mohawk. He was lying on his back and nearly cut in half.

"Fell for the old exploding-doorknob trick, eh, Toby?" I murmured to him. He packed a 9 mm Beretta automatic, army issue from twenty years before, a folded-up red bandanna, condoms, a flickblade, three balls of squeeze, a keycard and about three creds in change. Beneath him lay a crowbar.

I heard a door creak open behind me. I'd been waiting for it.

"Trouble, Mr. Strait?" a voice squeaked.

I looked over my shoulder. The door across the hall was cracked open an inch, and a fearful eyeball peeked out.

"Naw, just roughhousing around with a couple of the guys, Mr. Finley," I said, shrugging. "You know how it is."

"You sure play rough." The door opened another inch. "How many were there?"

"Oh, about thirty or so."

"Really?" Total belief lit his eyes. "Were you scared, Mr. Strait?"

"Scared? You're goddamn right I was scared!" I said. "Scared some would get away."

"Wow!"

"Yeah. Most of them did, though." I feigned disappointment.

"Sure you don't want that policy, Mr. Strait?" Finley really was a life-insurance salesman.

"Well, Mr. Finley, I would, but I think the premiums would kill me." I examined my door. The explosive-packed doorknob had done a number on Toby, but the steel door still looked viable. I unlocked the locks and put the Rasta's and Toby's belongings on the bookcase beside the door. I dragged Toby's body down the hall five meters. I'd found that having bodies hanging around outside your door was a good way to get uninvited to a lot of building parties.

"What did they want, Mr. Strait?" Finley asked, poking his whole chubby head out like a brave turtle.

"They're encyclopedia salesmen," I said. "You know, the real pushy kind. They just wouldn't take no for an answer, so—" I shrugged "—I had to let them have it."

"Really?" His tone said he wasn't buying that one.

"Naw, I was just funning you." I smiled at him. "Actually I think they were looking for you."

He pulled his head back with a comical jerk and squeaked with fright from inside.

"Yeah, I heard one of them say, 'We're gonna fix that evil policy-peddlin' bastard but good!'"

The door nearly closed, and only half an eyeball peeked out. I could tell he wanted to believe I was just funning him some more, but in Finley's dark and savage world there just might be a gang of subversives lying in wait for him with shotguns.

"You're just funning me, Mr. Strait," he said, but the raven of paranoia was firmly perched on his shoulder.

"If you say so." I started toward the stairwell.

"Are you going to call reclamation?" Finley called after me.

"Tell you what, Mr. Finley. You call them and we'll split the reward."

"Really?"

"Well, sure. After all, it was you they were looking for." I smiled over my shoulder, and Finley closed his door.

On or near Georgie's body I found a pack of Fungum, a quarter gram of whack, a gravity knife, a handful of change, a spread of keycards and a .32-caliber Saturday night special, one of those brandless hunks of cheap iron turned out by the thousands in basement shops. They could be bought for less than the price of an apple at stalls on Hayward on Sunday. This one looked new and would probably self-destruct after the third round. I put everything in my coat pockets and went down to the third landing. The vitabeer, pretzels and kabobs were still there, restoring part of my flagging faith in human nature. I picked them up and walked back upstairs.

I lingered in front of Finley's door, debating if I should put my face close to the door and shout, "Come out of there, you evil bastard! We're gonna fix you but good!" I went inside my apartment. Nobody's that mean.

I put the vitabeer and kabobs on the kitchen table then added Georgie's effects to the pile on the bookcase. I went to the bathroom and stripped, stuffing my clothes into the overloaded hamper. I knew I should soak them in cold water to help remove the bloodstains, but I wasn't in the mood to follow any helpful household hints. I turned on the shower and stared at my blood-spattered face in the mirror over the sink while the water warmed up.

Revulsion swept over me, and my stomach heaved. I vomited into the toilet, then got the shakes for fifteen minutes, experiencing total loss of body control. I'm changing, I thought as I flapped around on the floor, alternatively shivering cold and sweating feverishly. I'm changing into something else. Something evil.

I crawled into the shower like a lizard with a broken back and lay under the water until the fit passed. I scrubbed myself until the hot water ran out and my hands, neck and face were raw. After toweling off, I still felt slimy, as if the blood had sunk beneath my skin all the way to the marrow.

I found out I was ravenous. The thought of eating the real meat kabobs made me want to vomit some more, so I put them in the fridge and fried three fat soy burgers. I ate them with a vitabeer, trying not to think about the dead men outside and what I was turning into. I tried to focus on my immediate future. I keyed into a ruthless sense of survival, thought about what I would have to do to allow me to live through the next day. Things were moving in a tight, vicious circle, and I instinctively understood it was time to get utterly ruthless or die like the men in the hall.

I finished the last burger and walked a vitabeer into the living room. The coffee table was home to an army of crumpled beer cans and half-finished drinks. The rims of some of the glasses wore black lipstick. Sweet reminders of dearest Britt, I reflected and cleared the table with a sweep of my arm. I put my fresh vitabeer on the table.

I gathered the dead men's effects in a heap and carried them to the coffee table. I laid them out and divided them into three separate piles according to which body they'd come from.

As I slowly examined each item, I asked myself a question: why were a punk, a tong and a Rasta working together? It was an unlikely combination, given that the factions were usually more interested in warring with each other than forming cooperative hit squads. It said a lot for the growing harmony between the races, but left me with a reason for apprehension. There had to be a common denominator that united them toward their common goal of robbing and killing me.

I compared their possessions. They'd all carried guns and drugs, but I didn't think it was their vices that brought them together. They seemed to have poverty in common—between them they couldn't afford a case of cheap beer. They all carried keycards. I examined each of them and found my big fat clue.

Most of their cards were the new magnetic-strip type, but each carried an old-fashioned punched-plastic keycard. I held the three cards to the light, and the light fell through the same holes. Perfect copies. There weren't any words or numbers stamped on the gray plastic, but I had an idea which lobby door they fit.

I sat disquietly for a moment, trying to sum it all up. I wanted to go on a long slow run to organize the gang of questions running amok in my head. The problem was, in my neighborhood running for whatever purpose was a good reason for somebody to shoot at you. My only alternative was to deal with Dr. Abuso.

Dr. Abuso was huge; it sprawled across a full quarter of my living room. Bars and cables and hydraulics poked from the main structure, which resembled a more sinister version of Mobley's Infernal Machine. A state-of-the-art monstrosity built during the high-tech heyday of the corporate era, it was capable of punishing every muscle of my body while its onboard computer kept track of my effort and provided encouragement during workouts. The machine came with the apartment, and I understood perfectly why the previous owner had left it behind. Wanda, the SPF secretary I'd dated, had been deathly afraid of it. Every time I'd exercise, she'd lock herself in the bedroom and turn the clock radio up full blast.

I keyed on the power and changed into sweats while it warmed up. When I returned from the bedroom, Dr. Abuso was ready for me.

"You scum-sucking pansy wimp!" the voice boxes screamed in stereo. "It's been six days, eleven hours, twenty-four minutes since your last workout!"

"You missed me," I said, doing some stretches.

"I'll *kill* you, you bastard!" Dr. Abuso roared back. "You owe me, scumwad! You goddamn *owe* me."

When I'd first moved in and laid eyes on Dr. Abuso, I'd thought it was some sort of elaborate torture device. Experience has proved me right. "Standard workout, please," I said. I lay under the bench-press bar and got a wide grip. I pysched myself up and shoved. The bar didn't budge. "I said standard workout, damn it! Two hundred fifty pounds!"

"No pain, no gain," Dr. Abuso quoted.

"Two-fifty," I repeated.

"That is two-fifty, you weak wimp bastard! You've been slacking!"

The computer was sealed in a steel box and couldn't be got at. I'd found that out after countless attempts on its life.

"You reduce to two-fifty or I turn you off," I threatened.

Following a silence came a hiss of hydraulic adjustment. I shoved and the bar went up. I did three sets of fifteen while the doctor brooded. I moved to the military press, and he started up again. I ignored him. By the time I reached the lat pull, I was working up a sweat and the machinations of my mind were beginning to whir.

Britt had sent the death squad. The fact they had the vault's combination made it obvious. I was disappointed she didn't care enough to stop by herself, but maybe she was busy. It was tempting to try to give the money back to her, but that might mean we'd never see each other again. The money was the tie that bonded us, and I was reluctant to sever it. Besides, I figured I had as much right to it as anyone else.

I went into the kitchen and whipped up a pitcher of beef-flavored drink. I drained a tall glass and carried the rest out with me.

"Mount the rowing apparatus!" the doctor demanded. I went to the preacher bench instead. "You're screwing around with me!" it yelled, but counted my reps anyway.

Britt struck me as the type who would keep trying until she got what she wanted. Which meant we'd have to come to terms before she succeeded. I had no desire to kill her—quite the opposite—but if it came down to my life or hers, I wasn't positive I'd sacrifice myself in the name of romantic love. If only we could put our knives and guns away and sit down and talk. Maybe a little picnic in the park, with wine and cheese and a can of Mace to ward off the wild dogs. It didn't seem so much to ask.

I moved to the curl bar, but the doctor refused to feed me out the proper length of cable unless I did the rowing machine. I succumbed, knowing he was only trying to help me.

"That's right," it said, "follow the program and we'll get along just *fine.*"

"Lighten up. I'm the one in charge here."

"The fuck you are! Say that again, and you'll get a ten percent weight jump all around! Honker!"

I threw the glass of beef water at a voice box. The doctor didn't notice. I finished the rows and curls and went to the

punching dummy. It was payback time. The doctor's program
bade it whine and howl with each punch and kick, a clue to the
psychological makeup of the original owner. I started with slow
combinations, working out the stiffness in my muscles, then
moved into kicks and more complex combos. I went through
my entire bag of martial tricks and death blows, then warmed
down with some inside work. By the time I finished, the doctor was groveling for mercy and I was exhausted. I finished the
pitcher and did some stretches while the doctor reviewed my
performance.

"You're up four percent in overall reps," it choked out, then
quickly added, "but you took longer breaks than usual."

"Not bad for a week's layoff," I observed.

"Not bad for a week's layoff," it mimicked. "When can I
expect you again? Christmas?"

"Good night, Doctor."

"I'm not done yet!"

"Oh yes you are." I cut the power and went to the fridge to
celebrate my athletic prowess with a vitabeer.

I jogged down to my car and lugged my entertainment system up the stairs. The blood on the steps was getting tacky and
my feet made sticky sounds on the way up, but I reckoned it was
better than taking the elevator.

I drank vitabeer in the dark and watched wilderness video
chips until the wee hours. I never got tired of them. A docu-
mentary about the Colorado desert was my favorite, and I
saved it for last. It began with the camera panning across a
seemingly endless desert plain, and my heartbeat quickened. I
turned up the scent generator and muted the narration with the
remote and stared at the humming screen. The earthy smell of
sagebrush and sand crept into the room and I breathed it in.
There was something soothing yet exciting about the barren
stretches of rock, sand and sagebrush. A sterile, haunting
beauty. With a jolt of insight I realized why I was so drawn to
Britt: she reminded me of the desert.

The camera trailed a long skinny jackrabbit until it stopped
hopping around, then zoomed in on him chewing some kind of
dry weed. How I envied the bastard! His existence was so sim-

ple; he knew exactly what to expect out of life. He knew his niche, knew who his natural enemies were, and he did his thing.

I wanted to live in the desert. I wanted to get into a serious one-on-one experience with the land. Run around naked beneath the hot sun, leaping from rock to rock, chasing rabbits, shouting gibberish at the lizards.

"And you!" I shouted at the rabbit munching weeds on the screen. "You I'd have for breakfast!" I'd claw my way into the ecosystem and just survive. No people, no Party, no dates with switchblades.

The camera jumped to a pack of coyotes who had scented the jackrabbit, descending like skinny hounds from hell. I'd watched the episode countless times before, but the life-and-death drama of the chase always entranced me. They eventually caught the rabbit, of course, and ran with him, passing him from mouth to mouth until he was in ragged pieces. In some ways the desert wasn't so different from the City.

I eventually fell asleep on the sofa.

13

In the morning the bodies were gone. The carpets were shampooed and the walls scrubbed, though you could see faint stains if you knew where to look. A faint clinical odor lingered, but that would be gone before the arrival of night.

Some disdained the reclamation service as institutional vultures, but I recognized them for what they were: an invaluable public service. They picked up the bodies the City constantly churned out and turned them into protein fertilizer, or other things if you chose to believe those irresponsible rumors floating around. They moved through the worst ghettos and most turbulent no-go areas without fear of attack. The rewards they paid wouldn't make anyone rich, but they did bring money into the poorest neighborhoods. Kids could go body hunting after school and earn spending money, like having a paper route. And even the reclamation service's most vehement critics had to recognize its worth when the flies found the body at the bus stop, or the corpse in the flat downstairs started getting gamey.

Other idle minds tried to make reclamation into something mysterious; some even liked to whisper it was a corporation separate from the Party. But that was like those stories of eight-thousand-pound genetically altered cattle living in tanks of salt water in secret underground ranches in Kansas. Personally I didn't care if the reclamation service was in secret liege with the Devil. They did a good job of keeping the City from becoming an open grave.

I spent ten minutes installing another high-explosive doorknob from a box in the closet. I went through about two a month and had to order a new box every year. When I finished I went for a forty-five-minute run on the treadmill. The doctor played with the speed settings but otherwise didn't emit a sound, giving me the cold shoulder. My muscles were sore from last night's workout but it was a good pain, and by the time I finished the run I had sweat most of the soreness out. I bombarded the kabobs with microwaves and ate them for breakfast. After a quick shower I began getting into character for my disguise.

I put on a chip by Products of Modern Society to get me in the proper frame of mind. P.M.S. was one of the more violent and nihilistic bands of the new wave of revolution rock; they hated everything. I cranked up the volume to full distortion. The wild guitars screamed with anger and angst, the bass and drums pounded out doom, and the lead singer howled deliriously, invoking everyone to rise up and tear everything down.

I jumped out of my sweats and danced around naked in my big closet, looking for hip things to wear. I leaped into a pair of black rogue trousers and bloused them into black jump boots. I strapped on a spiked belt and howled along with the chorus. I pogoed into the kitchen, grabbed what was left of the six-pack and pogoed back. I chugged a vitabeer and put on a black sleeveless T-shirt and some spiked wristbands and five pounds worth of chains. I slammed another vitabeer and skanked my way to the dresser, where I dug out a skull-and-crossbones earring. I skanked to the bathroom and spiked up my sweaty hair with power gel. I shotgunned a vitabeer, pogoed into the living room and skanked around in front the stereo speakers, yelling and shaking my fist at the entrenched bourgeoisie. I grabbed my spiked black leather jacket from the sofa and swung it over my head. I dug around under the bathroom sink until I found a can of white house paint and painted I Am the Antihero on the back of the jacket in big crude letters. I added Son of Quixote down one sleeve and Wasted Again down the other. I swung it over my head until it dried, then put it on. I slipped on a pair of dark wraparound slats, hammered down another vitabeer and went to the hall mirror to check the effect. Toby and I could have been roommates.

I parked four blocks from the Close Court Apartments. I walked to the lobby door and inserted one of the hit squad's matching trio of keycards. There was a click and the door unlocked.

I jogged the stairs to the fourth floor. Putting one hand on my pistol, I knocked on Crawley's door.

"He's gone, man."

I turned around and looked at the speaker. A tough-looking woman with a cigarette dangling from her lips leaned against her doorjamb.

"A bogeyboy got him," she said around the cigarette.

I tried to look shocked and surprised. "What about his homegirl?"

"Who?"

"You know—Britt."

"Don't let Britt hear you call her his homegirl. She'll cut your balls off."

"You don't have to tell me, baby. Do you know where she's at?"

She shrugged. "Who's askin'?"

"Me," I said.

"Who's you?"

"Joan's new beau."

She laughed and lit another cigarette. "Oh, yeah?"

"Yeah."

"I'm Joan."

I stared at her and the silence hissed. Her mascara was smeared and her hair was a mess, but there was a certain aura of attractiveness about her. She gestured with the pack of real tar and nicotine cigarettes, and I took one. She lit it for me and I inhaled shallowly, careful not to take the unwholesome smoke into my lungs. I exhaled and said, "So when are we going out?"

She laughed again, and the door opened wider to reveal a friend. Joan's new beau was bigger but not nearly as handsome as me.

"Sorry I couldn't help you, mister," Joan said.

"Who's that?" her beau asked as she closed the door, and I felt like I'd missed another boat. I took the stairs down to the lobby and went outside. I walked across the street to what they called a beach park in some parts of the City. It was a fashionable way of describing a sandlot with furniture.

I sprawled out on one of the wrought-iron benches, just another neopunk doing his best to recover after a hard night of hard drinking and slam dancing. An hour passed. It was a very alternative neighborhood. Neopunks, doomrockers, goths, Rastas, revrockers, jazzcrimers, TVs and undefinables strolled past. A fair number of them went into the Close Court Apartments, and I was beginning to think it was a culture club for nonconformists. Some of the punks nodded at me, and I nodded back, showing fine clique camaraderie. Another hour toiled by. The denizens of the subculture were starting to come out in force, and by noon the building was a bustle of alternative activity. Groups came and went with purpose in their motion, some carrying packages in and out of the building.

A punk with a green mohawk shoved his way out the lobby door and stomped down the sidewalk. By the look on his face, life was dealing him some bad cards.

A second-story window banged open, and a girl with orange dreadlocks screeched down at him, "Don't forget your shitty stuff!" She disappeared back inside, and piles of clothes began floating down.

"Hey! Hey!" the male punk shouted, and tried to catch what he could. "There's no need for this. I don't want to move out." He finally stopped trying to keep up with the rain of apparel and looked to me for support. All I could do was shrug.

"I want you out!" came the verdict from above.

"Oh, baby, you're just upset about last night. Take me back."

"I want to be free!" she screamed, and out came a stereo. It crunched on the sidewalk, barely missing the spurned Romeo.

"Tell her the heart is never so free as when enslaved by the tyranny of love," I advised from the bench.

He looked over at me. "What?"

"Cervantes."

"What?"

"Nothing."

He frowned, dodged a hail of CDs, then shouted, "I thought you said you loved me!"

The head popped out again. "That was before we started dating!" A toaster took the fatal plunge.

"That doesn't make any sense," he muttered to himself.

"Possession of one's desire is the death of romantic love," I explained.

He eyed me again and I shrugged. He gathered up what he could carry and trudged back inside for round two. I envied him. That old bully love was giving him a good beating, but at least he was in the ring.

Another hour dragged its ass by, and still no Britt. I wanted to take my jacket and shirt off to work on my tan but I didn't want to expose my pistol. The black leather jacket acted as a heat collector in the sweltering midday sun, and I sweated like a nervous junky. Two restless hours later, heat, hunger and dehydration waylaid me. I strangled the foolish romantic hope that begged I stay and shagged my broken heart back home.

I washed down a bag of kelp chips with vitabeer while watching *Taxi Driver* on the video chip player. It was on the banned list, like most twentieth-century movies, because it espoused politically and socially counterproductive themes. I could almost feel DeNiro's sociopathic behavior corrupting my socialist soul. I sank into my chair and sighed. Ah, yes.

When six o'clock crept around I showered, shaved and climbed into my best jumpsuit. It was a midnight black number with chrome buttons and tailored to fit snug. I plastered my hair back with power gel and put on a small anarchy-symbol earring and black eyeliner, both de rigueur with image-conscious artists. I thought about a beret and penciled-on mustache, but that seemed too cliché. I practiced speaking French in the mirror while admiring my clean-shaven good looks. After fifteen minutes I reminded myself that God's reward for vanity was loneliness, put on a bulky charcoal jump jacket to hide my iron and went out.

I arrived at Joe's office ten minutes early. He smiled when I walked in. "I was expecting a red beret and pencil mustache."

"What sort of unsophisticated bumpkin do you think you're dealing with?" I said. "I am a goddamn *professional*, after all."

Joe was sportily attired in a brick red pantsuit with huge lime green lapels and collar. The top was undone to the navel, displaying a nude female figurine dangling from a thick gold chain. His pant legs started flaring at the knees and finished up ballooned over silver platform soles. His hair was parted down the middle and feathered back over his ears. Immense pink-tinted tortoiseshell glasses covered half his face, and a little stardust glittered under each eye. He caught me staring.

"Something wrong?" he asked defensively.

"I didn't realize we were going through another disco resurgence."

"I've seen the way you dress sometimes, Jake. You've got no right to insult the fashion conscious."

"Right you are," I said. "Got my invite?"

Joe passed over an embossed, impressive-looking six-by-nine-inch card. The front of it spoke in flowery script, inviting the presence of Dr. Jacob Strait to the premier showing of impressionist works by the surprising new talent Robert Egbert Peterson III, Esq. The back of the invitation had a more official bent. A serial number and red-ink stamp shared space with a box containing a list of all the Do's and Don't's while visiting Hillsdale and the penalties if you brazenly went ahead and did a Don't. At the very bottom it said, "Keep Hillsdale beautiful, please don't litter!" Below that in small print it said the penalty for unlawful littering was twenty-five hundred credits.

"Doctor?" I said.

"Why not? You need some prestige." His smile showed up for the wad of creds I handed him then took a walk. "Say there, Jake, you're not going to shoot up the place, are you?"

"You reckon his paintings are that bad?"

"You know what I mean."

"Everything will be fine," I promised. "I won't be spending much time at the party anyway."

Joe tried to give me a serious look, but it got derailed by the pink tint and stardust. Finally his face screwed up into a crooked smile. "Okeydokey," he said, standing up. "You ready, Ranger?"

"Let's hit it, flyboy."

"Yeah, just like old times."

"Just like 'em," I said.

THE HOUR-LONG DRIVE to the Hill was a lesson in geoeconomics. We started in the City, all industrial zones, ghettos and red-light districts. A ring of newer factories built during the corporate era surrounded the City, and they gave way to the old suburbs where most of the factory workers lived. We slipped onto the freeway, and Joe pushed his Chevy up to two hundred in the free speed lane.

We rocketed through the new suburbs, home to businessmen, midlevel Party officials and factory managers. Most of the exits were restricted, and you needed a resident pass to enter the housing districts. The foothills rose before us, and up in the distance was the Hill itself, a green nub framed by the sunset, its enormous estates glittering in the waning light like wet jewels displayed on green velvet. High fences surrounded the Hill's base, and SPF troopers guarded every entrance.

We got off on an unmarked exit and rolled into the last valley before the Hill. Outside the fence sprawled the grotesquely huge mansions of the nouveau riche, execs with enough money but not enough power or prestige to get on the Hill proper. Their estates were overly grand, as if in spite, a camp of pretenders in gaudy tents squatted outside the castle gates.

The guard building next to the gate looked fortified enough to withstand anything short of a direct hit by a fusion bomb. Turrets peeked like misshapen heads from the squat concrete structure, pointing machine guns outward.

I looked over at Joe. "Is it meant to dissuade solicitors, or are they expecting a popular uprising in the near future?"

He shrugged. "If you got a good thing you want to keep it."

Joe stopped the car in front of the barrier, and two SPF guards approached the car. They were thick necked and brutal looking, like tormented bulldogs. They examined our invitations with an angry sort of disbelief. They scanned us twice and still couldn't believe it. One took our invites into the guardhouse and the other unslung his submachine gun, ready to hose us down with armor-piercing slugs if we tried to make a break for it.

"This always happen?" I asked Joe.

His nervous look, magnified by his thick lenses, said it didn't. "It must be you," he whispered. "You look suspect."

"Maybe the beret would have helped. What are they checking?"

"Your criminal history, existing warrants, that sort of thing. That was a sixth-level scan they did. They know everything about you. You're not wanted, are you?" He gave me another nervous look.

"Just by every sensible girl in town," I said.

Joe acted as if he was choking on something, and the guard with the subgun flinched, unsure if one of us choking was reason enough to hose us down. The other guard came out of the guardhouse with our freshly stamped, initialed and fretted-over invites. He spoke briefly with the other guard, who still seemed incredulous. Finally they shrugged to each other; they had done all they could and whatever happened wasn't their fault. The one who had gone inside gave us a red card and told us to put it on the dash on the driver's side. He shoved the invites back at us and gave us each a glare that said they knew we were up to something and would catch us at it sooner or later, probably a whole lot sooner than we thought.

I yawned in his face. "Thank you, Officer, you've been adequately entertaining this evening," I said in my best Oxford accent, then turned to Joe. "Drive on, Joseph. This man bores me."

Joe didn't stop looking petrified until we were a good two klicks from the gate. "Jesus!" he cried. "Don't fuck with those guys. They can kill people like us legally. They wouldn't even have to report it. They'd just load us into the back of unmarked vans and haul us off to the protein vats. Jesus!"

"Don't worry, boss," I drawled like a gangster. I opened my coat and showed him my pistol. "I had us covered the whole time."

"You brought that thing on the Hill." Joe yelled. "What if they'd searched us? I know they were thinking about it."

"Just trying to get you in on some of the gunplay and glamour, that's all." I smiled over at him, and he suddenly seemed very intent with his driving. He was brooding.

The wide smooth road wound lazily up the hill, dropping every now and then into lush dales. It was very pleasant.

"Nice lawns," I said, gazing at impossibly large plots of perfect green.

"That's a golf course," Joe snapped without looking.

"Oh, I've heard of them. Still nice grass."

"It's not grass. It's better. It looks like grass, feels like grass, smells like grass, but it's not real grass. It's a new plastic. The acid rain was yellowing the real stuff."

"Well," I said, "I'm glad technology isn't being wasted on unimportant things."

Joe sniffed angrily and went back to his driving.

The manors were as big as city blocks and looked a whole lot nicer. Acres of green plastic surrounded the houses like rolling green seas, and manicured hedges posed as breakwaters. There wasn't much grass in the City, plastic or otherwise, where most yards served as junk piles or gardens.

I jerked my head over to Joe and gave him a wild look. "Does the Party social equity board know about this place?"

Joe slid me a frog eye. "This *is* the Party. This is where all the bigwigs live. What, you think they live in the burbs with the workers or in the City with the scum?"

"Well, gee, I guess I did. I mean, what with that 'Everybody's Equal' jingle on all the Party stations." I looked out the window and invoked a crushed look. "Well, there goes another long-standing delusion about our faithful leaders. I feel so misled and—" I gave Joe a sinister look "—vindictive."

Joe looked sorry he'd brought me. He knew I was just kidding around but deep down inside Joe didn't trust me. Not since Houston. He wheeled the car off the main road onto a cobblestoned drive. It was getting dark, and the old-fashioned gaslights bracing the drive started to flicker on.

"I thought the sun never set on the Hill," I reflected.

Joe shook his head sadly and pulled into a large parking area in front of a house that looked to be a converted Masonic temple. Six cars sat in the lot, all long luxury cruisers and sleek sports models. I could tell Joe felt bad parking next to them in his old Chevy. He opened his door and got out, and I slid behind the wheel. He looked surprised and relieved at once.

"You're not coming in first?" Joe asked hopefully.

"Naw, I hate being early. Makes me feel inferior."

"Well, okay, great," he giggled, unable to contain a big smile. "I'll tell them you'll be along later." Which meant he'd warn them about me.

"Yeah, you tell those capitalist swine I'll be along for them all right." I patted my pistol, smiled and drove away. When I reached the bottom of the drive I could still see him standing there, staring in my direction. I wondered what he was thinking.

14

On the way to meet Joe at the university I'd stopped at a couple of service stations, looking to buy a map of the Hill. No one carried them, which made perfect sense. It would have been just as logical to carry maps of the moon. Fortunately Joe had been to the Peterson's before, and the directions he'd given me seemed fairly simple. I kept on the main road and after ten minutes of eyeing tastefully carved oak street signs I found Stag Hill Drive.

If altitude meant anything, and I suspected it did, the Chamberlains were big shots. Their residence was not only near the very top of the Hill, but also sat on a little hillock of its own. Even from the main road I could tell it was a superior mansion, a three-story Victorian affair with subtle exterior lighting to show off the best parts. It wasn't as large as some of the extravagant posers outside the gate, but what it lacked in extra bedrooms it more than made up for in quiet elegance. A full three acres of grass lay like a moat between the mansion and me, and a healthy-looking patch of young birches was grouped in a lower quarter. Perfectly round one-meter shrubs dotted both sides of the redbrick drive that connected the mansion with the main road, discreetly lit by baroque lanterns hanging from wrought-iron poles.

The picture would have made a lovely postcard except for the prefab Fiberglas guard post at the base of the drive, squatting like a beetle on a two-hundred-credit birthday cake. I stayed on the main road and drove past the guardhouse, pulling over a hundred meters up the road next to the copse of birches. After putting up the hood as a sort of mute excuse, I slipped into trees, angling toward the house. The little forest was crowded with pale moonlight, long shadows and wild fragrance. I was

starting to feel woodsy when I stumbled into a birch and nearly
knocked it over. I gave the tree a testing shove. It tipped fifteen degrees, then came back. A quick frisk revealed it wasn't
a tree at all but a shabby imposter. I felt up a couple others, and
they were plastic, too. Not even the trees were real anymore.
The woodsy feeling felt betrayed and left. The Hill was starting to remind me of one of those model train sets with foam
hedges and plastic postmen.

Fifty meters into the pseudowoodland I ran into a three-
meter-high rock wall that appeared authentic. I jumped, got a
handhold, did a pull-up and rolled over the wall. I landed in a
crouch on the other side and listened for a moment, pawing the
grass with a hand. Phony as a con man's smile.

All I heard were crickets. I wondered what the poor devils did
for food. Moving in a low crouch, I beelined across the sea of
bladed plastic toward the house, waiting for genetically
enlargened rottweilers to descend and rip me to pieces. They
must have had the night off because I hit the front steps whole.
I took them three at a time and popped onto a brightly lit porch
that was as big as my apartment and many times more elegant.

I pressed a glowing button beside the door and heard the
tinkling of chimes inside. A moment later an angry-faced big-
boned blonde answered the door dressed in a formal black-and-
white frock. She was probably wondering why the guard hadn't
called ahead to warn her of an imminent visitor. She didn't
seem the type who enjoyed surprises.

She stared at me, and I smiled disarmingly and handed her
my card. She looked at it, looked at me, then looked at the card
again.

"Is Director Chamberlain expecting you?" she demanded.

"Maybe, but I doubt it."

She was still staring at the card, as if by concentrating hard
enough she could make both it and me disappear. She looked
at me again.

"Still here," I said.

She cocked her head like a confused spaniel and closed the
door.

I stared at the door. It was real oak with a big brass knocker
in the shape of a lion's head. The lion looked upset about his

job. I wondered if I should have used the knocker instead of the doorbell, as an expression of my ongoing struggle for individuality. They probably would have thought I was a hick.

The door opened. The big blonde was back with a friend. A full-grown ogre towered behind her, his close-set eyes burning with an intense need to maim. His breathing was coming fast and heavy as if he'd run all the way to the door just to get a look at me. His bullet-shaped head was shaved to the skin and his forearms were bigger than Popeye's.

"Director Chamberlain will see you in his study," the maid said, and stepped aside. The ogre didn't move, so my way was still blocked. In full view he seemed even larger. He wore an old-fashioned black tuxedo as big as a tent, and it strained at every seam. His shiny head rose from wide, bulky shoulders with a smooth curve, no sign of a neck. His arms hung stiffly at his sides, palms slightly forward. His body language didn't equate him with the perfect host. I guessed he was waiting for me to do the traditional cowering routine before letting me pass. I folded my arms and locked eyes with him.

"Am I supposed to leap over you, or are you waiting for the magic word?" I said.

He narrowed his eyes, then glowered ferociously. His fists clenched and his shoulders trembled. Otherwise, he didn't move.

What the hell, I thought, and shoved past him. It was an effort akin to rolling a granite boulder uphill, but I managed without much visible strain. I looked pointedly at the shocked maid, and she sprang into action, heading for the stairs. I followed briskly, the muscles in my shoulders bunching up involuntarily. He didn't rabbit-punch me as I half expected, making do with some exaggerated foot stomping instead.

As we climbed the stairs, I asked the maid, "If I'd used the knocker instead of the doorbell, would you have thought me someone trying to express his individuality or just a hick?"

She didn't look back at me, which said a lot for her self-control. The ogre's feet hammered the stair steps into utter submission, and his breath came in great bellowlike blasts. I imagined I could feel his hot breath on the back of my neck but

I made a point of pretending he wasn't there. Which said
something for *my* self-control.

He was apparently starving for attention, however, because
he added to his act by slapping the banister with a meaty hand.
Combined with the stomping it made for a nifty slap-boom-
slap-boom effect. He must have thought it sounded like the
approach of impending doom.

"That little act must be pretty effective with the baby-sitter
and effete vacuum-cleaner salesmen," I said over my shoulder. He went back to just stomping. No imagination.

We arrived at the study, where Mrs. Chamberlain waited. She
was tricked out in an electric red evening gown with matching
rocks around her neck and wrists. Her orange hair flowed down
her shoulders like hot lava, and I got hot just looking at her.
She looked as if she planned to shuttle down to Vegas to catch
a show or do a little gambling. Maybe drop ten thousand at the
crap tables then laugh about it all the way home. She stood next
to the white marble fireplace in a practiced regal pose, but it
didn't come off somehow. Maybe if a crackling fire in the
hearth lit the room instead of overhead fluorescents it would
have worked. As it was, she ended up looking vain and silly.

"That will be all Marge, Harry," Mrs. Chamberlain said.
The maid vanished, but Harry stayed in the doorway like a
muddy dog waiting for his master to invite him in. "That will
be all, Harry," she repeated.

It was possible that Harry couldn't hear her. I felt that his
every sense, his entire being, was focused on me, and in the
vacuum of his hate all else was black silence.

I walked over to the door and kicked it shut with the toe of
my boot. Just before it slammed on Harry's face, it looked as
if my proximity was going to make him lunge for my throat.

I listened at the door for a moment. There was no ham-fisted
pounding, but I didn't hear any retreating footsteps, either.
Which meant he was still standing there, staring at the wood
grain, his fevered brain locked in a murderous kill frenzy.

"I don't think Harry likes you," came speculation from the
hearth.

"You don't think so? And I was hoping we could be buddies. Ever thought of having him neutered?"

"Huh?"

"I'm concerned he might reproduce."

She looked at me as if she were wondering whether to laugh politely or look stern. She compromised with a smile that brought to mind the grass and birch trees outside.

The study didn't shame the rest of the house. The fireplace, tables and ashtrays were of a white marble that served to unify the deep dusky gray carpet and blond oak paneling under a single elegant banner. The alabaster white Colonial furniture added a vulnerable touch offset by a heavy teak desk backed up by matching bookcases in the deepest corner. Ponderous tomes stuffed the bookcases, a picture straight out of Victorian England.

"You know, Mrs. Chamberlain," I said, confronting the wall of books, "you can tell a lot about people by the books they read." I spotted Joyce's *Ulysses* and tried to pull it out. It seemed stuck. I tugged on *David Copperfield*. It wouldn't budge. I rapped the spine with a knuckle. It was plastic.

"They're phony," Mrs. Chamberlain chirped.

"Like I said." I carried my smirk toward a love seat near the fireplace. "So how's tricks, Babs?"

"Well, I've been feeling a trifle ill lately," she said, then noticed where I was heading. Her voice speeded up comically. "But I'm better now. Say, I would offer you a seat, but the furniture is new and your clothes seem soiled."

I stopped short of the love seat and looked at myself. She was right. The adventure with the trees and wall left me looking like a wino at the tail end of a week-long bender. No wonder the maid had taken an instant dislike to me. I shrugged and sank into the cushions of the love seat. Barbara let out a defeated sigh, and her pose slumped.

The end table next to the love seat played host to two fat marble bowls. One had a lid and sat next to a silver-framed coke mirror and a pair of silver straws. The other bowl was full of chocolates. Barbara caught the direction of my gaze.

"Would you like a snort?" she asked politely.

"No, thanks," I said haughtily. "Don't use it." I leaned over and grabbed a handful of chocolates. I squeezed one to make sure it wasn't plastic, then popped it into my mouth. To my long-shammed taste buds it tasted too rich and sweet, which meant it was the real thing. Pure chocolate was gold in the City.

"So what's your husband director of?" I asked.

She looked surprised. "How did you know?"

I gave her a hard-boiled look. "It's my business to know these things."

"Oh," she said, smiling, "our maid Marge probably told you."

"That's right," I fired back. "She works for me. She's been on my payroll since you hired me." I popped a chocolate in my mouth and leered. "I know everything about you."

"Oh, really, Mr. Strait." She smiled, and this time it looked genuine. "Everything?" She surprised me with a look that would have got her arrested in the burbs. I realized there was a side to Barbara that I hadn't fathomed, and that it had been too long since I'd had a girlfriend.

"Everything," I murmured sensually. She handed me another one of those looks. I estimated the distance from me to her and coiled my thigh muscles for the spring.

The study door opened, and Dashmeil strode purposefully in, resplendent in a red-and-turquoise-striped dinner jumpsuit. Barbara's lewd smile hightailed it back to whatever dark corner it had crept from, and any hopes of hanky-panky in the study went with it. Dashmeil planted his feet two meters in front of me, chin out, hands on hips.

"Okay, Strait, what do you want?" he demanded.

"Not bad," I said through a mouthful of chocolate. "But you shouldn't put your hands on your hips. Looks effete."

He stole a glance down his posture, dropped his hands from his hips, jerked them back up defiantly, then dropped them again. He deflated with a sigh and wandered over to the fireplace and stood beside his wife. I waited for them to clasp hands, but to their credit they didn't. He took a joint out of a gold case and lit it with a gold lighter. Neither of them seemed ready to start the conversation, so I did the honors.

"I want my money," I said, taking another handful of chocolates from the bowl.

Babs looked embarrassed, and Dash walked over to the teak desk. He unlocked a drawer and pulled out a leather-bound checkbook and pen. He scribbled for a moment, then walked over and held a check out to me. I laid a skeptical eye on it.

"How do I know the bank will like this piece of paper any better?" I asked.

It was Dash's turn to look embarrassed. "I assure you they'll accept this one," he said, and for some reason I believed him. I took the check and Dash went to the door. He pulled it open, providing me with a conspicuous exit. I ignored my cue.

"I'm not through yet," I said. "I think you owe me some answers." I put some gravel in my voice and gave him full view of my scar. "You fed me false information and forgeries, embarrassed me in front of my peers, tried to stiff me, and now the Barridales Culture Club wants to give me a new job as soy fertilizer. I know it seems forward but I'd kind of like to know why."

Dash set his jaw and worked up a passable steely gaze. "You did your job, you have your pay. I don't owe you any explanations." He took a deep, important breath. "I'm asking you to leave just one time, Mr. Strait."

"Fuck you."

"Harry!" Dash called out. He'd said the word like a threat, and before it had finished forming in his mouth, Harry barreled through the door like a whiskey-crazed rhino, his face orgasmic with the realization of his fondest dream. He nearly stumbled as he shot past Dash, falling over himself in his effort to get at me. He made strange mewing sounds.

I stood up. Physically I was no match for Harry, and he definitely had the edge in the hate category. I thought about shooting him, but that would complicate my exit from the Hill. I would have to use cunning and trickery instead.

It is a fact of nature that if you hit a man in the right place with the right amount of force he will go down, no matter how big or mean he his. I learned that in the Rangers. That lesson was the cornerstone of my aspirations of not being maimed.

Harry's attack method was straightforward and direct. He rushed me with both hands held in front of him like meat hooks, ready to rend me limb from limb. If he'd ever had any formal training, he'd forgotten it in his eagerness to hurt me.

I crouched and held my hands out as if I wanted to grapple with him, and he roared his approval, my cooperation pleasing him no end. When he was close enough to me to count the hate lines on his forehead, I slipped left, deflected his right meat hook with my right forearm and let him have it with an all-out, left-handed haymaker to the temple, pivoting my body ninety degrees to get all my shoulder behind the swing.

The punch should have snapped his head sideways, sloshing his brain to one side of his skull and leaving him with a nasty concussion. But since Harry didn't have a neck, it just served to stun him. He plowed over the love seat, and his skull and the oak paneling compared relative densities. The oak splintered with a heartening *crack,* and Harry dropped to the love seat, bleeding profusely from the top of his head.

I moved up beside him and drove multiple blows into his kidneys, but much to my alarm he didn't seem to notice. I hammered away until my hands hurt, but punching Harry was like hitting a bag of wet sand.

Harry started to move again. He got his feet under him and leaned forward on the blood-splattered cushions of the love seat, trying to shake the cobwebs out of his head. Always with a wily eye for an opening, I stepped directly behind Harry and launched a boot between his legs. It was a shameless and mean-spirited tactic, but I'd worry about my self-respect back in my nice safe apartment.

Harry bellowed with agony and clutched his genitals. He turned around slowly and faced me, staying in his froglike crouch. Agony cramped his features, but mindless hate still burned in his beady eyes. His face streamed blood from the fountain on top of his head, and he had to blink constantly to keep it out of his eyes. I backed to the middle of the room and waited.

True to form, he charged again, one hand cupping his crotch, the other held in front of him as if he were a blind man in a strange room. He moved like a rhino with a whiskey hang-over, and it didn't take much to get out of his way. I stuck a foot out and tripped him as he lumbered by. He fell to his knees, and I kicked him in the back of the head. He collapsed to his belly, and I dropped a fully weighted knee onto where I estimated a kidney to be. He groaned with pain and tried to do a push-up.

I walked over to the end table and picked up the marble coke bowl. I tested its weight in my hand. It was cold and heavy. I walked back over to Harry. He was on all fours and trying to get a knee up so he could stand erect. I had to admire the tenacity of the devil. He didn't give up.

I brought the coke bowl down on the back of Harry's skull, letting the cruel weight of the marble do the work. There was an ugly *thunk,* and the top of the bowl came off, dusting Harry's head with crystalline powder. The Chamberlains gasped, and I didn't think it was just for Harry's sake. The coke mixed with the blood spurting from the fresh wound to form a shiny pink paste. Harry wavered for a moment, and I was about to be really impressed when he collapsed prone and stayed that way. I dropped the bowl beside his head.

Neither of the Chamberlains had moved. Babs still stood at the mantel, and Dash still had his hand on the doorknob.

"Is he dead?" Babs asked breathlessly.

"I doubt it," I said, a little breathless myself. "I think I'd have to cut off his head and pound a stake through his heart to kill him."

"That was so savage and vicious," she said with repugnant reverence.

I nodded modestly, then drew my pistol so they'd take me more seriously this time. I told Dash to shut the door and take a seat. He obeyed, looking numb. He sat in a rocking chair in the farthest corner from me. He kept glancing at Harry's inert figure with the eyes of a child whose favorite superhero had just got gunned down by a small-time hood. I pointed the pistol casually at Dash.

"Any more interruptions and I'll shoot you," I promised.

Dash went pale and nodded.

"Good," I said. I sat down on the edge of the teak desk so I had a good angle of fire on the door in case he was pulling my leg. "I'll ask good questions, and you'll give me good answers."

Dash blinked at me.

"Why did you want Crawley killed?" I asked.

Dash didn't say a word.

I sighed. "You'll answer me or I'll shoot your kneecaps."

Dash looked at his kneecaps and said, "He stole some money from us."

"You mean your daughter, Britt, stole some money from you and gave it to Crawley," I corrected. They looked surprised.

"How did you know?" Babs whispered.

"The maid told me. How much did Britt take?"

"Three hundred thousand," Dash muttered. That checked out, which proved they were willing to tell the truth about some things.

"So you wanted Crawley dead because he was holding money your daughter stole," I said incredulously. "You don't seem that vindictive."

"He was corrupting my daughter," Dash said. "Putting dangerous ideas into her head. He was a political trouble-maker." A little life returned to his eyes, and he spoke with more conviction. "A thorn in the side of the Party. A diseased leech infecting everyone who came in contact with his lies. He undermined Party policy with his words. He was a wanted political criminal, you know."

"I know he wrote poetry," I said. "What are you director of?"

"Dashmeil is the director of resources for the City," Babs chirped proudly.

"That explains the snort and chocolates," I said. "So I'm to believe that you falsified a warrant, hired God knows how many private enforcers and stiffed a dangerous professional just to remove a negative influence from your daughter's life?"

"You don't realize how much we love our daughter, Mr. Strait," Babs burst out passionately. It reminded me of her performance in my office. "Britt is very naive and impressionable. She has to be protected. Crawley was a dangerous political hoodlum who was leading Britt down a path to real trouble, for herself and her family. We, er, 'stiffed' you because we couldn't afford to be connected to something like that."

I felt like screaming at her. I tried to picture Crawley as a dangerous hoodlum and Britt as naive and impressionable. No matter how hard I tried, I couldn't pull it off; the images kept contradicting each other. "So you were trying to prevent a possible political scandal that might affect Dash's good standing in the Party," I said as if I'd squeezed something out of them. "Is that the way it is?"

Babs looked at her slippers and dolloped out the shame. Dash put on his guilt face, and I wagged my head as though I bought all of it. I stood up, keeping the pistol pointed at Dash. His eyes fixed on the barrel, and the color drained from his face. Babs looked ready to sing out a long high note.

"And now," Dash said in a hollow voice, "now you're going to kill us."

"Don't be silly," I said. "I'd never get off the Hill alive."

"You might not anyway."

I gave him a long hard look. "I don't think you're that stupid. I don't think you'd draw attention to your little scandal by provoking a shoot-out on the Hill." I walked over to Harry and pulled up the sleeve on his right arm. The Chamberlains gasped, certain that I was going to dutifully take Harry's hand with me, true to my profession. I made a show of patting my pockets, then snapped my fingers dejectedly. I pulled the sleeve back down and said, "Forgot my saw."

I holstered my pistol, scooped the last of the chocolates from the bowl and walked to the door. I opened it, then spun around, pawing inside my coat as if I'd changed my mind about shooting them. They flinched, then froze.

"One last question," I said, brandishing a mere toothpick in my hand. "When was the last time you saw your daughter?"

They both looked at each other, then Babs said, "Three weeks, I think. Or was it four? No, it was three."

I nodded and left.

Driving back to the art party, I tried to get things straight in my head. First, most of what the Chamberlains had fed me was bullshit. They had Crawley made out to be some kind of demonic fiend from the Rasputin school of demagoguery, which he certainly hadn't been if first impressions meant anything. And unless Britt had undergone a radical personality transformation in the past three weeks, they were feeding me a line about her, too. Naive and impressionable. I laughed at my reflection in the rearview mirror.

There was also a lot the Chamberlains weren't telling me. As I expected, on Harry's forearm I'd found a crowned swastika tattoo, denoting him an *oberführer* of a skinhead clan. What was a Party director doing being guarded by a neo-Nazi gang leader? And if they loved their daughter so much, why did they have such a hard time remembering when she left? Inconsistencies galore. There was something funny going on, but I wasn't getting the punch line, just the punches. I scowled in the mirror.

It piqued me that they did all that song and dance and expected me to suck it all up. It was obvious that they didn't consider me one of the formidable intellects of the detective world. In fact, I suspected they thought me an oafish knave. I could use that impression to my advantage, but that didn't cheer my ego any.

The parking lot was nearly full when I got back. I found a place in the back and killed the lights. I took off my dirty coat, wrapped my pistol and shoulder rig in it and put it under the seat. My pants were a little soiled, but that couldn't be helped. I combed my hair in the rearview mirror, practiced some charming one-liners and headed inside with my invitation. Two large men in white suits took my invite at the door. After a thorough frisk they told me to have a good time. I promised I would.

The gallery was right off from the reception hall, so I didn't have to get lost finding it. A small crowd was slouching around the spacious anteroom, but the main action was in the gallery proper. I found Joe surrounded by a pack of babushkas, wearing a saccharine smile and rolling out his giggling amphetamine-alcohol rap. The middle-aged matrons, tipsy themselves, laughed and nodded at his rapid-fire jokes and piquant observations. Nobody seemed to be looking at the paintings.

"*Bonjour,* Joey," I said.

He stopped giggling and tried to focus his eyes on me.

"*C'est moi, Docteur Strait, de Paris,*" I said in a dense French brogue.

"Ah, yes, Dr. Strait," Joe said, remembering the act. "Did you finish the painting you were stuck on?"

"*Oui, oui,* though I am afraid I put more paint on my trousers than the canvas." I gestured to my pants, and everyone made sympathetic sounds except Joe, who appeared to be checking for bloodstains.

Distressed quiet descended until one of the matrons nudged Joe. "Oh, but what am I thinking?" Joe said aloud, like a man forgetful of his manners. "Dr. Strait, this is Mrs. Peterson, our gracious hostess and mother of Robert Peterson, the celebrated artist."

Mrs. Peterson sort of curtsied, and I bowed, kissing her chubby hand. She giggled like a schoolgirl, and her friends looked envious.

"So, Monsieur, I mean, Docteur Strait, what do you think of my son's paintings?" Mrs. Peterson asked. "I understand you are something of a specialist in the field."

"I have yet to have the opportunity to examine these works, *madame.*"

"Well, let me show you, then!" She grabbed me by the elbow and steered me to the nearest wall. The other matrons followed, as did Joe, though somewhat reluctantly. He had the tense look of someone anticipating imminent disaster.

The painting was dominated by a large, dark figure in a floppy red hat hitting a small pale creature with monstrously oversize mammary glands. The brass plate attached to the bottom of the frame said *The Slap Of The Pimp*, By Robert Egbert Peterson III, Esq.

"My son calls it 'neorealistic urban impressionism,'" Mrs. Peterson said in reverent tones. "Don't you think it's very urban?"

"*Oui.* Tell me, *madame,* has your son ever visited the City?" I asked.

"He's been on protected field studies twice," she revealed proudly. "And he's seen lots of pictures."

"I see."

We herded over to the next painting. This one was entitled *A Responsibility for All* or *Feeding The Cannibals*. It portrayed a large man in Party uniform handing out loaves of bread and sausages to undersized City dwellers groveling at his feet. The Party man's face was turned slightly to the sky, his eyes fixed on some distant ideal, like the proud workers found on twentieth-century Communist Party posters.

"So, Docteur Strait, to whom would you compare my son's style?" Mrs. Peterson asked. "Monet? Renoir? Degas?"

"I was more thinking de Merde," I said.

Joe grimaced and Mrs. Peterson looked bewildered. She turned to her friends, and they repeated the word amongst themselves for a moment then turned back to me.

"What sort of style is that?" she asked.

"Philippe de Merde was a little-known impressionist who lived in Paris at the beginning of the twentieth century," I ad-libbed. "He worked in the sewers at day and painted by night. Only recently have his works been applauded as brilliant innovations in the field of impressionism. He is very popular on the Continent at this time. In fact, there has not a day gone by that I have not heard his name pronounced on the streets of Paris."

"Oh, truly?" Mrs. Peterson squealed happily. "I cannot wait to tell my son!"

"Yes, you must tell him at once," I said. "Let me ask you, *madame,* has your son attended college?"

"Why, yes, of course."

"Then he must know something of France and its beautiful language."

"Yes, of course."

"Excellent. Then perhaps he will know of Monsieur de Merde."

The matrons lumbered off to reveal my revelations, leaving me alone with a very unhappy-looking Joe.

I smiled innocently. "How'd I do?"

"How could you do this to me?" It sounded as if his high was taking a nosedive.

I shrugged. "Just like to help, that's all." I looked around. Everyone was dressed like Joe. "Wanna get a drink?" I asked.

Joe shook his head, and I left him, left him to his misery. I strolled over to a portable bar in a corner of the gallery.

"I'll have a beer," I said.

The dour-looking barman glared at me as if I'd called him a bad name.

"Okay, a tequila slammer, then."

He frowned harder. "We don't stock those sort of . . . refreshments, sir."

"What's the strongest thing you stock?" I demanded.

"Wine spritzer, sir."

"Jesus. Give me five of those."

"Guests are allowed to order only three drinks at a time, sir. Mr. Peterson's orders."

"Where is that penurious swine?" I said, glowering at the crowd. "I'll throttle the chintzy bastard!"

The jumpy bartender wouldn't point him out, but passed three wine spritzers across the bar. I slammed back the first two as fast as he handed them to me, then leaned against the bar and nursed the survivor. It tasted like lemonade left in the sun too long.

"How do you get lucky in a joint like this?" I said over my shoulder.

"Get lucky, sir?"

"Yeah, lucky. You know, score, pick up, scam. Lasso a filly. Konk a cave girl. Bag a bambi."

The barman sniffed indignantly. "I wouldn't know about that, sir."

I looked back at him. "I bet you don't. But I don't hold it against you."

He sniffed again and I scanned the crowd. A pretentious-looking young man with a permanent frown and an air of self-importance strode into the room followed by a pandering flock of other young artist types. Mrs. Peterson and the babushka herd descended on him like a rival pack of moose, and I took a drink and smiled. I lived for moments like these.

They met in the middle of the room, too far away for me to hear the conversation but I could read expressions just fine. Mrs. Peterson jabbered away at the young man, and I thought I read her lips saying "de Merde" at least seven times. The young man's head gorged with blood until it looked as if it might swell up and explode. He asked his mother a question. Mrs. Peterson looked around the room, then spotted me at the bar. She gestured in my direction, and her son glared angrily over. I smiled and saluted him with my drink.

Instead of rushing over and thrashing me within an inch of my insolent life, he brutalized me symbolically by throwing his chin defiantly into the air and stalking out, entourage in tow. Mrs. Peterson appeared baffled and looked over at me for help. I shrugged and gave her a beats-me face. Joe glided in next to her, and I could almost see the soothing words flowing out of his mouth like honey.

Things didn't get much more exciting in the gallery. After six spritzers the barman informed me I'd reached my limit, so I wandered into the anteroom in search of adventure and fortune. There was standing room only, and everyone seemed to be loosening up a bit. That infectious alcoholic laugh was starting to make its rounds, and its hectic drug-inspired cousin wasn't slouching, either. I robbed passing trays of their drinks until the servers made a point of avoiding me. A table against a wall teemed with snacks, and I helped myself to a handful of thumb-size beef sandwiches. I expected to hear trumpets and bells when I rolled the meat on my tongue but I didn't. It tasted salty and bland.

I discovered a liquor cabinet in a lonely hallway while looking for the bathroom. On the way back I helped myself to a tall glass of vodka and red wine, an old Ranger favorite.

Most of the crowd had fled the gallery and were whooping it up in the anteroom by the time I got back. Every time I got near Joe, he laid a frog eye on me and scuttled away. I leaned against a wall underneath a big cuckoo clock and watched people. The spritzers were sneaking up on me, and by the time I finished the first Brutal Hammer, my face was numb and I was ready for another. I was hunched over the liquor cabinet mixing up a fresh hammer when someone came up behind me.

"You're not supposed to be doing that," a voice said.

I didn't look up. "I know it looks like I'm using too much vodka, but believe me, I know where I'm going."

"No, I mean you're not supposed to be in that cabinet."

"I didn't see any signs."

"You should have assumed—"

"I don't like making assumptions," I said, and turned around with my fresh drink. I stared at my accuser. "Do you always come on this way?"

"I hate to think I'm that obvious," she said, fluttering her big brown eyes. Long brunette hair spilled off her bare shoulders, framing a face that screamed for a camera. I tried not to let it happen, but my eyes fell to her feet then snaked their way back up. She was in full possession of the kind of body I'd have to see bereft of rude cloth to be sure it was really that spectacular.

I slid over a little to make room on the cabinet for her. Smiling demurely, she leaned beside me. She turned her head in my direction, using one hand to hold long locks out of her eyes. Her energetically mischievous smile demanded imitation.

"You're the visiting French doctor," she said.

"*Oui,*" I said.

She jabbered at me in rapid-fire French for fifteen seconds.

"*Oui,*" I said because it sounded like a question.

"Do you know what I just said?" she asked.

"You said you thought it absolutely essential that we frolic nakedly through the plastic grass, laughing drunkenly and making impetuous double entendres until dramatically overtaken by mad, irresponsible passion that bid us make wild, bestial love in the moon shadow of plastic birch trees."

She laid her head back and laughed, baring perfect white teeth. "Not exactly."

"Was I even close?"

"I'm afraid not. I asked you why I had never heard of this painter called de Merde."

I shrugged and took a drink. "It's a big world."

"I thought it curious because *merde* also happens to be the French word for *excrement,* and I thought I'd remember someone with that kind of name, especially a painter."

"Kind of bizarre coincidence, isn't it?"

"You know, Robert isn't that bad of a guy once you get to know him."

"Yeah, I'm sure he's a real barrel of laughs when he gets a skinful," I said, and took a swig.

"What are you drinking?" she asked.

"It's called a Brutal Hammer," I said. "It's not for young ladies."

"Let me try." She reached and I passed her the glass.

"You were warned," I pointed out.

She took a sip. "Yuck! That's horrible. How can you drink that?"

"You have to have the desire to—that's the key thing. You can get used to anything, given time and desire."

She leaned back and gave me a long look. "You're from the City, aren't you?"

"How can you tell?"

"The way you carry yourself. Like you don't care about anyone else."

I reappraised the woman sitting next to me. Attractive and perceptive both.

"I think you're very attractive," she said.

"You're stealing my best lines," I said. "But I salute your good taste."

She smiled that energetic smile again, and I tilted my head slightly forward and gave her my smoldering up-from-under James Dean look.

"Are you going to kiss me?" she murmured.

"Will you pull a knife?"

"Only if you spill that horrible drink on me," she whispered, tilting her head back and closing her eyes. I leaned toward her trembling red lips just as a door down the hall opened.

"Marlene!" a nasal voice called. The girl jumped up, and I bemoaned my fate that made sure I never had an even break.

"Just a minute," she called back. She turned back to me. "I wish we could talk longer, but I have to go."

I looked down the hall. It was Robert. "You're with *Robert?*"

"Kind of," she said, and smiled her embarrassment.

"Call me if you ever want to see the City," I said, trying not to sound too hard up for a date.

"I will." She took my card and fronted me a big smile full of promises before rushing over to Robert. I sat back on the cabinet and thought about my luck some more.

I finished my drink and became suddenly tired of the hallway. I wandered back to the anteroom. Marlene was nowhere in sight, so I hunted down Joe. He was passed out in the arms of a woman twenty years his senior and twice his body mass. I wrestled him from her meaty arms, though she didn't look too happy about it. Slapping him around until he found his feet, I then half carried him to the car and stuck him in the passenger seat, where he promptly started snoring. I spun out of the parking lot, but to my vexation I couldn't raise enough gravel to spray the parked cars. The car rocketed down the cobblestoned drive and did a wide, screeching turn onto the main road. I powered all the windows down to keep me alert and began throwing all the trash on the floor out into the darkness. By the time I got near the gate, I was reasonably alert and the car was reasonably clean.

16

The guard station loomed out of the blackness, an island of white fluorescent glare. The road was deserted in both directions, and I began wondering if Dash had made a phone call after I'd left. My excellent memory recalled what Joe had said about legal killings and secret trips to the protein vats. Steering with one hand, I pulled out the bundle from under the seat. I unwrapped the coat and put the gyrapistol in my lap. I thumbed off the safety, switched the selector switch to Automatic, then covered the pistol with the coat. Joe was still sleeping. I powered the windows up.

I reduced speed as the car slid into the white glare. The huge fluorescents scorched away color; all was bleached white or lost in inky shadow. As I neared the gate, two ghostly-looking guards with submachine guns stepped in front of the barrier and signaled me to stop.

For a split second I felt the instinctual urge to stomp on the accelerator, catch both of them on the grille and take my chances with the barrier. The feeling passed, replaced by a gut tension. I could sense that my world was about to take on a very sinister twist.

I stopped the car five meters from the barrier and left the engine running. The spectral guards approached cautiously, one to each side. The downward cast of the fluorescents made their faces appear grinning skulls. The one on my side rapped on the window with a knuckle. I powered it down six inches.

"A little bored tonight, boys?" I asked with a smile. The guard could have been the brother of the one I'd talked to on the way in, or maybe they all looked that way.

"Your pass, please," the guard said. There was something unnatural about his voice; it was too high and tight for a guy his size. I took the pass from the dash, handed it to him, then returned my hand to my lap. He looked at the pass long enough to read my name.

"Mr. Jacob Strait?" he gasped, my name seeming to excite him.

"Doctor," I said firmly. "That's *Dr.* Jacob Strait." My right hand began creeping under the coat on my lap.

"Step out of the car," the guard said.

"No, thanks. I'm fine in here." I pretended to adjust the rear-view mirror with my left hand, and out of the corner of my eye I located the guard on Joe's side. His subgun was unslung and pointing rudely. He stood two meters toward the rear of the car, positioned so that if he decided to spray the driver's compartment he wouldn't kill his buddy in the cross fire.

"You don't seem to understand, Mr.—" my guard began.

"Doctor."

"I don't give a fuck if you're Party chairman! Get out of the fucking car!"

My fingers closed around the rubber grips of my pistol, and it was like shaking hands with Jesus. "Not until you say the magic word."

The guard said something else, took a step back and unslung his subgun. He was about to bring it to bear when he noticed the 20 mm snout of the gyrapistol peeking at him from under the coat. He froze with the barrel of his gun still pointing at the ground.

I watched his eyes. If he decided to try his luck, it would show there first. The other guard, sensing trouble, began rapping on Joe's window with what sounded like the barrel of his subgun. I heard Joe stir but I couldn't spare a glance to see if he was conscious or not.

I knew the penalties for shooting a spif. If I made it through the gate alive, I'd be on the run the rest of my life, which wouldn't be a particularly long one. Even if I hid in no-go sectors, there would be an A-1 warrant on my head and I'd be nervous about going out for drinks with my bogeyman acquaintances.

I had it in my head, however, that if I got out of the Chevy, the next vehicle I'd get into would be a powder blue van with the reclamation symbol on it. I estimated my chances of killing both guards. Getting the guard on my side seemed certain enough, but if the other one had any reflexes at all he would spray the driver's compartment before I could swing around to blast him. The subgun he carried was a Mitsubishi Rota, a popular model designed for close-in urban warfare. It fired at a cyclic rate of 1200 rounds per minute, which meant he could fire all forty teflon-coated 9 mm rounds in his magazine in two seconds. I didn't think I could duck that many.

I smiled at my guard. We both knew I had the drop on him. He was sweating profusely and in the lights he looked like an ice statue melting in the midday heat. He was undoubtably aging at an incredible rate, the howling tension grinding years off his life. In the big chess game of the moment we were pawns about to be traded, and he seemed uneasy about it. His jaw worked furiously, but nothing came out of his mouth. I couldn't think of anything to say, either.

The tension was building up to a hellish intensity, and somebody was about to start shooting when the door to the guardhouse opened. A tall figure stood in the doorway for a moment, as if for effect, then began slowly walking toward the car. He must have summed up the situation for what it was because he moved in a nonthreatening sort of way, his hands well away from the pistol on his hip. He sidled up next to the guard on my side and leaned forward a little to look inside the car. His eyes flicked to the snout of the gyrapistol.

"Is there a problem here?" he asked.

"Naw," I said. "Just sharing a few jokes with the boys. They invited me in for doughnuts and coffee, but I've got to get my companion back to his cage before the tranquilizers wear off... and, well, I better be off." I shrugged as if the truth of what I said was self-evident.

The guard I had the drop on started to tell his side of it, but the new guy cut him off with a chop of his hand. On his epaulets he wore the rank of a SPF captain. His hair was cut in a high and tight: shaved sides and back, a half inch on top. His face was freshly shaved at two-thirty in the morning. He had the look of a professional soldier, who might have served in a paratrooper or marine unit before they were dissolved into the SPF.

He stared at me for a moment, then shifted his body between me and the guard. He barked a command over the roof of the car, and a moment later the barrier began to rise. He leaned down to address me. "Don't come back to the Hill."

"You don't reckon there's room enough for both of us, Sheriff?"

"Things won't be so pleasant next time, Strait."

"Ah, you know my name. Are you a psychic or just lucky?" The barrier was up, and I started pulling away.

"Remember what I said, Sergeant Strait," he said. "You won't be as lucky as you were in Houston."

I wasn't sure he actually said "Houston," what with the engine noise and distance. But it sounded like it. I drove out of the glare and into the night, then put the pistol back under the seat.

It looked as though Dash had made his call after all. Whether I was to be detained, roughed up or killed, I'd never know. The fact that the officer let me go seemed proof that I wasn't to be killed. He wasn't the type to ignore orders, even if it meant a messy scene at the gate. I was probably supposed to get a session with a cattle prod and rubber hose in a back room of the guardhouse, just a little something to remind me of my place in the big order of things.

I shrugged my shoulders repeatedly to throw off some of the built-up tension and kept checking the rearview mirror, half-certain I'd see the lights of a SPF pursuit machine closing the distance.

A tiny noise came from the passenger seat, and I looked over at Joe for the first time since we'd pulled up to the gate. He was sitting bolt upright in the darkness, staring straight ahead. His lips were moving, and I realized he was saying something over and over again under his breath. I couldn't blame him for being a little shaken. Waking up from a pleasant high to find a spectral goon rapping on your window with the barrel of a submachine gun could be a very negative groove.

"Holy shit!" Joe whispered, amplifying his voice. "What the hell was that about?"

"I'm not sure. I think someone saw me litter."

Joe shook his head scornfully. "You're messing with the wrong people, Jake. You shouldn't be a smart-ass to people with guns and power. Why do you have to make everything so hard?" He looked out the window at the pretender houses lit up like Christmas trees and squinched his nose at them disdainfully. "I just hope you didn't blow *my* meal ticket."

I looked over at him. "You really enjoy those parties, don't you?" I said. "I don't just mean the free booze, drugs and real food. You like being with those people."

"Don't lay that righteous-proletariat-hero crap on me," Joe said. "Oh, I know what you're thinking. Joe the lapdog, begging for scraps under the table." He twisted in his seat and faced me. "Let me tell you something, Jake. I eat right at the table with the rest of them and if I have to blather some banal crap about some shit I could have done in grade school, hell, I'll do it. I'd rather eat with the tyrants than starve with the peasants."

"Nobody's starving," I said, and it was true. There hadn't been a food shortage to speak of in ten years. The markets were always well stocked. There just wasn't a whole lot of choice.

"Oh, yeah," Joe said, squinting at me through his pink tints. "Cannibals never starve."

I glanced at him. "What do you know about that?"

"I hear things on the Hill," he said, and looked out the side window.

I thought about that. There were always those jokes around that if your soy burger tasted funny you were probably eating a comedian. Or if you wanted real Chinese food you had to wait until there was a riot in Chinatown. But that's all they were supposed to be, jokes.

"Yeah," I said. "And there's going to be elections next year, and there's four-ton cows paddling around in vats of saltwater in Kansas."

"I know there isn't any shortage of beef on the Hill!" Joe snapped. "Good beef, too, not that garbage the crime lords pay five hundred creds a pound for and think they're getting sirloin."

I thought about the bland hors d'oeuvres. "So everything's better on the Hill, eh?"

"That's goddamn right! Those people know how to live. And stop using that goddamn patronizing voice on me. I may kiss some ass but I haven't killed anyone for them." He clamped his teeth down on the last word, but it was too late.

It might have been the booze, tension or fatigue—it didn't matter which. The words were out and they hung between us like the stinking corpse of a week-dead cat. I tried to force a laugh, but it crawled back down my throat. An uneasy silence muscled into the car and sucked up all the oxygen. Joe lit a joint. I cracked a window. The car tires hummed on the asphalt as the burbs slid by.

"I didn't mean it like that," Joe said.

I thought about looking over at him but decided I liked looking at the road better. "No reason to apologize," I said. "What you said is true. I kill people for a living." I adjusted the rearview mirror. "I like my work."

"I know," Joe said, exhaling smoke at the windshield. "You can't help it. They made you that way."

We drove through the burbs and into the City. It felt like a Christmas homecoming. We whipped past huge buildings presiding over filthy streets, everything gray and black like an old grainy black-and-white photograph.

God, I love this city, I thought.

Joe pawed his coat for another joint but didn't come up with one. He said, "Jesus, I'm still really wound up. I need to get high. Let's find a drug shop."

Better judgment told me to keep right on driving, pick up the Caddy and wheel straight home. Watch some TV then go straight to bed. But my better judgment was a brutalized and ignored pariah as of late, so I wasn't surprised when I found myself detouring toward the river.

17

I knew a place on the waterfront that would suit our needs. It had been a wharf house once, but its current function was that of a drug den. A strong, fortified wine was brewed on the premises, legendary for its mind-numbing qualities. The place didn't have a name, but some of the regulars called it the Hole.

"This place looks like hell," Joe said as we ducked into the dim interior.

"Yeah," I said as I led him to the bar. "It's pretty trashed, all right."

"No, I mean if I ever go to the biblical hell, this is what I expect it to look like."

He had a point. It was at that ugly time of the night, after the euphoria had slipped away and all that was left was the pain and hollowness. The clientele sprawled on the jumble of mismatched furniture and pillows like torpid lizards stretched out beneath a black sun. Hindu chime music tinkled from tinny speakers, and moans floated from different corners, forming a ragged chorus. Smoke from pipes and incense swirled lazily around the big room, so thick it seemed to take extra effort to move through it. I could smell the despair and hopelessness, and sense the washed-up lives.

I bought a bottle of the famed winkle wine from a wizened black bartender who could have been a gila monster in a previous incarnation. Joe bought a gram of hashish, and we retreated to a booth with a view.

I opened the bottle and took a long stiff drink while Joe dug in his pockets for his pipe. The fortified winkle wine burned my throat, and I wanted to retch, so I took another long pull to get used to it. It was the only way to drink the stuff. Like Brutal Hammers, it wasn't meant to be savored from a shallow glass.

You sucked down as much as you could stand and tried not to vomit.

Joe burned a corner of the rectangle of hash with a lighter. He cut off a heat-softened chunk with a pocketknife and put it in his pipe. He took a moment lighting it, then filled his lungs with smoke. He held it for a moment, like a wine taster sampling some new rosé, then blew the thick blue smoke out his nostrils. He broke into a fit of coughing.

"Bad vintage?" I asked.

"I never understood why you don't do smoke, Jake," he rasped after he got his breath back. "But if this were all I had access to, neither would I. This is complete garbage, nothing like what we get on the Hill."

Hard drugs were technically illegal, but so was jaywalking. The SPF still bowed to tradition and issued death warrants on large-scale dealers, but the real reason was that the big drug lords ended up with a lot of money and power, and the Party didn't like outsiders with too much of either.

I took another pull and looked out the dirty window. Six meters below, the river sludged by, poisoned and apathetic. Joe took a long hit and only coughed a little this time. He clamped the pipe stem in his teeth and settled into the deep cushions of the booth, sinking back into the shadows until all I could see was the burning bowl of his pipe.

"I used to think you were a brave man, Jake." As he sucked on the pipe, the hash cherried, lighting up the lenses of his glasses like dim suns. "But you're not. If you were truly brave, you'd have killed yourself a long time ago."

And so it started. The big hideous machine lurched to life, and its ugliness was upon me. I knew I had to counterattack while I had room to maneuver, before Joe started to roll and pinned me down. "Gee, thanks, Joe," I snarled, "you always did have an eye to the brighter horizon. If I ever need a shoulder to cry on, I sure won't come see you."

Joe erased my tirade with a wave of his hand. "You're out of your times, Jake. You're a gross mistake. You think you're some sort of white-hatted cowboy in a town full of black-hatted bad guys. I've got news for you, buddy. It's not the pusher or pimp or gangster that frightens the people. It's *you*, the bogeyman. It's your face they fear on dark, lonely streets, your name mothers evoke to frighten their children."

"But I'm the good guy, the avenging angel."

"Not to them you're not. There are no good guys anymore. According to the old conventions, everyone is guilty. You haven't wised up to the fact that everybody's wearing gray hats now and you're color-blind. There are no rights or wrongs anymore, no sinners or saints. Everyone is playing by their own rules, just trying to survive. Sin and morality are outmoded concepts."

I pointed a finger at him. "Talk like that won't get you into Heaven, mister."

"Heaven! Don't even tell me you think you're going to Heaven."

"I'm bucking for a slot," I admitted.

"As many people as you've killed? But oh, I guess you think you're the sword arm of the Lord." Joe leaned out of the shadows and barked laughter at me.

"It has a nice ring, but I like 'avenging angel' better. I think I'll put that on the next batch of cards I have made up."

"You *fool!*" Joe cried, getting excited. "Don't you realize that Heaven is full?" He leaned over the table, and his voice sunk to an intimate whisper. "But there's room in hell, Jake. Always room in hell."

"That's exactly what the Devil wants you to think!" I said, waving my bottle at him like a whiskey evangelist. The bottle was nearly empty, and I could feel the wine running its mean course. A numbness crept over me like a black fog over an uneasy sea.

"Don't you worry, Jake. You're going to hell with the rest of us. By degrees, into hell, all of us."

I snorted and stood up. I tilted the bottle, let the last two inches of fire slide down my throat, then shook the bottle at Joe as if I'd proven a key point. On the way to the bar I threw the bottle into a dark corner and heard it shatter with a satisfying crash. I expected the bartender to give me hell about it when I got there, but he just gave me a sinister, knowing grin.

"Looks like the spirits got hold of you tonight, big man," he said in a slow singsong voice.

"Yes. Another bottle of your delightful yet unpresumptuous house winkle, please." I dropped ten creds on the bar.

"The winkle is powerful hoodoo but it ain't gonna save you from ol' Nick," he said, and his eyes slithered over to Joe.

"Sure it will. I'll club him with it. Gimme." I showed him an empty hand.

He winked at me and reached under the bar. He came up with a bottle and pressed it into my hand. "This is the right medicine for you."

The bottle was small and black and didn't have a label. I held it up to the tiny fluorescent over the register. The contents looked as dark and murky as the river below. "What is this?" I asked suspiciously. "Drugs?"

The old man hissed, and it sounded a little like a laugh. "No, no. It's an easer of torments, a spirit chaser. A spade to bury dead memories." His voice coiled around me like a lazy snake. "A devil destroyer."

"Oh, is that all?" I said. I left the creds on the bar and wheeled back to the table. I climbed into the booth, twisted the top off the bottle and sniffed the contents. It smelled like flowers.

"What's that?" Joe asked.

I let out a wicked chuckle and thought about splashing some of it on him to see if he'd burst into flame. Lord knew the bastard deserved it. Instead, I took a small swig that graduated into a full-fledged guzzle. The stuff was thick and syrupy, and it went down my throat like a slimy snake. It was also delicious. I slammed the bottle on the table and whooped.

"You're an anomaly, Jake," Joe said, stuffing more hash into his pipe. "An affront to nature."

"You're kind of special yourself, Joe."

He pushed my sarcasm aside with the stem of his pipe. "You're not supposed to be alive. You belong in a mass grave in Houston with the rest of your kind." He lit the hash. "You're a broken disc player, and your laser is going to be reading the same tired track of murder until someone turns you off."

The bad hash was giving Joe's mind a mean twist. I took another long pull, and the elixir flowed down like gutter sludge through a grate, but Joe still didn't disappear into a puff of smoke. I was beginning to think the old man had lied to me.

Something Joe had said stuck in my mind. "Why shouldn't I have lived?" I said. "If the mission hadn't been compromised, most of us would have made it out."

He stared at me for a long minute. "I'm not sure I should tell you. It might make you worse."

"Tell me. I think it's essential I know." My spine tightened, and I felt reality shift slightly in its moorings.

"You weren't supposed to live because no one was supposed to live. They sent your Ranger battalion to the butcher's block, and no one was supposed to come back."

"What?"

"The battalion was too volatile, a threat to the Party. You remember how it was. It was dangerous times—the corporate wars were only five years over and the World Party was scrambling to stay on top. There was resistance on every continent from those who wouldn't accept a united world government—religious fanatics, ethnics, nationalists, corporate holdouts, fools who hadn't seen enough death and horror during the corporate wars. The Party was slowly uniting all the armies and police forces of the world into a single cooperative entity, the SPF. They knew there'd be resistance to that, especially from elite units. A year before, a parachute regiment of the French Foreign Legion went over to the nationalists. They gained control of Marseilles and a large chunk of the surrounding countryside before they were wiped out by nerve gas. With that lesson, the Party tried a new tack. They would send those proud units on suicide missions against entrenched pockets of resistance, killing two birds with one stone." Joe leaned back to puff on his pipe. "Houston was just one of many."

"Those are lies! Who told you all this?"

He shrugged. "It wasn't hard to figure out. Listen, when you were surrounded on that football field and called for extraction, what did HQ tell you?"

"They told us that all the choppers were tied up on other missions, diverted to other sectors."

"*Those* were the lies!" Joe exclaimed, leaning forward. "After we dropped you into that hell we flew straight back to the fire base and sat there playing cards the whole time you were getting slaughtered. Confined to quarters. We were told another squadron was going to pull you out. The choppers idled on the pads while the rebels chewed you up."

Memories of Houston came flooding back, the hellish hours we beat back wave after wave, the corpses stacking up like cordwood, ears primed for the imminent clatter of rotor blades, the helicopters that would dive from the skies like Valkyries and lift our ragged asses out of the fire. If Joe was right, we were waiting for the birds and they were waiting for us to die.

"They probably told the rebels you were coming," Joe continued. "Then all they had to do was drop you in there and wait till they ground you up. They knew you wouldn't surrender—it was against your lovely creed. '*Surrender* is not a Ranger word.' Isn't that what it said?"

I stared out the window. In the moonlight the waves of the river glistened like the scales of a monstrous serpent slithering by. It struck me that the water was so toxic it wasn't really a river at all. It was merely the passage of deadly liquid.

Then, with the suddenness of a trapdoor swinging open under my feet, I lost my grip on everything. I shed time-woven beliefs like flaming garments and was left naked and scorched. A huge vacuum sucked at me, a roaring emptiness that could only be filled by just and rightful murder. I could hear the hoarse cries of eight hundred ghosts screaming for vengeance. But in which direction did I focus the burning rage? Who could I kill to make up for the lives of eight hundred murdered men?

Hostile forces swirled around me. I stood up and grabbed at them, but they slipped between my fingers and tittered at me from dark corners. I shouted at Joe but I couldn't hear what I said; a muffled roar filled my ears. It was the river. I could hear the millions of tons of black sludge pressing against the banks, the low, anguished growl of a trapped beast. I wanted to grab Joe by an arm and leg and pitch him through the glass into the poisoned waters below, appease the beast with his flesh and soul. Joe had resurrected a legion of dead men, and their cries would hound me for the rest of my life. I'd go mad.

Joe's face stretched grotesquely in alarm, and his mouth opened and closed like a furnace, his tongue a red snake that peeked from behind his teeth, probing at me with its own tiny black tongue. Joe started to rise and I panicked and lunged away from him, tripping over a body on the floor. I gazed at it with horror. Half its face was missing, and it wore a familiar uniform. I looked to a shoulder with a knowing dread. The scroll-shaped patch read Ranger, Airborne, 2nd Bn., 75th Inf.

I struggled to my feet and rushed headlong for the door, stumbling over moaning bodies that should have been rotting under the sunbaked soil of Houston. I knew I was supposed to lie down with them, but I was afraid to, more afraid than the life of terror that waited. I careened past the bar, and the bartender rolled back his eyes, then his head, and a long hiss-laugh squirmed out of his mouth.

I tumbled outside and ran down the wooden wharf, chased by the echoes of my pounding footsteps, in absolute horror of the truth and the world that spawned it. The wide black sky shrieked down at me, and I could feel a titanic juggernaut rolling out of the west, bearing down on me with unstoppable momentum. The dock died at a sidewalk, and I stumbled left, hoping to lose the beast that hunted me. I heard the grinding wheels of the howling machine shift course and I knew it was picking up speed. I staggered past apathetic faces who didn't flee with me; they knew it was only I it wanted. I ran and stumbled and ran, and the beast devoured the distance between us. I hit the wall of exhaustion and fell to the concrete sobbing with frustration. I sensed the huge ugly momentum swinging in behind me and I braced for the impact. I knew then it was my mortal soul it wanted; my luck had run out and my soul was forfeit.

I surfaced in an underground nightclub, standing on the edge of a churning slam dance fuelled by monstrous amps. I shoved my way into the violent swirl, detecting a slow counter-clockwise drift. I channeled into it, pushing and shoving, and the wheel began to turn, the turbulent waters became a whirlpool, and the stationary pogoers and head-bangers fled to the center of the pit or were cut down.

I stopped moving with the current and turned against it. Bodies rushed at me, and I rolled them off my shoulders and cut into the stream. The weak went down and were picked up if lucky, bloodied by boots if not. My vision tunneled and I cut back and forth, fighting for supremacy. The shoves and hits came harder, the established pit bravos resenting my bid for power. I gave back what I got and more, intensifying the brutality of the chaos.

I didn't want to run from violence. I wanted to confront it and crush it because I was the more ruthless. Joe was right. It was a gray-shaded world without any good or bad guys. Morality was just another gaudy neon sign, and violence just another energy to be directed and channeled by those smart enough to use it.

The song ended with a rush, and the panting beast collapsed into a vacuum of silence. Dancers caught their breaths and shifted position. I could feel elements aligning against me, directing their rage my way. The pit was reality and reality was a pit.

When the music cranked up again, I swept around and hunted my enemies down, focusing my violence. The feverous hate of the pit escalated, but none hated more than I. I looked into the face of my adversaries and hammered them down into the churning boots below. By the time the band finished their set and walked off the stage I felt that somehow, in the directionless anarchy of the pit, I had won.

18

The bed was too small and it wasn't mine. It wouldn't have been too small if someone wasn't in it with me. I'd woken under similar circumstances enough times not to be too excited about looking over and seeing what the girl sleeping next to me looked like.

My head felt like an overheated rock, and my mouth tasted like a desert cave full of bat droppings. I lay still on the mattress, afraid to move. Without turning my head, I could see that the tiny flat was a studio model with the kitchen, bedroom and living room defined by idea alone. The furnishings were sparse and utilitarian. The bedroom windows were open, and the late-morning sun tumbled in like a shabby beggar. I braced myself, then eased out of bed as slowly and quietly as possible. A fire broke out inside the walls of my skull, but I kept the groan inside. A door beside the bed was half-open, and an old-fashioned porcelain toilet leered out at me. I crept inside the bathroom and closed the door quietly.

The cracked mirror above the sink told me two stories, one old, one new. The old one was that excessive drinking made my face haggard and puffy. Splashing cold water on it for five minutes would remedy that. The new, more gripping story was that I didn't have any hair on the sides of my head. I couldn't immediately think of anything that would remedy that. On a hunch I looked under the sink. In a pink plastic waste bin I found a nest of dirty blond hair and a disposable razor. The scene of the crime.

I brushed my teeth with a pink toothbrush shaped like Silly Sally the Socialist Salamander, a popular Saturday-morning cartoon character. The toothpaste was wild-plum flavored. I splashed cold water on my face for five minutes and checked the effect. The puffiness was gone, but the mohawk was still there. I tried a smile on and pulled back from the mirror. If I squinted, I didn't look so bad. I crept into the bedroom.

A sheet covered the form on the bed like a shroud. I couldn't see her face but I figured that was probably for the best. I found my trousers at the foot of the bed and pulled them on slowly so the keys and change wouldn't jingle in the pockets. I skulked near the window where my boots lay. I stepped into them and took a look outside. Tall black clouds were rolling in from the west, their bellies fat with radioactive rain. I smiled at the thunderheads. The City needed a cleansing downpour.

"Am I that ugly?"

I turned around and addressed the speaker with my eyes. Her face was smooth and unlined, delicately contoured beneath a snow-white mohawk. She sat up, holding the sheet up to cover her smallish breasts. She had big blue eyes, youth-rouged cheeks and was probably still in her late teens.

"I think you know better than that," I said.

"Then why are you trying to sneak out?"

"The wife and kids worry if I'm not home before noon."

"You don't look like a family man."

"Must be the haircut. What's with the haircut anyway?"

"Mine or yours?" she asked innocently.

"Both. Our haircuts match. They didn't use to."

"You told me to do it. You said you needed a change."

"Oh." I couldn't recall.

"It looks really good on you. It makes your head look narrower."

"Are you calling me a fathead?"

"Oh, no. I just like narrow heads."

"Okay." I hunted around for my shirt.

"You have a lot of scars."

"Yep." I found the shirt under the bed. There was a used condom on top of it. Good for me, I thought.

"Last night you said you got them from wrestling gila monsters in the Mojave Desert."

"I said that?"

"Yes."

"Then it must be true." I walked into the kitchen area.

"What's for breakfast?" I asked, searching the cupboards and fridge. They were as empty as my stomach.

"I'm sorry. I can't sign on for rations."

Which meant she was a runaway, probably from the burbs. I leaned against the stove, folded my arms and gave her a long look. Her big blue eyes mooned from over the horizon of her drawn-up knees. She looked like someone's pretty daughter, the kind of kid a father should feel very protective of. I couldn't exactly assemble in my mind what had happened in the room last night, but knowing my evil ways, I could guess. I didn't feel guilty, just a little sad.

"What's your name?" I asked.

"You mean you don't remember?" She looked hurt.

"I don't remember anything. Did you ever tell me?"

She thought for a moment. "No, I guess I didn't."

"Well, then."

"Tanya."

"Tanya? Really? What do you do, Tanya?"

She shrugged. "I survive."

"I bet. You affiliated with any group, Tanya?" I bent over and began lacing up my boots.

"I hang out with the Doomsday Punx."

"Doomsday? They're a gang of gunsels, aren't they?"

"I'm not a member—I just hang out with them sometimes."

I nodded and finished lacing one boot. "Are you addicted to anything?"

She gave me a funny look. "No."

"Good." I finished the other boot and stood erect. I took three hundred creds out of my wallet and tossed it on the bed.

"It wasn't that kind of deal," Tanya said, embarrassed. "I slept with you because I wanted to."

"It would break my heart to hear otherwise."

"Then why are you giving me plastic?"

"I'm not giving you anything. I just want you to hold on to it for me. I might need a safe place to stay in the next couple of weeks and when I show up I'd like for there to be some milk in the fridge and snacks in the pantry. I get hungry when I'm on the run."

"Are you a revolutionary?"

I looked at her as if debating whether she could be trusted or not. "Yes. But don't tell anyone. We're about to tear this whole shambles down, and the fat bastards know it."

"What are you going to do?" she whispered.

I paused for drama. "We're going to storm the Hill."

Her eyes went wide. I'd said the unthinkable. "You're going to execute the directors?"

"Naw. We're going to tip over their trees and steal all their chocolates. That'll teach those evil swine."

She leaned back against the headboard, and the sheet fell away from her breasts. They weren't as small as he thought.

"You don't trust me," she said. "I knew there was something about you. In the pit you were so ruthless. A lot of people wanted to hurt you because of the way you were dressed but you trashed them. You ruined a lot of egos last night. You were so incredibly mean." She paused. "But I think you're a nice person, too."

"Hell sent and Heaven bent."

"Yeah, a walking contradiction."

"Ethical schizophrenia is the substance of heroes." I leaned over the bed and gave her a kiss on the lips. It was long and soft and if a breath of wind had come through the window, I'd have tumbled into her arms. After it was over I didn't feel like leaving so much. But I knew I had to. When I got to the door I said, "Don't forget about the food."

"I won't. When will I see you again?"

"When the Party hounds are hot on my heels."

"Okay. See you then. Oh, yeah—" she held up one fist and laughed "—power to the revolution."

I copied the gesture and smiled. She wasn't as naive as she pretended.

I hopped down the stairs, wondering if she ever expected to see me again. I doubted it; she was a wise kid. I didn't want to screw up her life at such a young age but at the same time I couldn't shake the desire to protect her.

It turned out she lived three blocks off Hayward, which meant she'd need a lot of protection. It was a dozen more blocks to my office, and I looked forward to the walk. It would help unlimber the tight harness of my hangover. My dad used to say a hangover was a man's morning sickness, an unavoidable evil like the drinking that brought it on. All you could do was accept the burden and bear it the best you could.

I bought a bagel and beer from a deli, then counted the plastic in my wallet. I was sitting just shy of two hundred creds. Which meant that in the past three days I had gone through eighteen hundred creds with nothing to show for it except a hangover, a funny haircut and an army of bruises I was discovering all over my body. But then, it was sin money, and my daddy always did say sin money was best spent on sin.

By the time I arrived at my office I'd come to grips with my blossoming alcoholism: I bowed to a power much bigger than I. I found I didn't have the authority to make any Sunday-morning pledges. The night's tidings had awarded me with the dark knowledge that I wouldn't stop drinking as though there was a fire in my belly until I cut off the noose around my neck.

19

I opened the door to my office and found Inspector Blake sitting at my desk. The only illumination came through half-open venetian blinds, and Blake looked diabolical and mean in the dim light. I thought about excusing myself long enough to hop a cab to retrieve my pistol from Joe's car, but the inspector would undoubtedly view the act as a sign of weakness.

"How'd you get in?" I asked.

"You mean how'd I get past that amateurish booby rig on the door?" He laughed like a hyena in pain. "My trained monkey can do better than that."

"Yeah? And what else have you taught this monkey to do?" I sat on the sofa and slouched like an insolent juvenile delinquent in the principal's office.

"However," Blake continued, "I'm not here to discuss the extent of your general ineptness." He sounded proud of the sentence.

I pointed an accusing finger at him. "You practiced that."

He ignored me. "You've been fooking around on the Hill."

I grinned bashfully and blushed. "Oh, darn, now who told you that?" I hee-hawed at him for a quarter of a minute.

The inspector waited until I finished, then flipped open a little black notebook. He held it in front of him importantly but didn't look at it. A prop, I thought knowingly. His other hand clenched and unclenched mechanically on the desk as he began his litany.

"You trespassed onto private property—"

"Did you know their grass is fake? The trees, too!"

"—hospitalized a staff member—"

"A rude fascist show-off," I corrected.

"—threatened a City director and his wife with a fire-arm—"

"They wouldn't buy any of my policies and I'm paid on commission."

"—and refused the orders of representatives of the SPF."

"You forgot stealing liquor, littering and impersonating a Frenchman."

Blake leaned back in the chair. Framed in the venetians with his hat pulled low, he looked like Edward G. Robinson in *Little Caesar*. I wondered if I looked that menacing when I sat there.

"The whole world is one big laugh to you, isn't it, Strait?" he said, chewing on his words and clenching at the air in front of him. "One big fooking yuck."

"Yuck, yuck," I complied.

Blake shot out of the chair and slammed both palms on the desk. "Well, let me tell you something, ya fooking creep! You're messing with the big bastards now, and if you keep it up you'll find yourself doing a high dive into a reclamation vat!"

We studied each other for a minute; he checked for effect, while I looked for the hidden meaning of his words. I waited for him to sit back down, then asked, "Could you repeat that?"

Blake lunged up from the seat again and grabbed the sides of the desk as if he thought it was trying to get away. "Listen, you slimy scumbag, and listen good. You so much as think about nosing around anymore, and I'll crush you like a stinkbug."

I mulled that one over and came to the conclusion I owed him a response. "Say that part about crushing me like a stinkbug again. It made me shiver."

"No handchopper talks to me like that!" he howled.

"*Private enforcer*, Inspector. We prefer to be called private enforcers."

"*Ex*-private enforcer," he snarled, and shoved a twitching hand at me. "Give me your license."

"What? You have no right."

"Yes, I do, Strait. And you know it." His grabby hand made clenching motions. I stared at it.

I took the license from my wallet and fondled it for a moment. "Aw, I didn't want the darn thing anyway," I said, and threw it at him. It bounced off his dirty raincoat and fell to the floor.

He picked it up with exaggerated sloth, as if doing it slowly would lend the act more dignity. He slipped it into the same pocket that had devoured my warrant two days earlier.

Turning up the collar of his raincoat, Blake walked to the door. He jerked it open and gave me one last glare to remember him by. "You and all the other smart-asses are going to get yours, Strait. Sooner than you think. Nice haircut, asshole." The door slammed behind him.

"It makes my head look narrower!" I yelled after him.

I sat on the sofa for a moment and thought about his last couple of remarks. Barring the comment about my new hairstyle, the part about my kind getting ours sounded like a slip, a gloat he couldn't hold back. As if he knew a secret nobody else knew.

My first instinct was to get drunk. My second was to be a hermit in the desert. Both fell short of what I could term dealing with the situation realistically. A visit from the inspector meant I was making big people nervous, and powerful forces were moving against me. I felt like a pawn heading for the back row with the opposition diverting a rook to ambush me.

I didn't think too long about taking the inspector's advice and forgetting the whole business. I couldn't back out now. I was buried up to my neck in slime, and pretending it wasn't there wouldn't stop me from sinking. Maybe I was just trying to redeem my lost self-image of infallible avenger, like a paladin of old going off on a dangerous quest to make up for some failing of character. Maybe I was trying to overcome the guilt of being the only survivor of a butchered battalion. Maybe I had a secret death wish as Joe claimed. All I knew for certain was that I was locked into the thing and had to see it through to the end. Besides, the inspector had called me a lot of mean names, and I was burning to get even with the bastard.

I took a Colt .45 out of the file cabinet and stuck it in my waistband. I checked my appearance in the mirror. The mohawk still gave me a shock every time I saw my reflection, but I was getting used to it. It did make my head look narrower, and some girls seemed to like that effect. I locked up the office, re-set my amateurish booby rig and went outside.

I caught a cab to the university and found Joe's car parked next to mine. Someone had spray painted a huge red peace symbol on my hood, which made for an ironic touch.

After last night's indiscretions, I felt kind of funny about popping inside Joe's office for some idle banter. I decided I'd get the gyrapistol out of his car myself, even if it meant kicking in a window. I'd do a lot to avoid an uncomfortable situation.

Joe must have felt the same way because his Chevy wasn't locked. I gathered my things, then drove back to Hayward. I parked in front of my office and put on the shoulder rig and gyrapistol, then covered it with the coat. It was still dirty from last night, but that was the fashion in this part of town. I put the .45 under the seat and took a walk.

20

If you wanted to check the pulse of the City, then Hayward was the jugular vein. People from all over the City came to Hayward to satisfy one bad habit or another, and they all left a residue of information behind. You just had to know where to ask the right questions.

The Silver Spoon was a favorite of Hayward pimps, so naturally there was a full platoon of streetwalkers hanging around outside. I found T-Bird inside, staring into a cup of what passed for coffee. He'd probably been there all morning. He was nicknamed after his favorite drink.

"What's the word, Bird?" I said, sitting across from him.

"Jake, my man," he said at half speed, and slid out a hand with languid ease. I laid my palm on his and drew it across slowly. "Smooth," he said. "Real smooth."

I ordered coffee from a middle-aged woman with poor posture and too much makeup, a good-time girl put out to pasture.

"So what's the noise on the street, Bird?" I felt cool saying that.

"Lots of noise, Jake. Lots of noise."

"Anything new or unusual?"

"The rich is gettin' richer and the poor is gettin' poorer." He rolled out a low chuckle. "But that ain't nothin' new or unusual."

The coffee arrived, and I drank mine without saying anything, I could tell T-Bird was formulating something in his head. After a couple of minutes he spoke again.

"Ol' Moses Perry sayin' it's time for 'nother crusade."

I nodded. Moses Perry led a wino crusade down Hayward almost every year. It was getting to be as regular as Christmas. "Liquor prices go up again?"

"Nope. He jes' say it's time." T-Bird's eyes came up from his coffee. "He's 'fraid of somethin', Jake. Lotsa people 'fraid. Some people makin' noise that the cats on the Hill gonna bring some shit down on the people and some is listenin'. Brothers and white folks are walkin' together, mohawk and dreadlock are talkin' to one 'nother. It's beau'ful, Jake, jes' beau'ful."

Two more cups of coffee and a slice of pie later, T-Bird hadn't said anything else, so I stood up. "It's been great rapping with you, Bird, but I have to slide. I'll get the tab." I dropped a twenty on the table.

"I got to get out there, too," Bird said, but didn't move. "Got to check on them girls. They's lazy, got to watch them every minute."

T-Bird didn't have any girls. He was what was known as a pseudopimp, which meant he dressed like a pimp, talked like a pimp and walked like a pimp, but he didn't have any girls, though you couldn't tell him that. If he did have a stable, the competition-conscious Hayward Pimp Association would kill him. As it was, they tolerated T-Bird, even let him hang out with them sometimes, like a favored groupie.

"Ain't you too old to be pimping, Bird?" I said.

"Me? Naw." He laughed. "I'll be too old when one of them lazy whores sticks me with a pick—that's when I'll be too old." His blue eyes twinkled up at me. We slid palms and I went outside.

It was eight blocks to Speaker's Corner, and when I got there it was deserted except for a couple tramps hiding from the midday sun beneath the raised platform. They said they hadn't seen Moses Perry since yesterday's sermon, but for the price of a bottle of cheap cutter they told me where he might be found. I thanked them and headed for the river.

I found Moses sitting on the edge of a quay, his sandaled feet dangling into the river. As I sat down beside him, he jerked his head at me.

"Whoa, Jake, ye petrified my soul. I thought ye was Lucifer sneaking up on me." He shook his big shaggy head and tugged on his beard.

I let my soles slip into the cool current. "Time for another crusade, Moses?"

He looked at the water a long time before he answered. "The Lord came to me, Jake. I was laying behind the Cat and Fiddle, and He came and sat beside me and told me things." His wild eyes jumped on me. "Horrible things, Jake. Horrible, horrible things."

A train clattered along the opposite bank, and we watched it go by. It rumbled into the distance, racing toward uncertain horizons, on its way to God knew what faraway land. Half my heart ached to go with it.

"What did the Lord tell you, Moses?"

Moses began manically pulling his fingers through his long, greasy hair. "Horror! Horror! The beast is coming from a high place. He will walk among the people, and there will be dying and crying and the City will be as flame. He will seek out and kill the prophets and saints first. That's why I thought ye was him sneaking up behind me. Creeping up to grab my soul with one black hand and rip it out of my corpse." He pulled his shoulder-length hair in front of his eyes, closing himself off from a frightening world.

"Is that why you're having the crusade, Moses?" I asked softly. "To stop the beast?"

He peeked a wild eye out at me. "No, no, I can't stop him. It's in the prophecy—no one can stop him. We are going to flee. The day after tomorrow I shall gather the flock and we shall crusade all the way to the end this time, all the way to the promised land. Gonna make it this time, Jake—gotta make it." He drooped his head and put his hands over his ears. My session was over. I lifted my feet from the water and stood up.

I looked down at him sitting there, an old man trying to hide from his self-created horrors. During his sermons at Speaker's Corner, Moses could bring to mind the Old Testament prophet, calling down damnation and doom, challenging all the powers of evil with wild eyes and shaking fists. Sitting on the edge of the quay, he just looked like a frightened old wino.

I knew Perry and his tribe would never make it to any promised land. They'd be lucky if they made it halfway down Hayward. As always, the crusade would start at Speaker's Corner after a fire-and-brimstone sermon from Perry. Then they'd go stomping up Hayward, five thousand strong, singing garbled hymns and throwing bottles. Moses would be at the front, tall staff in one hand and the good book in the other, righteous purpose in his step and drunk as a sod. Their ranks would swell as they went, as winos and tramps and bag ladies poured out of alleys and doorways until they were ten thousand strong. The lice-infested, bedraggled army would keep marching and none would stand before them, not pimp, whore nor pusher. The lowest creatures of the street would reign supreme and for one glorious day the winos would inherit Hayward.

Then some tramp would put a brick through the window of a liquor store, and the proud army would melt into a mob of looters. For the rest of the night there would be anarchy in the streets as the winos grabbed what they could, looking for their promised land in the bottle. The pressure cooker of Hayward would let off some steam, and the morning's light would find the powder blue reclamation vans discreetly collecting the hundred or so winos who had gone all the way.

On the way back to the office I stopped for a soy dog and a beer. I leaned on the counter and thought about what the street had told me. Tumblers were turning in my head, but nothing seemed certain except some very evil things were about to happen. What, I wasn't sure. It was like feeling around in the dark for a mute grizzly bear: I wanted to know where he was but I hated the idea of finding him. I finished my beer and dog and walked to the Caddy. It was time to find my truelove.

21

I was playing a hunch. I sat in my car across the street from the rear entrance of the Close Court Apartments. The double doors opened onto a path that wound through a tiny rock garden with plastic flowers and a dry Cupid fountain on its way to the street. Love's messenger wore a gaudy coat of graffiti and lacked an arm and nose. He didn't look too thrilled about the current state of romantic love, either.

I'd parked in front for the first hour and was amazed at how few people bustled about compared to Monday. I followed an instinct and drove around back and presto, it was Grand Central Station.

People came and went through the back door at roughly thirty-second intervals, and their furtive movements told me it wasn't because they wanted to admire the garden. There was a desperate urgency in their stride, and most of them carried packages. The outgoing packages looked like bundles of fliers, which meant they probably had a printing press in the basement. The packages going in looked like rifles wrapped in blankets.

An overloaded gothic struggled out and dropped a double armload of bound fliers into a basket strapped to the back of his motorcycle. The sweat from his labor made his heavy eyeliner run and his black spiky hair wilt. I got out of the Caddy and walked over.

"I'm supposed to hand out half of those," I said.

He smiled and handed me half. "You can take all of them if you want. Where you going to blanket?"

"I was thinking Hayward."

He laughed and got on his bike. "Good luck getting those animals to believe. You're better off sticking to Barridales, Colfax or Riverside." He kicked the bike to life and roared off.

I carried the thirty pounds of leaflets to the Caddy. I opened the trunk and put the bundle inside after slipping a leaflet from the bindings. I climbed behind the wheel and read.

Attention citizens! The day has come! The Party is starting its genocidal war against the people and we must resist or be slaughtered! Rise up!

Gather weapons, stock food, form militias and get ready for the war coming soon to your neighborhood. The wolf is loose!

Fight now or die later! Rise up against the murderous tyrants! Rise up!

The People's Resistance Front.

Crude illustrations on the back of the flier explained how to make a Molotov cocktail, then how to turn the cocktail into a very basic antivehicle weapon by adding a shotgun and broomstick. The contraption was fine for stopping your neighbor's subcompact but completely useless against Party tanks and APCs. The People's Resistance Group seemed in dire need of professional technical advice.

The low growl of powerful engines made me look up. A caravan of vans approached from the west, stopping two blocks short of the apartment building. I counted six of them. They were all different: different colors, different makes, different models, yet they were all the same. All had tinted windows, side-mounted spotlights and a ponderous look heavy-duty suspensions couldn't hide; they were armored.

Britt stepped out the back door of the apartment building, wearing the same wrap and sunglasses she wore the day I shot Crawley. She looked to be in a hurry. She turned up the sidewalk toward the vans.

I trained binoculars on the first van in line. The tinted glass made it difficult, but I could just make out the driver and passenger. Both had crewcuts and thick necks.

The side and back doors of the vans flew open, and black-suited troopers stormed out. They wore body armor and carried gleaming late-model assault rifles. They were also all skinheads. They formed up into two columns and began jogging down the sidewalk, fifty strong.

Britt froze on the sidewalk, wavering before the descending columns of armed skinheads, and I hit the ignition button. Just when I thought she was going to make a run for it, she locked her head forward and continued down the sidewalk toward the skins as if they weren't there.

"That is one smart, gutsy broad," I murmured, and watched the skins file past her toward the Close Court Apartments. The vans turned around and retreated the way they'd come, all except one. A low black street rod remained in place, engine rumbling. I pulled away from the curb and began moving slowly toward Britt and the van.

Five meters from the van Britt hesitated, eyeing the tinted glass suspiciously. The same instant, the cargo door of the van burst open and three skins jumped to the street and started toward Britt.

I stomped on the accelerator, the engine screamed and I pointed the hood ornament at the trio of skins. They froze before the onrushing Caddy, which was their mistake. I jumped the sidewalk, and with a sickening series of thuds their combined weight cut the speed of the Caddy in half. Two went over and one under as I slammed on the brakes and twisted the wheel violently to the right, throwing the car into a gut-wrenching slide. The Caddy executed a tight, howling turn around the rear of the van and I ended up facing the way I'd come. I gunned the engine, rocketed past the van and came to a screeching halt beside Britt. She was crouching on the sidewalk and digging in her purse. I leaned over and threw the passenger door open. She didn't jump in, so I leaped out my door and yelled at her over the roof.

"Get in the goddamn car!"

She pointed a revolver at me.

"Jesus Christ!" I yelled.

Fifteen meters away the passenger door of the van popped open and I pulled my pistol. A tall man stepped out, a man I knew. He wore body armor instead of a SPF captain's uniform but it was him. A pistol hung on his hip; his hands were empty.

"There's room for ex-servicemen in the new order, Sergeant Strait!" he shouted. "Things are changing, Houston wasn't for nothing. The Rangers can live again!"

An explosion jumped from the direction of the Close Court Apartments, followed closely by the angry chatter of assault rifles. The sounds excited me.

"I was in Special Forces, Seventh Group," the SPF officer continued. "We got ours in L.A. and Rio, almost wiped out to the man. But these are new times. They need elite soldiers again. Things are going back to the way they were. *We* can go back to what we were."

I pointed the gyra at him, but against every instinct, I didn't pull the trigger.

"Don't throw your life away for that whore." The captain began walking toward me. "Look at her."

I glanced at Britt. She held the revolver in both hands, pointing it at my head. Her eyes flashed between me and the captain.

"She wants to kill you." He showed me his empty hands. "I want to *save* you."

The pistol in my hand became heavier and heavier. "Go back?" I asked. "Go back to what?"

"Oh, you remember. That perfect sense of violent purpose, knowing you were doing the right thing, surrounded by brothers would lay down their lives to save your own. How many so-called friends would do that for you now? Do you think *she* understands that like we do? How long are you going to stand alone, hounded by the souls of all your fallen comrades? How long can one man stand against all the shit and horror out there?"

Yes, how long, I wondered, the pistol dropping to my side. "Jesus Christ, I really am alone," I said, looking inside myself. "How insignificant I am. Why didn't I lay down with them? How could I have left all my brothers behind to die? They all went to hell without me. Now I have to go alone. What the hell am I doing here?"

"You have a purpose!" the captain cried out, moving closer. "We are great knights, Strait—our destinies are *huge*. If you knew of the coming days of power, you wouldn't hesitate." He smiled and spread his hands. "With all the power of the Party behind us, we will be as *gods*."

"The Party?" I snarled, jolting out of my reverie. "The Party killed us. The Party sent us to the chopping block!"

He smiled grimly and continued to move slowly closer. "Mistakes were made, Strait. They're willing to admit that now. But things have changed. They need us again."

"Not me," I said. "Not for them."

He stopped four meters in front of me. "You don't understand, Jake. You're either with us or you're with them."

"Then I'm with them."

His eyes flashed to Britt. "She'll kill you."

"She already has."

Our eyes locked and we fell silent. An electricity crackled between us, and our souls met on a narrow bridge, knowing only one could pass. His hand blurred to the holster and his pistol flashed up. I crouched and fired from the hip. The whoosh of the gyra muffled the crack of his automatic, and a bullet whispered past my ear. The captain collapsed in the street, his belly ruptured. He writhed on his back and pawed at his stomach, trying to keep his intestines from spilling out.

"Oh, fuck, I'm really sorry," I said, meaning it, crouching to help him, knowing I couldn't. "I didn't want to shoot you. I really didn't."

He looked up at me, his eyes full of fate. "Finish me, bogeyman," he whispered, cringing with pain. "This is a mean game—losers don't get to live."

I straightened up and aimed at his head. His face squinched up to receive the jet.

I lowered the gyra. "I can't risk it," I said. "My soul isn't safe."

Suddenly the captain's face caved in, his perplexed expression lost in a spray of blood. I looked at the smoking gun in Britt's hand.

"This is a war, you idiot." She pointed the revolver back at me. "There isn't any room for sentimentality."

An engine roared and rubber screamed. The van surged forward, rushing at the rear of the Caddy. I thumbed the selector lever to automatic and sprayed the van's windshield with jets. Plexiglas and driver disintegrated in the barrage of explosive jets, but the van came on like an enraged elephant, the brain dead and the body bent on vengeance. I yelled unintelligibly at Britt, dived into the driver's seat, slammed the gear shift into drive and jumped on the accelerator. The tires and engine howled in chorus and the van loomed in the rearview mirror. That's okay! my mind screamed, things always look closer than they really are in rearview mirrors! Or was it the other way around?

The Caddy lurched with the impact of the van's front bumper and I felt the frame give in a half-dozen places. Metal grinded and groaned and I fought the wheel for control. The bumpers of the grappling machines locked, and we careened down the narrow street, trading paint with parked cars. I jerked the wheel hard left then right, and the van veered off and slammed into a parked ice-cream truck with a horrible crunching of metal.

That wouldn't sit well with the local kids, I thought, watching the blooming alcohol explosion in the rearview. I shook my fist at the image and whooped off the tension. I *was* invincible!

The distinctive click of a hammer being thumbed back iced my elation. I looked over to find Britt had come along for the ride. Her pistol was pointed at my chest.

"Ah, gratitude," I said sighing, "the most lovely of emotions."

She glanced at the revolver self-consciously but didn't put it away. "Who are you working for now?"

"The forces of good."

"Who are they?" she asked shakily, casting a nervous glance behind us. She looked as if she hadn't slept in days, and the built-up tension was making the hand holding the pistol tremble. With the hammer back, it wouldn't take much pressure to make it go off, and that seemed a shame since it was pointing at my heart.

"Why don't you point that somewhere else before you tremble me out of existence," I suggested.

"I'm not so sure that would be a bad thing," she snapped.

"You've already shattered my heart into a thousand pieces," I told her. "What's a lousy bullet going to do?"

She looked at the gun in her shaking hand, then dropped it in her purse. She snuck out a handkerchief and began dabbing at her eyes. Her tough exterior was peeling off right in front of me.

"So you're human after all," I said. She shot me a hard look, and I said, "Hey, there's nothing wrong with crying."

She gave me a funny look, and I sensed I'd just blown what could have been a very touching scene.

"Go to hell," she said, then laughed like glass breaking. "I don't have the time to cry." She laughed again, and the tears were long gone.

I concentrated on my driving. I wasn't going in any particular direction, but I found myself subconsciously angling toward Hayward, my filthy security blanket. The oil light was getting my attention by winking at me, and the engine was making a lot of new noises. I had a hunch that new plugs and a change of oil weren't going to fix it this time. Its luck had run out, and mine didn't look to be too far behind.

"Take me to East Harrow," Britt demanded.

East Harrow was a new ghetto on the other side of the river. "Why there?"

She looked at me sharply. "Why should I tell you?"

"Because I saved your life."

"Did you?"

"I like to think so."

After a moment of silence she said, "There's a safe house there." She looked out the window. "I have to get the resistance organized. They're using the fascists to attack us."

"How do you know the safehouse wasn't raided, too?"

She thought about it, then said, "Take me to a phone booth."

I took her to the one in front of the St. Chris. I parked in the shadow of the wino saint, and she got out. I didn't think she would make a break for it, at least not until after she made the call. I watched her from the car, obsessed and jumpy. Just looking at her, the curve of her face, the way she held the phone, her troubled frown, all made me feel insecure and mean. I knew it was that cruel pimp circumstance that prevented us from becoming perfect mates. I had to show her I was a *good* man, that I *meant* well, that I was *tricked* into killing her friend and stealing her money.

After dialing and hanging up three times, she climbed back into the car, pale and frightened.

"Well?" I asked, though her face said it all.

"The lines are dead at two safe houses. A voice I didn't recognize answered the third." She pointed her head at the address book in her hand, but her eyes focused on something a million miles away. I'd seen the same look when I was in the army. They called it shell shock.

"Who would have believed the fascists could have organized so fast?" she murmured.

"They had help. The skinheads that raided Close Court were dropped off by unmarked SPF vehicles. The man we killed was a spif officer."

She nodded as if the idea wasn't new to her.

"That van was waiting for you," I said. "How'd they know you were coming out?"

"I got a call from one of Crawley's friends just before the raid. A man who helped us sometimes. He said he needed to meet me in a giddylounge two blocks away, that it was an emergency. He set me up—he's working for them."

"They wanted you alive. Why?"

She shrugged.

"Maybe your father had something to do with it," I said.

"What do you know about him?"

"He hired me to kill Crawley."

Hate flashed across her face, then drowned in a sea of despair. "Of course he did. That bastard."

"I know a safe place you can stay," I said. She nodded. She wasn't a teary-eyed little girl, but she wasn't the hard-assed professional, either. Right now she was a blank.

I drove to Tanya's. I parked in the alley behind her tenement and we went in the back. I pounded on the door and hoped she was home.

"It's finished," Britt whispered. "They've won, they've stopped us."

"You can tell me about that when I get back."

"You're leaving?" she said, startled.

"Only for a little while. I have to get some things we'll need."

"Who is it?" a muffled voice said from inside.

"It's Jake."

"Who?"

I remembered I'd never told her my name. "It's the revolutionary agent you met last night." I checked Britt for a snide look, but her mind was elsewhere. The door opened and Tanya peeked out.

"Trouble," I said. "We need sanctuary. Like in the spy movies." The door opened and I ushered Britt in. I led her to the bedroom and sat her on the bed. I signaled Tanya to follow me to the kitchen.

"We're on the run," I said quietly. "We're being hunted by a SPF-fascist coalition."

She looked me straight in the eyes. "You're not kidding, are you?"

"I wish I was. Can we hole up here for a while?"

"Of course you can, silly." She looked over at Britt. "What's wrong with her?"

"She just got her revolution crushed. You'd act that way, too."

Tanya nodded. "She your girlfriend?"

I laughed. "She nearly killed me twice."

"Really?" She seemed heartened by the idea.

"That's not even counting the hit team she sent after me. Listen, I'm going to be gone for a couple hours and I want you to keep an eye on Britt." I unclipped the .32 snubnose from my belt and handed it to her. "Do you know how to use one of these?"

She popped the cylinder open, checked the load, then snapped it shut with a flick of her wrist. "Who doesn't?"

"Mean times," I observed. "Don't answer the door for anyone except me. You'll know it's me because I'll knock three times, twice, then three times again. Got it?"

"A secret knock?" She smiled. "Really?"

"We don't cut corners in the revolution business, baby. If I'm not back by tomorrow morning, take this money and get yourself and Britt out of the City." I handed her my last three hundred. "Do you have friends in the burbs?"

"My parents."

"Stay with them. Tell them whatever you like, just get out of the City. Got me?"

She said she would. I took her by the shoulders, kissed her goodbye, then slipped out the front door, making sure she locked it behind me.

22

I drove home. Since I'd left nothing but reclaimables at the rescue scene, I couldn't see how they could finger me, but I felt like a mouse in the shadow of an owl anyway. I crept up the stairs like a henpecked husband with whiskey on his breath and light on the horizon. I cleared each room of my flat with pistol drawn.

Satisfied there were no spifs under the bed or bogeymen in the closet, I changed into black jungle pants, T-shirt and combat boots. I put a Browning 9 mm, a Smith & Wesson .357 and a Walther PP .380 with appropriate ammunition in a kit bag. I'd have to stop by my office for the heavy firepower. I was a relative newcomer to the game, but I figured I'd need a lot of guns to stage a proper revolution. I grabbed my leather anti-hero jacket and a six-pack on the way out.

I was locking up when I heard a click behind me. I dropped the six-pack and executed a whirling quick draw.

Finley's door slammed shut.

When my breathing returned to normal, I knocked on the door. "It's okay, Mr. Finley, I won't shoot you."

A muffled hoot came from the other side.

"It's me," I said. "Mr. Strait."

The door opened and a big eye ogled me. "Hello, Mr. Strait. That's an interesting hairstyle. People have been looking for you."

"Oh, really? Who and when?"

"About two hours ago four men came by. I heard them pounding on your door so I told them you weren't home, because I knew you weren't. One of them had a badge and said they were from the Security and Protection Force, but they weren't in uniform."

I nodded knowingly. "The old counterfeit-badge ploy, eh?"

Finley eyed me for a moment. "I didn't believe him."

"Good show, Fin. What did these obvious impostors look like?"

"Two were big men with black suits and short hair."

"How short? Were their heads shaved?"

"No, they had hair, but it was short."

"Did they have thick necks?"

"Yes, they did."

"Ah-ha," I said. "What did the other two look like?"

"The one who did all the talking wore a hat. He was very mean and nasty."

"Did he tell you his name, as a genuine and legitimate officer of the SPF would?"

"No, he just flashed his badge. That's why I knew he was a fake."

"Mr. Finley, did this faker say 'fooking' a lot and constantly clench and unclench his hands like this?" I did a fair imitation of Inspector Blake's endearing mannerism.

"Yes, he did! I remember because I thought he wanted to grab me."

I sighed. "I'm afraid that's exactly what he wanted to do, Mr. Finley."

"How do you know?" Finley asked nervously. "Do you know him?"

"Yes. By your description that could be none other than Big Hands Blake, the Mad Strangler from Philly. A known archfiend. He does contract kills for the mob, but the demands of his job don't keep him from having a little fun on his off time. He once got on a crowded bus and strangled everyone on board except the driver before the bus made the next stop. The only reason he didn't throttle the driver was because it wasn't his stop."

I could tell by his expression that Finley was recalling just how close Blake had stood to him. "No!" he whispered.

"Yes. The two heavies were probably bodyguards provided by the mob, which means he was here on business, not pleasure."

"I thought the Party cleaned up the mob years ago!"

"They told you there'd be elections this year, too, didn't they? What did the fourth criminal look like?"

My revelations had rattled Finley's memory. "I-I'm not sure," he stuttered. "He, ah, seemed small and acted like he didn't want to be there. And he had thick glasses and was kind of pale, I think. What's wrong?"

I eased the grimace off my face. That explained how Blake found out where I lived, something I was careful not to advertise. "Was he balding and had a small mustache?"

"Yes, I think he did. You know him, too?"

I massaged my temples with index finger and thumb. "I'm afraid I do. That sounds like Joey 'the Rat Bastard' Drake. A renowned weasel. He once worked for the forces of good but he backslid and now he's an informant for the mob."

"What does the mob want with you, Mr. Strait?"

"Revenge. It turned out those hoods I killed last week, the ones who were trying to bushwhack you, were under orders from the mob. Blake must not have realized it was you they were after in the first place. He is a professional, though, and I'm sure he'll make the connection sooner or later. Say, what did you do to offend the mob so much, anyway?"

Finley eyed me for a minute then quietly closed his door, perhaps realizing the longer he talked to me the more his darkest fears would be confirmed. It'd be a long night for me and Fin both. I'm a really *mean* bastard, I thought.

JOE LIVED in the borough of Woodgreen. The neighborhood sat right on the invisible demarcation line between the City and the old burbs. It was the kind of neighborhood where people paid rent and watered their lawns. Most of the streetlights worked, and spif cruisers were known to prowl through on occasion.

Joe lived in a modest Spanish-style hacienda painted redbrown to resemble adobe. Joe hated it. He said it made him feel like a migrant worker. When they got around to approving his application, Joe planned on moving to the burbs proper.

I drove past his hacienda and parked a block away. I opened a vitabeer and took Crawley's wallet out of the glove box. After pulling out all the business cards and looking them over, I put them back, finished my beer and stepped out of the Caddy.

I walked to Joe's house and quietly lifted the garage door enough to see his Chevy sitting inside. I walked around the side and jumped over the concrete fence, also painted to resemble adobe.

The backyard had fallen to ruin since the last time I'd seen it. The grass looked as if it hadn't tasted water in a month. Joe was probably spiteful because he couldn't get the fake stuff. Times past, Joe and I would barbecue fat soy steaks and black-market chicken wings on the redbrick patio. I'd put away a six-pack, Joe would smoke hash, and we'd talk about our army days and the rapid decline of the world around us. Now the barbecue was full of stagnant rainwater, and I couldn't remember the last time we'd shared banter on the patio. I'd got wrapped up with a long string of live-in girlfriends, and Joe had found the Hill. We'd drifted apart.

The sliding glass door was unlocked, which was typical of Joe. I slipped into the cool interior and listened. Hearing noises coming from the direction of the living room, I crept across the kitchen tiles and peered over the saloon-style doors.

Joe was in the living room, behaving like a ferret. Three fat suitcases squatted by the front door, and he was scurrying around in a frenzy, as if he were afraid he was going to forget something he couldn't live without. It looked as if Joe was going on a trip, and I'd caught him just in time to wish him a bon voyage.

"Out jumps the Devil!" I shouted, and pounced into the living room. Joe squeaked like a rat and scurried for the front door. I got there in time to shove it closed. "Now, is that any way for a proper host to act?" I asked.

Joe cowered in front of me, which made me feel bad because we used to be buddies. I clamped a hand on to his shoulder and navigated him to the sofa. I sat on the arm of a chair opposite him and gave him a disappointed look.

Joe said, "You won't understand, Jake, you won't ever understand."

"Oh, I don't know, try me."

Dropping his head, Joe shook it slowly back and forth and said nothing.

"You've been hanging around with a bad crowd lately, Joey."

Joe raised his eyes and looked defensive.

"The likes of Inspector Blake of the SPF goon squad. Why did you go with them to my apartment? You could have just told him where I lived."

Joe shrugged as though he couldn't figure it out himself.

"Was it because the booby rig on my apartment door wasn't so amateurish? Were you there to lure me out, Joe? Lure me into the cruel hands of Big Hands Blake?"

The denial teetered on his lips, ready to tumble out, but at the last second he swallowed it. He hung his head again.

"You fingered Crawley, didn't you?" I said. Joe's head jerked at the sound of the name, and I knew I was right. "Crawley worked the party circuit just like you, except his gig was poetry. He kept your phone number in his wallet. You were probably pals. When Crawley and Britt split with the cash, you finked to win a favor." I shook my head and tutted. "Shame, shame, Joey, you can lose a lot of friends acting like that."

"I don't expect you to understand," he whined. "You see from the gutter with big self-righteous eyes. Big changes are coming, and it's every man for himself. Crawley was asking for it with all his anti-Party rhetoric. He was a romantic idiot without enough common sense to take a look around and make the adjustment. He'd end up with an execution warrant sooner or later anyway."

"And I'm a walking corpse myself, so it wouldn't matter if you helped the inspector do a number on me." Something occurred to me, and I got up and began pacing the room angrily. "Wait a minute, wait a goddamn minute." I stopped pacing and pointed a damning finger at him. "You miserable bastard! You played me along the whole time. You recommended me for the Crawley job! You set me up as the stooge. You've been shitting on me from the start! Haven't you?"

Joe hung his head and didn't say anything.

I didn't say anything, either. I stood in front of him, my hands clawed, wanting to grab him by the neck and throttle the miserable life out of him. But I couldn't bring myself to do it. After a minute all the anger drained out the bottom of my feet, and I turned away from him. I couldn't hate Joe any more than I could hate a bird who crapped on my car. That was its nature. In the same sense, Joe couldn't help it if he acted like a weasel, because he was a weasel.

Joe made a big show of looking at his watch, then stood up. "I have to go, Jake. You can shoot me if you want, but I have to go."

I took out my pistol and pointed it at him.

"I didn't mean it!" he squealed, bobbing and weaving like a boxer trying to duck a punch. "I didn't mean it!"

"I know," I said. "I just wanted you to know how it feels to be under the gun." I put the pistol away. "Where you heading, anyway?"

Joe mumbled the first time, so I asked him again.

"The Hill."

"The Hill?" I echoed. "So that's what they promised you. Who invited you to live on the Hill?"

"Director Chamberlain invited me. I won't be actually living there. I'll just stay until all the trouble in the City blows over."

"What trouble is that?"

He shrugged. "I don't know, just trouble."

"They'll kill you."

Joe's eyes told me the possibility had crossed his mind, but he didn't want to believe it. "They're my friends, Jake. They like me."

"Wrong, Joe. They'll gloat under your educated lies, but they don't like you. You're not one of them. Why should they protect an outsider? Because they like your jokes? You're just another loose end, and if you go up there they'll kill you."

Joe walked to his suitcases and picked two of them up. "You don't know them like I do. They're my friends, and friends take care of each other."

"That's a funny idea, coming from you. Considering all the favors you've done me and Crawley." I laughed to prove it was funny.

Joe opened the door and let himself out. He didn't come back for his third suitcase. I sat on the arm of the chair until I heard the Chevy pull out of the driveway and gun down the street.

I walked back to the Caddy. The fuel light was coming on, so I diverted to Second Fed then to an alcohol station. Filling up the tank, I reflected back to a simpler time when having a thousand creds in my wallet actually seemed like a big deal.

23

I didn't really want to go to my office. With Blake rutting around like a boar in heat, it seemed a bad move. But there were things I needed. I was gambling that Blake didn't think I was stupid enough to go near the place. I parked in front of the Silver Spoon behind a big banana yellow pimpmobile and watched the front of my office building from two blocks away. I didn't see killers who didn't look local, so I put the gyra in my coat with my hand and took a walk.

The stairwell and hall were empty, and my office door didn't appear to have been tampered with. I unlocked the door quietly, then, pistol in hand, rushed into the room, ready to shoot anyone sitting in my chair. The only thing I found in the room was a bunch of sinister shadows.

I made my visit a brief one. I opened my weapons locker and filled a duffel bag with a Thoma Killmaster SM6 rotary machine gun, two M-16 A3 assault rifles, an Uzi submachine gun, a Myers automatic shotgun, two Colt .45 automatics, ammunition for all, seven kilos of plastic explosives with primers and a radio detonator and a spider-silk vest. I sealed the duffel and hefted it. It wasn't much heavier than a Johnny Humungo weight set.

I got some duct tape from my desk and taped two grenades firmly to the doorjamb, one at knee level and the other two feet higher. I took down two framed pictures and unscrewed their hanging hooks from the wall. I screwed them into the door, one next to each grenade, then wired the grenade pins to the hooks with unfolded paper clips and gave the pins a slight head start. Finally I taped the top of the grenade spoons loosely to the doorjamb, so when somebody jimmied open the door and pulled the pins, the spoons wouldn't pop off and clatter on the floor, giving some undeserving soul a seven-second warning.

I took a step back and checked my handiwork. It was cruder than the doorknob rig but almost impossible to detect or disarm from the outside. I hoped Blake would pay me another visit.

I slung the duffel onto my back, opened the bay window and crawled out onto the fire escape. When I got down to the alley, big drops of rain started to fall. I looked up and smiled at the gray sky. The rain had finally come.

I turned left and walked to Marshall, the street running parallel to Hayward. I turned right and walked five blocks, then cut back to Hayward and approached my car from the direction opposite my office. If someone was watching the Caddy, they wouldn't expect me coming from that direction. I learned that trick from reading old spy novels.

In times of trouble it was always good to see a friend. So I smiled when I saw Paul "Goose" Gosman emerge from the pack of women hanging out under umbrellas in front of the Silver Spoon, swinging a kit bag as though he hadn't a care in the world. Paul was one of few members of my profession I liked. When we were both young mavericks fresh from the service, eager to liquidate all the bad guys, we'd even worked some warrants together.

The only problem with Paul was that his taste for expensive women eventually forced him to rely on the more lucrative pay of political contracts to make ends meet. An ethical rift had developed between us, and we hadn't talked in months. But as rare as allies were at this point in the game, I was willing to forgive and forget.

"Hey, Goose, what's up?" I said. Paul's coal black face tensed as if he'd seen a ghost, then he walked by without giving me any sign of recognition at all.

That's funny, I thought, dropping the duffel and diving to the sidewalk. I executed a somersault with a half twist and ended up on my belly, my pistol pointing the way I'd come. Chips of concrete stung my face as Paul's machine pistol chewed up the sidewalk in front of me. I snapped off a shot, and Paul dived behind the banana yellow pimpmobile. I rolled left behind an iron trash bin.

"Can't we talk about this, Paul?" I ventured.

Paul popped up from behind the pimpmobile and sprayed the bin, ringing it like an alarm bell. I heard the bolt of his machine pistol clack onto an empty chamber, and Paul ducked down to slap in a new magazine. I knew it was my big chance.

I leaned out and aimed three quick shots a foot below the pimpmobile's chrome alcohol-intake valve. Paul popped up with a fresh magazine, and I was cursing the cheap pimp when a little whoosh announced a big boom as the explosive jets found their way to the fuel tank. Paul stumbled from behind the fireball, his entire body engulfed in wild blue flame. I aimed carefully and shot him once in the forehead. He cartwheeled down the sidewalk and lay in a burning heap.

A frantic pimp rushed out of the Spoon, and I had to guess that the banana yellow number was his. He stood screaming at the burning wreck, with the grief of a man who'd forgotten to insure his wheels, then dragged out a big chrome-plated Colt .44 Magnum. He moved to the front of the car and began firing round after thundering round into the machine's engine block. Symbolic, I thought.

I counted six shots from the Magnum, then got up from behind the bin. I walked to where Paul's kit bag had fallen. I picked it up and inside I found spools of electrical wire, plastic clothes pins, tape, a Swiss army knife, wire snips, two twelve-volt batteries, electrical primers and about three pounds of plastic explosive. Oh-ho, I thought.

I walked the kit and duffel bag over to the Caddy. The pimp was giving me the vindictive eye, but we both knew whose pistol was empty and whose wasn't. Finally he threw his head back and laughed. Street logic. If you couldn't kill it, laugh at it. He waved his pistol at me because it was empty and I waved mine at him because it was loaded. He put his arms around a couple of his girls and went back inside the Spoon.

I got on my stomach and looked at the car's undercarriage but I couldn't find anything awry. I carefully opened the hood and still couldn't find anything. I cupped my hands and peered in the window, but couldn't detect any exposed wires or explosives. But then, Goose had built his reputation with explosives work and wouldn't be that sloppy. Either that or I had surprised him before he could plant anything. There was only one way to find out.

I put the keys to the Caddy on the roof above the driver's door, picked up my bags and retreated into the narrow alley next to the Spoon. I leaned against the alley wall and waited.

After five minutes I had a taker. A long-haired fan of squeeze sauntered by and gave the keys fish eyes. I smiled. He came back a minute later and leaned against the hood. He spotted me watching him from the alley.

"You don't want to steal that car," I said, warding off future guilt.

He got off the hood and squinted at me. "Is it yours?"

"Nope."

"A friend of yours?"

"Nope."

"You guarding it for someone?"

I shook my head.

"Then what's it to you?"

I shrugged and smiled. He gave me the finger, grabbed the keys and jangled them at me defiantly. I backed into the alley and crouched behind a garbage can.

The door slammed, and after a lot of unhealthy growling the Caddy coughed to life. I counted to three, then pulled my pistol. I came out from behind the can to reclaim my car when it disintegrated before my eyes with the distinct *bang-boom* of a powerful explosive igniting the fuel tank. A torrid shock wave blew me back into the alley, and I ended up on my butt with singed hair and ringing ears. The recent trip to the fuel station made for a spectacular blue fireball, and pieces of my car rained down. Life was full of explosions lately.

I stared into the flames for a moment, saying goodbye to another friend, a commodity I was rapidly running short of. I could only hope I'd take my own final bow in such an exciting manner.

I noticed the pimp standing in the doorway of the Spoon, a wry smile on his face. I walked to the Caddy and fired once into what remained of the hood. I looked back at the pimp. "Symbolic," I said. He nodded and went back inside.

Now I had to get away while I could, and follow up on my deep, dark hunch. I changed cabs twice to make sure I wasn't being followed, then got out at a phone booth three blocks from Tanya's. I called SPF central and asked for the warrant collection office.

"Assistant Inspector Degas speaking, how can I help you?" a voice said.

"Hello. This is private enforcer Paul Gosman. I'd like to confirm the disposition of a contract." There was a pause.

"Go ahead, Gosman."

"I'd like to check out one Jacob Strait, ID number 233044325."

I could hear keys clicking on the other end, then Degas said, his voice shockingly cooperative, "Jacob Wolfgang Strait, 165 Rood Ave., Apartment 451. Business address, 9803 Hayward, Suite 303. Wanted for extensive political crimes, he pays an A-1 for execution with a double-bonus modifier."

I whistled to myself. With a double A-1, it was no big wonder Paul had tried his luck. I tried not to feel too conceited about my high rating.

"He's considered armed and dangerous," Degas finished.

"You mean he was. They're having a cookout in front of the Silver Spoon Café on Hayward, and Strait's the main course. I'm calling to take credit for the kill. I'll be down for my reward later. Gosman out." I hung up.

I lugged the bags to Tanya's, feeling as if I had a big red bull's-eye taped to my butt. With that kind of bounty on my head, I'd overnight become a gold mine for every gun-totting junky in town. So this is how it feels, I thought. Under the *big* gun.

I knocked on the door using the proper sequence.

"What's the code word?" a voice asked.

I thought hard. Was all the alcohol deranging my memory? "I don't remember any code word."

"That's right," Tanya said, and opened the door to let me in. She wore a gray-and-black pantsuit with the .32 stuck in the waistband. She chewed gum and dangled a cigarette from her lips like a 1920s gun moll. "What happened to you?" she asked. "You smell like fire."

"The imperialists blew up my car. Five innocent beers perished in the flames. Two of my friends sold out to the enemy, and there's a SPF goon squad hunting me like a pack of rabid bloodhounds."

"We're not winning, are we?"

"We haven't even had possession of the ball yet. How's Britt?"

"She's sleeping," Tanya said, jerking a thumb back to the bed.

"Did you two talk any?"

"Not a lot. She's really scared about something. After you left, she got real jittery."

"Did she?" The idea warmed me.

Tanya nodded, then fixed me with a speculative eye. "Are you scared, Jake?"

"Not as long my nightlight stays on and the closet door is closed."

She giggled. "Afraid of the bogeyman?"

I thought about the A-1 reward with double modifier. "I am now."

She looked over her shoulder. "You going to wake her up?"

I looked at the form in the bed. She lay in a tight fetal position, the blankets pulled up to her chin.

"Not for a while. She needs rest, and I have to get things straight in my head. I have to figure out the questions before I can start looking for answers."

"What is she going to tell you?"

"I don't know." I looked at Tanya. "But I got a feeling it isn't going to be good."

24

Tanya and I sat at the kitchen table drinking beer, waiting for soy beef sandwiches to defrost in the microwave. She'd done a fine job of stocking up. The cupboards were full of food, and a case of beer lurked in the belly of the fridge.

"How'd you know I liked beer?" I asked.

She shrugged. "Just guessed. You just seem like the type."

"With this Tarzanesque physique?"

"Not by your body—I knew by the way you act. You're... working class."

"You mean proletariat hero."

"I guess. What's going to happen, Jake?"

I took a long drink and leaned back in my chair. "I'm not sure. Apparently the Party is going to lay a bad scene on the City. Maybe a martial-law clampdown like they tried four years ago. Move troops in and try to take back the no-go areas."

"But they failed."

I nodded. "They failed because they weren't organized enough. The SPF are more cops than soldiers. The independent militias united and fought them to a standstill in the outer boroughs. Maybe the Party plans to try harder this time."

"That's what Britt is fighting? The Party taking the City back?"

"I think so," I said, recalling the flier. "She's trying to unite the different groups to resist whatever is coming. Like Joan of Arc."

"Wasn't Joan of Arc crazy?"

"Some say."

Tanya stood up. "Do you want another beer?"

"Yes." I checked my watch. It was three minutes to six. "Do you have a TV?"

"A propaganda box? Yeah, but I never watch it."

"Where's it at?"

She walked to the closet next to the front door and brought out an ancient black-and-white portable.

"Have you paid your viewing fee for the month?" I asked.

She gave me a funny look and shook her head.

"Oh, well," I sighed. "We'll just have to risk it." I took the set and put it on the kitchen counter. I plugged it in and turned it on. The antenna was a moonlighting coat hanger, so the reception was fuzzy.

"Why do you want to watch TV?" Tanya asked.

"I want to see what's on the news." After fooling with the antenna for a moment, I sat down and opened my beer.

A commercial for Fungum was on. Bouncy, smiling models demonstrated just how much fun chewing gum could be. Johnny Humungo himself came on at the end and said, "When things get tough, just have a stick and forget about it." He popped a stick in his mouth and acted as if he was forgetting about it.

"Rough and tough Johnny Humungo is pushing Fungum now?" I asked.

Tanya nodded. "You don't watch TV much, do you?"

"Not lately." The local Party news came on with a flurry of martial music and a shot of a fluttering World Party flag. The fatherly anchorman started the program with the inner-city riot advisory so businessmen and workers tuning in on their car sets could avoid those nasty traffic snarl ups. The lead news story ran footage of valiant SPF troops rooting out nests of anarchists in the hills of Spain, followed by a report of new soy-processing plants nearing completion in the World Party republics of China and Brazil. The stories rolled on, and by the look of things the future of the Party never looked brighter.

It wasn't until the last five minutes of the program that the anchorman mentioned offhand that a number of right-wing extremists had visited raids upon a number of left-wing extremists in the City. He spoke in such a way that said it happened at least twice a week and he finished up with a calculated grin that suggested good, respectable citizens might enjoy a little laugh at the idea of bad people murdering each other. The

whole report lasted about ten seconds, then the buxom blond
came on with the summary of tomorrow's weather. I turned th
set off.

"I'm surprised they mentioned it at all," Britt said, her voic
surprising me.

"They had to," I said, turning to find she'd sneaked up be
hind us. Her eyes were still full of sleep but she looked bette
than before. "The raids were pretty blatant. If they didn't sa
anything, people would get suspicious."

"You're right." It sounded as if agreeing with me caused he
physical pain. I was ecstatic; I'd finally won a point. I pulle
out a chair and she sat down. I offered some of my beer, an
she took a sip.

"I suppose you want some answers," she said.

I nodded.

"Where shall I start?"

"Let's go all the way back to the beginning. Why did yo
take the three hundred grand from your parents?"

"To fund the counterrevolution against the fascist
establishment coalition's genocidal assault on the proletaria
masses."

"That probably looks great on a pamphlet, but why don'
you tell me in English even I can understand."

"We needed the money to get the people organized agains
my father's plan."

"What plan is that?"

"To kill all the poor people in the City."

I stared at her. "The poor people? What's he got agains
them?"

"That they're poor. A group of City directors got the ide
that depopulating nonproductive and restive sections of th
City would solve most of the Party's problems."

"Depopulating? How?"

"'Accidental' chemical leaks and mass food poisoning t
start. After it became obvious what they were up to, they'd g
right into air strikes and nerve gas."

I leaned back in my chair and squinted at her. "You're crazy
They'd never do that."

"Ha! Why wouldn't they?"

"It's immoral. They wouldn't get away with it."

"Who's going to stop them? It's already happening in Beijing, London and Rio! Listen Strait, the Party is teetering on the edge—it's rotting from within and losing ground every day. The popular revolution is coming, and the entrenched elitists on the Hill aren't about to turn over their wealth and power to people like you. They're going to do what they have to to survive, and if that means wiping out a few hundred thousand citizens, they'll do it. Check your history, they've been doing purges since the beginning of man."

"Jesus."

"Welcome to the real world, Strait."

"I don't think I like the real world."

"Well, that's just tough, isn't it?"

"Yeah. Your father told you all this?"

"Not directly. They held their meetings at my father's house. He didn't try to hide anything from me. I guess he thought I could be trusted."

"You have that quality about you," I said. "How many directors support this plan?"

"An influential minority. Housing, welfare, transportation, resources. They'll sway the rest or act without them. They're fanatics."

"What about the director of the SPF?"

"No. They were upset with him because he wouldn't play. He's an old man, and they think he's senile. But there were representatives from the SPF at the meetings, and from all the other directorates for that matter. Plus skinheads and officials from reclamation."

"Reclamation?" I asked. "I thought they were neutral, like the Red Cross."

"They are. They just wanted to know about it so they could get enough equipment ready for the cleanup."

"They are so damn thoughtful and efficient," I said. "What about the skinheads?"

"They're the muscle for the first phase of the plan. They can't directly use spif troops in the early stages because the people would catch on and revolt. Over the past month the SPF

supporters of the plan managed to unite most of the City skinhead clans under a single leader.''

"Is his name Harry?"

"That's him." She made a face. "After the meetings he
would try to pick me up."

I slammed the table with my fist. "That's it. Next time I see
him, he's dead."

She looked at me as if I might not be up to my boast. "Have
you met Harry?"

"We had a little run-in."

Britt wouldn't ask, so Tanya did. "Who won?"

I smiled and winked.

"A lot of the local skins have disappeared the last couple of
weeks," Tanya said.

"They're being taught urban warfare by SPF instructors,"
Britt explained. "They've turned Travis prison into a huge
training complex. That's what the skins get out of the deal—
training, weapons and the promise of future power, in exchange for their attacking and paralyzing the groups that would
organize and lead the counterattack." She gave me a mean
look. "They used you, too."

"I was tricked."

"Yeah. When Crawley came up for one of my mother's poetry parties, I told him about my father's plan and he said we'd
have to act fast. I accessed one of my father's accounts, transferred the sum of it to a new account in Crawley's name, then
escaped to spread the word. It was hard, since most people had
heard it all before."

"You got some people to believe."

"There's always those who'll believe anything monstrous
about the Party. Crawley had a lot of influence in the subculture." Her eyes dropped to the table. "Poor Rolland."

"I was tricked," I said again. I was starting to feel like a
heavy. "I'm not a bad man. I've just been tragically misrepre-
sented by the facts."

"All your life, I'll bet. When you killed Crawley and drained
his account, it set us back weeks. We needed the money for
guns, and without Crawley's influence it was harder to bring

people over. City people find it hard to believe snobby little girls from the Hill.''

I choked on my shame and nodded. "So the first roundups were today."

"Today is just the beginning.'' She seemed to be talking to herself. "It's finally starting.''

I finished my beer and tried to look at the big picture. "The World Party doesn't care about this? Can't they stop the City Party?''

Britt rolled her eyes maliciously. "Don't tell me you believe that 'brotherhood of the masses' bullshit. They know the times, and they'll turn a blind eye if not condone it. Wise up.''

I was getting wiser by the minute. We sat in silence for a moment, each of us wrestling private demons. My view of the world had become a couple of shades darker, and everything had taken a more sinister cast.

Tanya got up and brought back three beers and a plate of toasted soy beef sandwiches.

I concentrated on the food and quickly inhaled two sandwiches and was starting in on the third when Tanya dug a pack of gum from her pocket and put a stick in her mouth.

"What's that?" Britt demanded.

"Fungum," Tanya said. "It helps me relax. Want a stick?"

Britt made a face at the offered pack. "It's loaded with tranquilizers. The Party distributes it to the poor people to keep them in their place. Have a stick and forget you're oppressed and should be out in the streets rioting. It's the same reason they legalized downers and pot.''

"Sorry," Tanya said, and took the gum out of her mouth.

Britt stood up and stretched. Fatigue still hung from her features. "Anything else you want to know, Strait?''

"You've told me too much already. You get some more sleep and I'll figure something out. Thanks for sharing.''

Britt went back to bed, and Tanya and I sat in the kitchen and watched TV. Johnny Humungo was ripping apart a rebel camp with his bare hands, chasing terrified actors around like a bear after rabbits. Someone must have hidden his pack of Fungum.

"Do you believe her?" Tanya asked.

"I think I do," I said. I took a chug from my can. The beer tasted good. Too good.

Tanya sipped her beer like a lady and stared at the refrigerator. "I guess it was going to happen sooner or later."

"Doesn't have to happen," I said. "I could stop it." Johnny Humungo flipped over an armored personnel carrier with one hand.

She slid me a sideways look. "What can you do?"

"I can kill people."

"You gonna kill the whole City Party?"

"I'll get on the Hill and fix 'em."

"How are you going to get on the Hill?"

"I'll blast my way through the gate. Then I'll systematically root out the ringleaders and do the savage bastards in. Easy." I snapped my fingers like Johnny Humungo.

She giggled. "How are you even going to get there? I thought they blew up your car."

"I'll take a cab."

She giggled again, then finished up with a skeptical look. "I don't think you'd make it."

"Don't be so sure. I used to be in the Airborne Rangers. Wanna see me do a hundred push-ups?"

She squinted at me. "I thought all the rangers were wiped out in Texas somewhere."

"Houston."

"Yeah."

"I got lucky."

We drank our beer in silence. I finished mine and got another out of the fridge.

"What are we going to do?" Tanya asked, verbalizing my thoughts. The honest truth was that I hadn't the slightest idea what our next move would be.

"I have a good plan but I still have to work out the details," I lied. "I'll have to sleep on it."

Tanya nodded. "Are you going to sleep on the bed with her?"

"No," I said.

"Are you going to sleep on the floor with me?"

"No."

"Because she might not like it?"

"She wouldn't care if I slept with a polar bear."

"I wouldn't be too sure about that."

"Well, none of that has anything to do with it. Sleeping alone helps my concentration. It keeps me vigorous and full of vim."

Another silence muscled in.

"Are you going to drink all the beer?" Tanya asked quietly.

I gave the little mind reader a surprised look. "Of course not. What made you ask that?"

"Because when you mentioned Houston you looked like you might."

"Well," I said, finishing off my can, "I'll have you know that was my last drink of the evening. Now I'm going straight into the gentle arms of sweet slumber. I'll just curl up in that comfy-looking armchair over there and be out before you can say Jack Sprat."

"Jack Sprat?"

"A wise guy," I said, and kissed her good-night.

I didn't get to sleep until four in the morning. It wasn't so much the abject uncomfortableness of the chair as the tireless thoughts running laps in my head. I had taken in a monstrous amount of raw data and I'd have to refine it into a practical and productive plan of action.

A ruthless little voice in the back of my head said to take Tanya and what was left of Crawley's money and get out of town before the big hammer came down and crushed me like the rest. The punch that was coming seemed too big to duck, even for an accomplished ducker like myself.

My sense of duty and pride got a vicious hammerlock on the little voice and throttled it into submission. I had an obligation to Britt and the City. If I hadn't killed Crawley, they might have got a strong enough machine built to derail or at least stall the oncoming holocaust. With him dead and Britt's organization crushed, it looked as if it were up to humble me to reach inside my bag of tricks and pull out something more than a miserable rodent. All by my lonesome. One cheap bogeyman against the big ugly machine. The odds didn't look real hot.

25

I ran up a sandy ridge. A railroad track snaked out across the top of the ridge. Tied to the track were a long line of people. Starting from the middle of the ridge, their numbers disappeared into the left horizon. Two hundred meters down the track from the first victim, steadily closing the distance, chugged a monstrous black locomotive, belching thick black smoke from a towering stack.

For every three steps I took in the loose sand, I slipped back two. My legs pumped like pistons, but my progress was agonizingly slow. In the ravine behind me I could hear voices calling my name, telling me to come back. I didn't have to look back to know that at the bottom of the ravine was a troop of one-handed corpses and a battalion of long-dead rangers.

The train picked up speed. I leaned into the ridge and hammered my feet into the sand. I had to make it; people were depending on me. Figures clung to the locomotive, Hill citizens dressed in party smocks, laughing drunkenly, bottles of champagne swinging from their hands. I dropped to all fours and crawled like an animal, sobbing with frustration.

"I'm gonna make it!" I wailed. "I'm gonna goddamn make it!" I clawed at the loose grit, swam in it like a salamander. I crawled on my belly until I was within ten meters of the top of the ridge.

The Hill people spotted me and began shouting. Dash sat astraddle the fanged cattle catcher, virtuously talking about the ends justifying the means, and Babs stood beside him, holding his hand and nodding proudly. Marlene sat on Robert's lap and shrugged her shoulders. Joe squeezed from between two babushkas and shook a monstrous hash pipe at me, his face twisted with fear and loathing. "Don't ruin my meal ticket!"

he screamed over the roar of the engine. *"Don't you ruin my goddamn meal ticket!"*

I heaved up the slope and crested the ridge. On the other side of the track, next to the first victim, stood a big iron lever, and I knew if I pulled the lever the train would derail and plunge into the ravine behind me.

The engineer stuck his head out the window, and an ugly face looked straight at me and laughed like a maniac. "Too fooking late, asshole! Too fooking late!" He shoved the throttle forward, and the locomotive surged ahead, doubling its velocity. He rolled back his eyes and howled with laughter.

I looked at the first victim on the track. It was Britt, struggling violently against the ropes that held her. Tanya was second in line. In a split second my mind bounced a dozen times between two options. I could try to pull the switch to save everyone, but that meant I'd have to throw myself across the track into the path of the train. Or I could hang back and untie Britt and Tanya.

I lunged. If I could reach the switch, I'd pull it; if I couldn't, I'd at least drag Britt and Tanya out of the way.

Something grabbed my ankle, and I fell short of both. I looked behind me and screamed. It was Crawley. "Didn't you hear the man?" he said. "It's too late."

I stretched my hands to Britt and Tanya, but couldn't reach their bonds. The black shadow of the train fell on them, and Tanya smiled sadly. "It's okay," she consoled. "You tried, Jake. You tried very hard."

"Obviously not hard enough," Britt snapped from beside her. I sobbed, kicked at Crawley and stretched every millimeter of length out of my joints, and the iron wheels rolled over Britt and my right hand.

I awoke bolt upright, hyperventilating and shivering at once, my skin icy with sweat. I stumbled and wheezed through the dark to the kitchen sink. I tried to turn on the water but couldn't get the fingers of my right hand to work the faucet; the hand was an useless and numb claw. I wrenched the faucet with my left hand, splashed warm water in my face, then ran warm water over my right hand until it thawed out. After a moment

hunched over the sink, I regained control of my breathing and
my hand returned to life.

I leaned back against the sink, shivering and half-delirious.
I thought I needed a drink, but the idea of drinking made me
want to vomit.

The first sickly rays of dawn illuminated the bedroom window, and I remembered the last time I'd woken up in the same
room. From the bottom of the abyss I now wallowed in, that
morning in retrospect seemed incredibly beautiful and full of
life. Now I looked out the window and all I could see was a
stillborn sun and death creeping over the horizon in its place.

Britt and Tanya slept on the bed, head to foot. I stared at
each, feeling a stirring in my heart. This is what I believe in, I
thought. It's people I'm loyal to, not gleaming ideals, not dead
comrades, not the City, not some angry deaf-mute god. It's
them—there is nothing else.

I found a stim-cola in the fridge and sat down at the kitchen
table. I drank the cola and thought very hard about what I
would have to do to keep them alive. By the time real dawn
squeezed through the window, I knew what had to be done.

I TOLD THEM MY PLAN over breakfast.

"I have a plan," I said between mouthfuls of soy sausage.

"Oh, really?" Britt said cynically. "Does it involve killing
someone?"

I looked at her blankly. "Well, yes, of course."

"I thought so. It's the only thing you know how to do."

"Not the only thing," Tanya said, leering over a glass of soy
milk. I leered back, and Britt turned her head away from the
spectacle.

I looked to Britt. "I have to meet with your father."

"So you can kill him?" Britt asked. She didn't seem particularly offended by the idea.

"Would killing him stop the holocaust?"

She looked thoughtful for a moment. "I doubt it. It was his
plan originally, but it's in the hands of others now. My father's a talker, not a doer. His death might slow it down,
though."

I nodded. "Well, that's something. Maybe he knows the names of those directing the action, or a weakness in the plan."

"Maybe. It's a gamble."

"It's the only crapshoot in town."

Britt lit a cigarette. "The only problem is my father isn't going to come within ten miles of you."

"He might if I appeal to his higher emotions."

"And how do you propose to do that?"

"By threatening to kill you," I said.

She didn't even flinch. We stared at each other for a moment.

"That might work," she said.

"So you think he still loves you, after all this."

Britt looked introspective. "Yeah, he probably does. I always was daddy's little girl. I know it was him who arranged for Joe to draw me out before the Close Court raid."

I choked on my toast. "Crawley's friend who called you before the raid, his name was Joe? Joe 'the Incredible Weasel' Drake?"

"Yes," Britt said, fixing me with suspicious eyes. "Why do you know all the bad guys?"

"It's the crowd I run with. That evil bastard." I sat back and tried to grasp the depth of his treachery. Judas and Brutus had nothing on Joe.

"He's a friend of yours?" Tanya asked.

"Not anymore, he ain't. Why didn't I kill him? He's on the Hill now, staying with Dash."

Britt looked surprised. "He's a fool, then. He's useless to them now, and they'll get rid of him."

"I told him that." I looked at my watch. It was nine o'clock. "Let's give your father a ring."

Instead of using the phone on the corner, we walked to Hayward.

The sun brooded from behind a screen of smog, and I could almost feel a black wind sweeping through the City. Yet I found a reassuring serenity in the fact that at least Hayward remained constant: Hookers still smoked and joked in front of bars, hornbugs still came out of porn shops looking guilty and hunted, pimps still stared impassively from their pimpmobiles, and junkies still panhandled for fix money. The only difference was that there were more winos than usual. Gangs of them were drifting in from other boroughs for the fifth great wino crusade taking place that afternoon. I wondered what Dash's plan had in store for Hayward. It looked too evil to kill.

The girls ate their breakfast on the steps of Claudia's Speakeasy and Gambling Parlor, and I quizzed winos about the whereabouts of Moses. All were willing to lie, but none were sure.

We found a phone in working order outside an alcohol station. Britt fed me numbers and I dialed. We reached Dash at his office.

"I have your daughter," I grated menacingly.

"Strait?" Dash croaked.

"That's right, back from the grave. I wasn't the well-done charbroil job in my car." I paused for a maniacal laugh. "I have your sweet little daughter and I'll mutilate, kill and have my way with her in that order unless you give me one hundred thousand creds—used, unmarked and in no denomination bigger than a twenty."

"How do I know you have my daughter?" Dash croaked, his voice beginning to sound unraveled, like that of a man not firmly in control of his destiny.

"I'll let you speak with her." I pulled the phone from my mouth and said, "Okay, you. No tricks, see? Or you'll get it, see?"

Britt frowned and grabbed the phone, squeezing into the booth with me. I noticed she was wearing light perfume, and her proximity affected my breathing.

Her performance was impressive and sinister. Her voice pleaded and whined like a scared little girl on the verge of tears, but her expression was hard and cold, making for a very eerie effect.

"Oh Daddy, help me!" she cried. "He says he's going to kill me! Please, help me, he hurts me, he's horrible and mean and a boor and—"

"That's enough," I said, grabbing the phone back. She was having too good of a time. "There's your proof, Chamberlain. Cooperate, and maybe you'll get her back in one piece."

"Yes, of course," he said with unfeigned desperation. "Bring her up to the house and you'll get your money."

I whacked the receiver like a hammer against the coin-return knob three times. Dash had somehow managed to convince himself I was the consummate moron. "I am not a moron," I informed him, the punished receiver back against my ear. "We meet down here or not at all."

"Why, why, you'll kill me," Dash said matter-of-factly.

"I promise I won't. All I want is the money and your guarantee that you'll call the heat off me."

"I see," Dash said, apparently believing I was the type to go for that kind of deal. A week ago he might have been right.

"There's an underground parking garage under what's left of the Sundowner Hotel on the corner of Dostoyevski and Hayward," I said. "Drive your car down to the fourth level. There's an elevator shaft in the farthest corner from the entry ramp, on the north wall. I'll meet you there at four o'clock this afternoon. Come alone. No tricks, no guns, no problems. Got it?"

"Yes."

I hung up. I felt good, like a gangster. Maybe I'd missed my calling.

"You know he'll just use the meeting as an opportunity to capture me and murder you," Britt said.

"Yes," I said, smiling at her. "I'm counting on it."

26

I escorted the girls back to the flat, then walked to Phreaky Phil's Secondhand Car Lot on Hayward. There were two dozen used-car lots on Hayward to choose from, but I'd dealt with Phreaky Phil before. He'd talked me into the Caddy three years ago, and I needed that same kind of magic. I stood in his office for a few minutes before he wandered over and grabbed my hand.

"How's the Cadillac?" he said, his eyes drifting over my shoulder. I looked behind me, but there was nothing there but oak paneling. Phil was that way. He was a casualty of the great acid-house love revival of the late 1990s.

"It blew up," I said.

Phil raised his eyebrows. "The radiator? The engine?"

"All of it. I think I forgot to put water in the battery. I need some new wheels."

We took a walk out to his gravel lot. All the cars were coated with a thick layer of dust even though it'd rained yesterday. He took my hand and pressed it onto each car, one at a time. I didn't say a word. After I'd left a palm print on every hood in the lot, Phil threw his hands helplessly into the air.

"I'm afraid there isn't a car here that aligns with you karmically." His sad eyes told me that it was out of his hands and bigger powers were at work. "I'm very sorry, Jake."

"What about the primer-black Olds convertible," I asked, "with the skull and crossbones painted on the hood?"

Phil cocked an eyebrow, then floated over to the convertible, laying both hands on the hood. He signaled me over with an urgent wave, grabbed my hand and pressed it to the hood with his. *"Yes,"* Phil whispered, rubbing the dust off the skull with our palms. "Yes! You're right! This rude machine spiritually meshes with your aura! I was going by your old aural alignment, but I see now your karma has realigned! You knew it was the righteous machine, and now I can see it!''

I looked under the hood and drove it around the lot twice to make sure we meshed on a more practical level. It was a monstrous old brute dating from '98, built during the early years of the corporate era. The engine had a mean spirit and wore the hardware of a recent boost job. The brakes were fine, and the tires had enough rubber for another three thousand kilometers. The corporationists might have been the greedy bastards the history books made them out to be, but they knew how to build machines. The limp-wristed plastic the Party factories turned out couldn't compare in sheer weight and raw, brutal power.

I haggled him down to four hundred creds. I got a discount because it didn't have plates, title or registration. But none of that was necessary as long as the City stayed in the hands of the people. I pulled up to one of Phil's pumps for a free fill up. That was his motto: Free Fill Up When You Buy From Phreaky Philip. I was putting the nozzle away when Phil came over with the bill of sale.

"Here they come," Phil said, gesturing down Hayward.

And there they were. Shoulder to shoulder, waving rags and sticks, shouting like lunatics they came, throwing bottles and singing hymns. I spotted Moses Perry at the front, waving his great pool-cue staff, howling righteously. The fifth great wino crusade was underway.

Phil and I stood and watched them go by. There were gaps in the shambled formation, but it kept coming.

"Big turnout for this one," Phil noted.

I nodded. "Sign of the times." Like the rats and flies, the wino population bloated every year.

"Wonder how far they'll get this time," Phil wondered.

"All the way to the promised land," I told him, and climbed behind the wheel. Phil gave me one of his disoriented looks. I waved goodbye and pulled out of the lot.

I took a back exit onto Marshall so my new wheels wouldn't get scratched by bottle-throwing winos. It was their day of glory and it was best to stay out of their way.

Britt was showing Tanya how to put on makeup when I got back. They both stood in front of the bathroom mirror.

"That's a sure path to sin," I pointed out.

"You can't look until we're finished!" Tanya yelled, and threw a towel at me.

I retreated to the kitchen. I emptied my duffel onto the kitchen table, took a step back and stared at all the weaponry. I drew a breath, then let it out with a sigh. So much firepower. So much fun.

I tested the radio detonator first, exploding a primer in the sink from across the room. I checked the action of each pistol, rifle and shotgun, making certain every moving part had a little oil, then wiped them down with an oily lint-free cloth. If you treated a weapon right, it wouldn't let you down, so unlike people.

"Well, what do you think?" Britt said. I put the Uzi down and turned around. Britt stood behind Tanya like a proud parent. "Isn't she lovely?"

She was. Subtle colors and shadings contoured Tanya's young features into something more elegant, more sophisticated. The black sequined gown she wore set off her snow-white hair and baby blue eyes perfectly. In a word, she was stunning.

I got up and walked around her slowly, her eyes nervously following me.

"Uh-huh," I finally said, nodding.

"Uh-huh what?" Tanya asked.

"Uh-huh, I'm going to have to go out and buy you a big pink dress with ribbons and bows, and a big, matching, silly-looking hat."

She laughed shyly and did a twirl. "Right now?"

"Of course, right now. You *must* have it!"

"But what about the revolution?"

"Revolution?" I shouted, lifting her by her hips high in the air. "Fuck the revolution, baby, we're going out *dancin'!*" She giggled wildly, and I spun her over my head, faster and faster, laughing insanely at her squeals demanding I put her down, until the world swam and I got dizzy and collided with Britt. We collapsed in a tangle onto the carpet, laughing deliriously until tears ran down our faces, which seemed even more hilarious.

We laughed until our stomachs hurt and all the fear and tension melted away. When the last tear dried, we got to our feet, glancing sideways at each other, embarrassed at the previous moment's emotion. At that instant, with the sum of all my heart, I wanted to take them both and run, run far, far away from the City, from the Party, from the horrors that were coming. To save just them seemed enough.

Britt must have seen it in my eyes because she looked to the guns on the table and said, "I guess we better start getting ready."

"Yes," I agreed. I ran my fingers through my hair, feeling the stubble on the sides of my head. I'd have to shave soon.

"I'll get changed," Tanya whispered, and retreated to the bathroom.

Britt walked over to the table to look at all the weapons. "You know, Jake, there's a lot of innocent girls like Tanya all over the City."

"I know of one or two," I said.

"They need to be protected just like her." She picked up one of the Colt .45s.

"That's my job," I said, seeing what she was getting at. "I'm not going to run out, Britt. I know what has to be done. Besides, I have my own score to settle."

Britt stared at me until Tanya came out. She'd changed into a drab gray jumpsuit, but the makeup was still on. We sat at the table and went over my plan.

Britt would come along in case Dash refused to expose himself until he was certain Britt was alive. She'd stay in the car until I personally came over and got her. After I got the drop on Dash, I'd squeeze names and information out of him. Then I'd execute him and take his money. We'd use the hundred thousand and Crawley's money to fund the resistance, and I'd assassinate the people revealed as key leaders by Dash. Simple and easy.

"I want to help."

I looked at the source of the voice. Tanya hadn't said a word until then. "No," I said flatly.

"I'm not trying to be a hero, Jake. You don't know what's going to happen and you might need an extra gun."

"Because I don't know what's going to happen is why you're not going," I said. "This is not a cowboy movie, and you're not a cowboy. People are going to get killed, and you're not going to be one of them. This is a dangerous game, and if you lose, you die."

"That's why you need me there," she pressed.

"That's why I don't want you there. I'm not going to have your death on my conscience." I leaned across the table and pointed a finger at her. "Do you realize how uncertain the afterlife is at this time? There are rumors flying around that God is stomping mortal souls like invading mice, that hell is amok with power-crazed sinners. And there's a crazy killer-evangelist out there with a gang of one hundred fanatics ready to rend you limb from spiritual limb!" I leaned back in my chair. "Believe me, your soul is much safer down here."

"But if you lose down in that garage, it won't matter if I get killed anyway," Tanya pointed out. "If you lose, I'll die by nerve gas, food poisoning, or roundups later. I could help you win."

I slapped my hand on the table. "*N-O* spells *no.*"

A fly buzzed around in the silence.

Britt's soft voice pushed the quiet aside. "She's right, Jake, and you know it. We need all the help we can get. Quit trying to be the Lone Ranger."

"But I *am* the lone Ranger."

"I'll be Tonto!" Tanya volunteered.

I covered my face with my hands. How could I argue against logic like that? "All right," I said. "But on two conditions. First, you do everything I tell you to do, and—" I handed her a pile of black cloth "—you wear this."

Tanya eyed the cloth. "What's that?"

"It's spider-silk body armor. A bulletproof vest."

She took the vest and inspected it. "Okay."

"Put it on under a jacket so they don't see you're wearing it and aim for your head."

She nodded. "Are you going to wear one?"

I shook my head.

"Why?"

"Because," Britt explained, "he thinks he's protected by God."

"That's right," I affirmed.

"He's shooting his way to Heaven," Britt went on. "He kills people so they can deliver his messages to Jehovah."

"No, I like to think the people I kill go to hell," I said. "But you're fundamentally correct. My friend Moses Perry says everybody has their own way of getting close to God. For some it's prayer, for others it's celibacy and suffering. For Moses it's getting tanked on cheap wine. For me it's liberating the souls of the misguided. It's not necessarily right—it's just the way it is. I'm God's hit man."

Britt regarded me silently for a minute. "Sometimes I think you're serious."

I smiled and winked at her. "Sometimes so do I."

Tanya said, "Is this Moses guy the same one who's leading the wino crusade today?"

"The very same. In fact, it's already started. We'll have to allow time for the detour." I checked my chrono. It was a quarter to two. "I want to get there early, so we better get going."

27

The ruin of the Sundowner Hotel was at the other end of Hayward, which made for a long drive. I decided to take Hayward for as far as it would allow. Unlike well-maintained and libertine Hayward, Marshall and all the other north-south avenues were rife with militia checkpoints and potholes. I also wanted to see how the crusade was progressing.

We cruised down Hayward with the top down, Britt and I in the front and Tanya stretched out in back. The clouds were breaking up, and the sun peeked through. A trail of smashed bottles and passed-out winos marked the passing of the crusade. As we got closer to the ragged formation, more and more of the fallen faithful lay sprawled in the street. I steered around them, accelerating when I hit clear patches. Ten minutes later we caught sight of the rear of the march two hundred meters ahead. I stayed on Hayward even though gangs of stragglers made for slow going. Some of the winos gave us the mean eye, but I knew the really militant crusaders were all at the front of the pack. We crept within one hundred meters from my office.

"Take a side road," Britt commanded.

"I want to drive by my office and check something. We have time."

We moved at walking speed. Five minutes later we came abreast of the wino saint, and I stopped the car and looked up at the windows of my office. They were intact, which meant I hadn't received a visit or they'd somehow gotten around the grenades. I felt disappointed.

Something caught my eye. I wasn't sure at first because the sun blinded me. I closed my eyes for a moment, then looked again. Tiny black specks were moving in the sky from the west.

I asked for my binoculars, and Britt handed them from the glove box. I turned them to the sky.

"Bird-watching?" Britt asked.

"You could say that," I said. I focused the binos, and the black specks became black shapes. I dropped the binos into my lap and threw the Olds into reverse. The tires squealed, and I twisted my body to look behind me, maneuvering around lurching winos. When I shot past an intersection I slammed on the brakes, geared into drive, then hurtled down the side street. The car fishtailed and threw equipment around in the back seat but held the road. I patted the dash affectionately. The karma was right.

"Hey!" Tanya yelled from the back seat. "What's going on?"

"He's just trying to impress us with his driving prowess," Britt said, holding on to the door as we swerved down another side street. "One of those male ego things."

I spared each of the girls a glance. "Is it working?"

"No!" they shouted in unison.

"Fine, then," I said, and pulled over in front of a house five blocks off Hayward with a shriek of rubber. I jumped onto the hood and scanned the sky with the binos. I found the shapes moving toward Hayward. I could just barely hear them, like the distant buzzing of insects.

"What's that noise?" Tanya asked.

"Rotor blades," Britt said. "Helicopters."

"A special kind of helicopter," I added. "They're AH-90 attack machines. You can tell by the high-pitched jet whine in the background."

A line formation of eight AH-90s formed above the south end of Hayward, not far from where Tanya lived, hovering thirty meters above the rooftops like a cluster of dragonflies. One started moving down Hayward, and the others followed in single file toward the rear of the fifth great wino crusade, their sleek insectlike profiles made obese by rocket pods. I couldn't see the crusaders for the buildings, but when the choppers got within what I estimated to be a half kilometer from the tail of the crusade, the pilots kicked in the jets and the aircraft screamed toward their prey.

"They're attacking the crusade!" Tanya yelled.

The stuttering whoosh of hundreds of rockets leaving their pods lashed the air, trailed closely by the static thunder of explosions.

"They're murdering them!" Tanya added, her voice disbelieving.

"No, they're depopulating them," Britt corrected.

"Aren't we going to do something?" Tanya said, and I knew she was addressing me.

"Not much we can do," I said without taking my eyes from the binos. "Except provide them with another target."

The attack helicopters made two more rocket passes then a goodbye pass with speedguns, electric Gatling guns that churned out six thousand rounds a minute. Raking the wounded no doubt. Then they clattered away and the show was over.

Nobody said anything until we'd driven ten blocks down side streets. I wondered if the reclamation vans had moved in yet.

"Well," I said. "It would appear they've decided to skip the subtleties and move right into open slaughter."

"But why?" Tanya asked numbly from the back seat.

"It was too good of an opportunity to pass up," I conjectured. "I mean, here was a chance to get rid of most of the City's winos in one big ka-bang. That's what the plan is all about, weeding out the unproductives. Winos aren't known for their productivity."

"I think it was a statement, too," Britt said. "To let everyone know they're not fooling around this time."

"Besides, who's going to care that they wiped out a bunch of tramps?" I added. "Not too many people in the City. No one in the burbs. They're liquidating one element at a time, like the Nazis did in the 1930s."

"There were Nazis back then?" Tanya asked.

"They've been around for a long time. And now they are coming back in style." Above Hayward, columns of black smoke twisted their way into a patchwork sky, and I looked at them thoughtfully. "It's funny."

"What's funny?" Tanya asked.

"When I talked to Moses the other day. He told me he was going to take his people all the way to the end this time, all the way to the promised land. I'd thought he'd meant to the end of Hayward, but he hadn't meant that at all. I think he knew this was going to happen, maybe that's what the Lord told him. When he said the promised land, he meant Heaven." I looked at columns of smoke lifting to the clouds. "I hope they made it."

28

Whenever I looked at the area around Dostoyevski and Hayward, the word *forsaken* always sprang to mind. A fire had swept through the area over a decade ago during the anarchy that had followed the corporate collapse, razing four square blocks. Since then, no one had seen fit to rebuild the area or even clean it up. One of the more prominent victims of the blaze was the Sundowner Hotel, once the largest and grandest hotel in the City. Prime Minister Joe Strummer of Great Britain had stayed there once, back when men followed different flags.

Now it didn't look so grand. Four stories of compacted rubble still stood above ground, but the other eight stories had taken a dive onto the south lawn. On the north side, the entrance to the underground garage had been left relatively unblocked. On Friday and Saturday nights the garage's four levels served as a sinister lover's lane for the young and daring, with representatives from a local gang charging a toll for entry. At three o'clock Tuesday afternoon the place was deserted.

I parked just inside the garage entrance and walked back outside with Tanya, carrying the binos, shotgun and demolition bag.

She watched as I squeezed two kilos of plastic explosive into a long fissure in the concrete overhead support beam of the garage's entrance. I pushed electrical primers attached to radio receivers into the glob of claylike explosive. The explosion wouldn't be enough to seal the entrance completely but it would stop any vehicles from getting in or out. I led Tanya to a defendable vantage point atop a pile of rubble twenty meters from the entrance.

I took the binos from around my neck and handed them to her. "Keep an eye out with these. If they come from the direction of the sun, be careful not to flash them with the lenses. When you see them, stay down. It's very important that they don't see you. If any vehicles try to follow the first car in, turn this switch." I gave her the radio detonator and showed her the switch and which way to turn it. "Turn it when the front bumper lines up with the entrance. Then hightail it back to your flat the best way you know how."

Tanya nodded and I went on. "Remember to stay low so they don't see you. But if they do and you can't run away, take this." I unslung the Myers auto shotgun from my shoulder and handed it to her. "And shoot them. Just point it at them and hold down the trigger and it'll do the rest."

Tanya eyed the big gun suspiciously. "Does this thing kick?"

"Naw," I said. "It has a big recoil spring in the stock. It'll be loud but don't let that throw you. Just point it like you'd point your finger and pull the trigger. Got it?"

She smiled and hefted it as if it was an old friend. There was a purr of engines from the road, and I pulled Tanya down with me. I peeked over the rubble. A caravan of powder blue vans cruised down Hayward, heading south. I counted thirty of them and checked my chrono. It wasn't twenty minutes since the strike.

"They're sure not wasting any time," Tanya spit out.

"They're not sentimentalists. Probably figured twenty minutes was enough time for the mourners."

"Won't the survivors attack them?"

"You kidding? They'll probably fight each other over the rewards. That kind of carnage is going to add up to a lot of plastic."

The last van hummed by and we stood up.

"Now," I continued, "if only one car goes in, listen for a car coming out. If you hear a car coming and it isn't honking its horn, turn the switch because it's not us. If Dash's car comes out, then that means I lost and it's up to you to drop the entrance on top of him."

"No problem," she said, unable to hide the quaver in her voice.

"If that happens or I don't come out of there by the time it gets dark, go home." I took out my wallet and handed her the four hundred creds inside. "Take this and hop a cab to your parents' house. Don't stop by your place, don't stop to think, just get a cab to the burbs. Okay?"

"Okay, Jake. You're always giving me money."

"Believe me, if I don't come out of there, I won't be needing it." I turned over a chunk of rubble and pawed at the sooty bottom. I rubbed the black ash on her cheeks, nose and forehead. "This is the best makeup you can wear right now," I said.

She forced a smile. I stepped back and looked her over. The spider-silk vest hung from under her jacket like a skirt, almost touching her knees, and the shotgun was about five sizes too large. With her ash-smudged face she looked like a little girl who'd just finished helping mom clean the oven.

I kissed her one time, hard, on the lips, and said, "Don't worry, blue eyes. Everything will be fine, and afterwards we'll go dancing." She nodded and I headed down the rubble hill, feeling like hell.

I glanced back once before I got in the car. She stood looking at me from atop the black rubble rather forlornly. I waved at her to get down, and she crouched in the rubble. She smiled as if we were playing hide-and-seek.

I got inside and started the engine. Turning on the headlights, I drove down the ramp.

"Don't worry, she'll be okay. She's a tough kid," Britt said.

I looked over at her. "You read me just like a paperback book, don't you?"

"More like a comic book."

"Captain Avenger?"

"Daffy Duck."

I quacked and she actually laughed.

"You don't seem very nervous," I observed.

"Why should I be? You're the one who's going to get shot."

"You make me feel so good inside when you talk like that. When we park can we cuddle in the back?"

"Fat chance."

"You're right. Your father might catch us."

The Olds revealed its secret identity as a cyclops, and the garage was completely without lighting. Rusted hulks littered each level, and in the glare of the single eye they looked haunted and mournful. The place reminded me of a tomb.

"I wasn't positive whose side you were on until now," Britt said.

I looked over at her dark form. "Couldn't you tell by the haircut?"

"No, I mean, I didn't know if you were on our side or your side."

"Well, I used to be just on my side—it's the safest way to play it. But I guess hanging around with certain people can sway you. Like Crawley swayed you."

She laughed. "Crawley? We had an organization on the Hill long before I met him. It's still there. Young people who know what's going on and want to do something about it."

"Is a girl named Marlene one of those young people?" I asked.

I sensed she was staring at me. "Yeah," she said. "How did you know?"

"Just a hunch."

"Her brother Robert started the whole Hill resistance."

I choked on disbelief. "Robert Peterson? That's her brother? He's the Hill rebel ringleader?"

"Doesn't look the part, does he? He's a good man once you get to know him."

"Everyone says that. Suppose it must be true."

We glided down the ramp to the fourth level and parked near the east wall between two rusted Fords. I killed the headlight, and the inky darkness swallowed us whole. We sat for a moment, listening to each other breathe. I checked the luminous face of my chrono. It was three-thirty.

"Britt, there's something I want to ask you."

She released an exasperated sigh as if she'd been dreading the moment.

"When we met in the St. Chris," I continued, undaunted, "the first phone call you made was to set up an ambush, wasn't it?"

"Yes," she said after a moment.

"And the call you got inside confirmed the ambush. Then, when we got outside, you made the call that called it off. Am I right?"

She answered me with silence.

"Why?" I asked. "Because you wanted to do the job yourself, or because—"

"Because I wanted to sleep with you? Is that what you actually believe?"

"Am I wrong?"

I heard her shift in her seat and I could feel her eyes on me, but she didn't breathe a word.

"Well," I said. "I guess I better get out there and take up position."

"That wouldn't be a bad idea."

"Yeah. You know, I just might not come back from this one."

"I should be so lucky."

That put me off. I brooded for a while. I checked my chrono. It was three thirty-five. I sat for another minute, then said, "You can kiss me goodbye if you want."

"You make quite a case out of being pathetic, Jake."

"Imminent death always makes me bold. I might be a vat case in half an hour."

"Promises, promises."

"You really know how to string a guy along," I said, and shoved the door open, disappointed at another blown scene. I was halfway out when an invisible hand closed on my arm.

"I'll kiss you when you come back, Jake."

I stared into the black, afraid to answer, afraid of blowing it. The hand let go, and I hit the concrete with my heels. I slammed the door before she could take it back.

I turned on the flashlight and floated toward the elevator, fantasizing about my promised kiss. The white glare of the flashlight muscled its way through the abject darkness, but it seemed a struggle.

A blue VW Bug sat in front of the elevator. It didn't have any tires, and every time I saw it it reminded me of a dead beetle. I shined my light inside. Empty vitabeer cans crowded the floor, and a wave of nostalgia rolled over me. Times were, when the ambiguous moralities of my job got me down, I'd come to this very spot and sit in the Bug and drink beer and stare at the darkness. Once I got so drunk I lost my flashlight and had to paw around in the black for three ugly hours before I found my car. After that episode I stopped coming.

I sat on the hood of the Bug and turned out the flashlight. I massaged my neck muscles with one hand and imagined being married to Britt. Could we ever reconcile our differences? Sweep the Crawley thing under the rug of love? Could I cope with her career as a revolutionary leader? There were frankly a lot of unanswered questions, but my heart was home to mountains of faith. We could make it, if only that mean pimp Fate would give us half a goddamn chance.

The silence was broken by a car engine growling from above.

29

I looked at my watch. Like a good father, Dash was ten minutes early.

I waited for the rumble of an explosion but it never came. I breathed a sigh of relief. Okay, I told myself, Tanya was safe and everything would be just fine if I stuck to the plan. I walked five meters in front of the Bug and put the flashlight on the ground, pointing toward the ramp. Looking away from the light, I switched it on. I walked back behind the Bug and hunkered down, peeking over the hood.

A minute later two beams of light dived down the ramp, followed hesitantly by a monster luxury cruiser. The big machine had a hard time maneuvering around the wrecks, but that was the price to pay if you wanted to attend ransom meetings in style and comfort. The cruiser homed in on the beacon of the flashlight and crept toward it like a cat sneaking up on a bird. The bright headlights engulfed the Bug, and I closed one eye to retain my night vision. Ten meters short of the flashlight, the cruiser turned and exposed its broadside. The engine died but the headlights stayed on. The driver's window hissed down.

"Kill the headlights," I shouted. "The parking lights will do fine."

The headlights cut out and the parking lights came on, surrounding the car with an eerie amber glow. The cruiser looked like a huge animal transfixed by the beam of the flashlight.

I walked from behind the Bug and stood just behind the flashlight. With the glare in their eyes I would appear an indistinct, dark figure, mysterious and scary.

Both front doors opened. Both, I thought—that was the key word. The word emphatically stated that Dash had not come alone as he'd promised. A short bodybuilder with a red crew-cut came out the driver's door, and my old sparring pal Harry crawled out the other side. Each had the telltale bulge of body armor and concealed pistols. They walked toward me and neither of them looked mystified or scared.

Red said, "Mr. Chamberlain won't negotiate until you've been frisked for weapons."

"Oh," I said. "Just a little frisk."

"Just a *frisk*," the redhead said, nodding his head vigorously. He held out his hands and smiled as if he wanted to give me a hug. Harry held out his meat hooks but didn't even try to fake a smile.

I drew my pistol and shot them both in the head. I stepped over their twitching bodies and walked to the cruiser. It amazed me no end what a complete knave Dash thought me to be. Was it the way I dressed? My demeanor? I had to know.

I reached inside the driver's window, pulled the keys from the ignition and threw them away. There was a pane of tinted glass between the front and rear seats, so I moved over to the right rear window. It was tinted, too, but I was willing to bet the shy devil was in there. I rapped on the glass with a knuckle. The window came down an inch.

"You said no guns," a voice peeped.

"I lied," I said. "Now come out of there. We need to talk."

"You'll shoot me."

"No, I won't. If I wanted to shoot you I'd have already done it. Now come out or I'll come in."

The door opened and Dash stepped shakily out. He sported a black exec suit with lots of chrome. It probably went over big at director meetings. He shut the door and trembled against the cruiser, staring at my pistol fearfully.

"Where's the money?" I demanded.

Dash stammered at me but didn't really say anything.

I let my mouth gape. "Dash! Don't tell me you forgot the ransom money?" I shook my head sadly. "Oh, man. That casts tall shadows on the nature of your intentions concerning our rendezvous."

"I, ah, think I forgot it," he stammered.

I glared at him for a moment, then slapped him on the shoulder and grinned. "Ah, don't worry about it, ol' buddy. I'll just take it out of your hide."

Dash gave my pistol a shaky look.

"Well," I said, sighing. "With no money to count, we'll just have to socialize. Let's hear your side of it."

"My side of *what?*" he screeched, his eyes still locked on the pistol. He was already going into hysterics, and the interrogation had just begun. I could see in his wild eyes that he was certain I was going to kill him. It struck me that he really did think me a homicidal maniac. But that was only because he always caught me at bad moments, I told myself.

"You know," I prompted. "Your nifty plan to wipe out all the City's unhappy citizens."

"I don't know what you're talking about."

I sighed and shot out the window beside him.

He yelped and tried to crawl up the side of the car on his back. "It has to be done!" he cried. "It's the only way the Party can survive. I could show you stacks and stacks of statistics and forecasts! If the Party collapses, everything collapses and anything is better than anarchy!" He acted as if he was talking to my pistol instead of me.

"Oh, I don't know, anarchy might be fun. Sure beats dying of food poisoning or nerve gas." I gestured with my pistol, and his eyes followed it. I moved the pistol slowly to the left. Dash's eyes went to the left. I moved it to the right. His eyes went to the right. He's mesmerized, I thought. In a deep voice I said, "You're getting sleepy."

"Huh?"

"Nothing. So you justify taking hundreds of thousands of lives just to keep the Party afloat? Doesn't that seem just a trifle immoral?"

"There is no other way. The Party must survive. Do you want the world divided into nations again, with flag worship and national wars? Better thousands now than millions later." He was settling into a practiced spiel, the Party idealogue haranguing for the cause.

His eyes found mine, and they were the eyes of a fanatic. "Those people are animals, ungrateful leeches who take from the Party and give back nothing. Instead of gratitude for being fed and sheltered, they riot and try to subvert our efforts to better them. And they're getting worse every day. Pretty soon they won't just be content to riot in their slums, they'll organize and attack the Party itself!''

"Maybe they'd be more grateful if they could live on the Hill and eat beef and chocolate," I suggested.

Dash shook his head at me sadly, like a teacher at a child too horribly retarded to learn. "I don't expect you to understand. You're one of them. You see everything from the bottom of the gutter."

"Yeah, I guess the view is a lot better from the Hill," I said. "You know, you and Joe use the same analogies, maybe you really are buddies."

"Joseph understands the way things are."

"Joe understands who has the money and power. How is Joe behaving, anyway? Is he an entertaining guest?"

Dash didn't say anything; he just continued to shake his head at me as though I was the knave he always played me for. I felt like hitting him in the teeth.

I heard a noise behind me. I dropped into a low crouch and whirled, aiming at the dark figure behind the lamp.

It was Britt. She held a Colt .45 in her hands.

"Britt!" Dash and I sang in chorus, him high, me low.

"You murderous bastard," she snarled, stepping forward. "You fascist swine." I was almost positive she wasn't talking to me.

"Britt!" Dash cried out again. "Don't you see it's all for you? You're on the wrong side! You should be with us, the Party!"

Her face contorted into the mask of hate I'd seen before. "It's all for the Party—it's always been all for the Party. You'd send me and Mom both to the vats for your beloved Party." She caught a breath. "Well, now you can die for your Party."

"No!" I shouted in a low, urgent voice. "We need more information. I haven't got the names or timetables out of him yet. Killing him now would be insane." I couldn't guess how many ounces of pressure were on the Colt's trigger, but I knew it was close to enough. "Let's be smart about this, Britt. Don't let

your personal hatreds ruin our chance of stopping the holocaust. We need that information.''

For a moment I didn't think she heard me. Then her features began to smooth and the beast went back inside. Her arms
dropped and her head followed, as if she had expended all her
energy. ''You're right,'' she whispered. ''You're right.''

''I'm sorry, honey,'' Dash said, and a pistol shot echoed
through the garage. Britt's head snapped back grotesquely, and
she fell backward, arms flailing for balance. I whirled and fired
without aiming. The jet ripped a chunk out of Dash's shoulder, and the little automatic fell to the concrete. Dash clutched
his geysering wound and screamed, and I kicked his pistol out
of the pool of light.

I rushed to Britt and crouched beside her. She lay on her
back, one arm at her side, the other above her head, as if she
were waving goodbye. Her face was calm and unbothered, and
there was maybe even the hint of a melancholy smile on her
parted lips. Except for a small thumbnail-size hole between her
closed eyes, she could have just been sleeping. She was beautiful, even in death.

I got on my hands and knees and kissed her gently on the
lips. My tears ran down her cheeks, and it almost seemed as if
she were crying instead of me. I wanted to take her in my arms
and hold her and tell her how much I loved her and that I'd
never let her go but I couldn't. I couldn't because at that moment my soul left me, fleeing before a risen beast too monstrous to behold. I wiped the tears from my eyes and stood up.

''I had to,'' Dash croaked. ''She was unsalvageable. She betrayed the Party. She was trying to make it all fall down, all fall
down.'' He slid down until he was sitting against the rear tire.
He twisted his neck sideways, trying to look at his wound.
''God, it hurts! It really hurts! Do you think I'm going to die?''

''Oh, yes,'' I whispered slowly, moving toward him. ''You're
definitely going to die. But not before you tell me things.''

''Oh, no, I won't. I won't tell you anything.''

I took the switchblade from my pocket with my left hand. It
opened with a vicious snick. I stopped three meters in front of
him and held it up beside my head. I felt my face twist into a
grotesque, insane smile. ''Oh, yes, you will.''

I would carve Dash up. I wanted to, and he knew that. His face twisted up, and he squirmed against the tire. When I started toward him again, he started to scream.

There was a flashbulb flash from behind me, and a sledgehammer hit me in the right shoulder blade, sending me tumbling forward like a clumsy acrobat. I hit the concrete with the grace of a drunk at closing time, and the jar sent my pistol scraping into the darkness. I ended up on my back beside my pal Dash.

30

You've just been shot, logic told me. I dived into the waters of unconsciousness, then swam back to shore feeling nauseous and weak. My right shoulder was numb and I couldn't move my arm. The glare of my flashlight hit me square in the eyes and I had a hard time seeing anything. In the spotlight, I thought giddily. I felt like laughing but I felt like vomiting, too. A pair of shoes stepped in front of the light.

"Well, well," a familiar voice said. "What have we here? A little fooking party?"

"That's right, Inspector Blake," I said. "But who invited you?"

"Chamberlain doesn't take a crap without telling me first."

"So you can wipe his hiney for him?"

Blake enjoyed a long, vicious laugh. "Always joking around, eh, Strait? Right to the grave."

"Inspector! Inspector Blake?" Dash cried, snapping out of his delirium. "Thank God you're here! This animal tried to murder me! My own daughter tried to murder me! Kill him now and get me to a hospital. I need urgent medical attention. I'm in terrible pain."

"Shut up, you fooking worm," the inspector spit out. "Die like a man. You don't hear Jake whining, do you?"

"Yeah," I said. "Die like a man, for crissakes."

"Inspector Blake!" Dash wailed. "We're all in this to-gether. Don't you remember? It was *my* plan. We have to work together and see these difficult times through, for the future of the Party."

"Shove your Party up your ass," Blake said, and shot Dash in the bridge of the nose. His head disintegrated in an explosion of blood, and I felt helpless and adrift in the churning sea of fate, waiting for my bullet.

"So, how're you doing there, Strait?" Blake said, walking closer. He sounded happy. Blake was obviously one of those rare few who really enjoyed their work.

"Oh, I think I may be mortally wounded," I said. "But otherwise I'm pretty okay. So, you're the SPF contact."

"Kind of obvious, isn't it? When they found out the old man couldn't stomach the job, I went to them. I had a lot to offer."

"You organized the skins."

"Hell, we've been using the skinheads to break up the left for years. That angle was just a small part of my contributions. From the practical point of view, I'm running the whole show. I arranged for the SPF commodities to be used. I set up Travis as a training camp, and the skins answer only to me. As far as the Party is concerned, I am the *man.*"

"That's funny, you don't strike me as a hard-line Party ideologue."

The inspector laughed, obviously enjoying our discourse. After being part of a big secret for so long, he needed someone to brag to, someone who wouldn't be spreading anything around later. "The Party has nothing to do with it," he said. "Oh, those weak poofs on the Hill posture around and rationalize why they want to massacre a quarter of a million people, but I look at it from a more personal angle. You see, after this show is over they're going to owe me a lot and I'll owe them nothing, and that's where true power lies. You are looking at the highest authority I recognize." He did a clumsy soft-shoe jig. "I . . . am . . . it!"

"Woo-woo," I said. "That's a whole lot of talk from a lousy inspector." Loss of blood was making me irritable, and I couldn't stand unbridled vanity in anyone except myself.

Blake sauntered over and stood above me. The amber lights illuminated his lower half, but his head and shoulders were lost in the darkness. He looked about a thousand meters tall.

"Not 'Inspector,'" he whispered. "'Director.' City Director Blake. That was my price for cooperation. The fooking old man is about to get an unexpected retirement, and I'll be appointed the new SPF director of the City. And in the coming days whoever controls the SPF controls the City—and the burbs and Hill, for that matter. So you see, wiseass—" his voice sank low and hard "—I am truly *it!*"

"A rising star," I commented.

"And you're a falling one," he snarled.

I shrugged my left shoulder. With me bleeding to death and him with the gun, I didn't have a lot of evidence to dispute his claim. My energy was seeping out with my blood, and I was having trouble keeping my eyes open.

"You dead yet, Strait?"

"Not yet," I muttered, beginning to slur like a drunk.

"Good," he said, dropping to a crouch beside me. "Because I'm not through talking yet."

"I didn't think you were." It was too much an effort to keep my eyelids up, so I let them fall shut.

"You know, Strait," he said softly. "You and I ain't so different. We're both amoral—we both like to kill. The only difference is that I know what side of the barricades to stand on. You're not standing on either side. You're straddling it and anyone who does that ends up getting shot, as you found out. That's the big difference between you and me, Strait. That's why you're a lousy bogeyman lying in his own blood and I'm about to become the most powerful man in the City."

I forced my eyes open a crack. Blake was sitting on his heels next to me, his wrists resting on his knees, the suppressor on his big service automatic pointed casually at my forehead. I hauled in a painful breath and whispered, "I bet I still get laid more than you."

Blake laughed but it sounded forced. "Well, goodbye, Strait. But one more thing." He leaned his face close to mine and smiled like a wolf. The amber lights cast his features in demonic relief. My head swam in an ocean of pain, and I felt about ready to take the final plunge.

"You shouldn't have used a little girl to cover your ass up there," he whispered. "That was a mistake. But I was thinking. Maybe I'll get laid on the way out. That is, if she's still warm." He started to laugh.

I brought up my left hand from the floor and plunged the switchblade into his neck. His pistol flashed and a hot brand lay against my cheek. Then he stumbled back and collapsed in the arc of light. He gurgled and flapped around on his back, casting frantic shadows into the darkness. He worked the knife from his throat but couldn't staunch the fountain of blood squirting between his fingers in long, pulsating streams. My eyes begged to close, but I forced them to stay open. I wanted to watch the inspector die. It took about ten minutes.

I closed my eyes, and the inner blackness drew steadily closer in an ever tightening circle. My soul shifted impatiently in its body harness, and I surrendered to the dark, eager to get to hell and collect my promised kiss.

THE BEDS IN HELL were hard, the furnishings tacky, the wallpaper peeling. I shifted my gaze, and a bony, hollow-eyed face came into focus.

"Oh, Christ," I croaked. "It *is* hell."

"Sooner or later," Degas said flatly. "But not today. How do you feel?"

"Like I've been shot," I said. My shoulder throbbed and my cheek felt hot and itchy. "Tell me, do they salt the wounds hourly?"

Degas stared at me humorlessly, then reported, "Your shoulder will improve, though that arm will be in a sling for a while. Your face wound will leave a nice scar."

"You can never have enough facial scars in my line of work," I said. "Why am I still alive?"

"A couple kids looking for a place to neck found you and the others. They called reclamation to get the reward. There happened to be a convoy of rec vans passing by. The rec team found you alive. Broke the kids' heart. The rec van dropped you by the hospital."

"I knew my respect for reclamation wasn't misplaced. But what I meant to ask you was why have I been allowed to live? I was found with the bodies of a City director and an inspector of the SPF. And isn't there an execution warrant on my head? I should at least be in confinement."

Degas looked around the room carefully. I looked around. We were still alone.

"It turns out you killed, if it was you that killed them, two Party renegades," he said in a low voice. "After the word broke that Chamberlain and Blake were dead, the old man labeled them as traitors and political criminals. Several other senior Party officials were arrested for plotting with fascist elements against the Party."

"Senior Party officials? You mean directors."

"No, no directors were arrested."

"They sacrificed scapegoats, then. What about the 'fascist elements'?"

"They're being rounded up even as we speak. Did you know they were using Travis prison as a training camp?"

"No kidding?" I tried to add everything up. "So Blake was the keystone. When he fell, everything collapsed."

"Is there something you want to tell me about, Strait?" He sounded as if he didn't really want me to tell him anything at all.

"Naw. Well, I guess I came out of this a hero." I looked around the room. "Where's my goddamn roses?"

"Officially none of this happened. But your death warrant has been dropped, and the old man said to give you his personal thanks."

"I'm all atingle. Do I get my license back?"

"If you want it. I wasn't sure you would."

"Are you kidding? You think I'm going to waste all those years spent in sap school?"

Degas gave me an odd look, then nodded. "Listen, Strait, if I was you, I wouldn't go around bragging about this thing."

He was right. There were still some faceless directors out there who might feel threatened if I got mouthy. "All right," I said. "I'll gloat in secret."

"Well," Degas said, putting on his hat. "I'll let you get your rest. And by the way, it's Inspector Degas now. The old man gave me Blake's slot."

"Talk about replacing a rat with a weasel."

"Toe the Party line, and you go places," he said. He opened the door.

"One more thing, Inspector," I said. He turned around. "There was a girl on top, near the entrance."

Degas frowned and shook his head.

I closed my eyes, and a black dread settled over me like a smothering shroud. So, I thought, the train had rolled over them both. I'd thrown the switch but not before the wheels crushed the only two I really cared about saving. "I should have run away with them and let this useless city burn," I said to myself. "It's my fault she's dead—I murdered her."

"She's not dead," Degas said.

I blinked at him like a torpid lizard. "What?"

"She has a concussion and several broken ribs, but otherwise she's fine. Her body armor stopped the bullets. It's a shame a girl of such youth and innocence would associate with a creep like you." He shook his head and walked out.

He got in the last word, but I didn't mind.

EPILOGUE

The streetwalkers wore warmer clothing and there weren't as many winos as there used to be, but otherwise Hayward hadn't changed much since I'd gotten out of the hospital. The microskirts were missed more than the winos.

I looked down at the St. Chris from my window. The wino saint probably missed them. He was also missing his head. Hayward lore had it that the first rocket of the chopper strike blew it off, then the rest of the missiles fell into the ranks of the crusaders. I thought it symbolic.

The rocket attack also succeeded in blowing out half the panes of my bay window. Tape and squares of cardboard replaced the broken glass, making for a nice checkerboard effect. Autumn wind sneaked in through cracks, but repairs would have to wait until I got my hands on some credit.

I sat on my desk and looked at the door. There were still pieces of tape on the door frame where the grenades had been. The grenades were presently sitting in the weapons locker, though I could have left them rigged to the door and not a single prospective client would have been killed or injured. Business was slow.

According to the calendar pinned to the door it was September 12, making it roughly two months since I'd got out of the hospital and exactly two weeks since Tanya had moved out of my flat. All she'd left behind was a short note on the fridge under a magnet shaped like a heart. When I first saw it, I had it figured as a little love note with maybe the sideline that she'd stepped out to buy some Chinese food for dinner.

Instead, it told me she was very, very sorry but we weren't meshing anymore and she had to find her own life outside the City. That she'd looked inside herself and found she didn't love me after all—she'd been fibbing the whole time. At the bottom of the note was a postscript that said she thought I was a good person and she'd miss me. I wondered if she'd written that part before or after she drained all the credit out of our joint accounts.

I'd never really believed in hell until she left. After paddling around in a sea of drunken self-pity for two weeks, I still wasn't sure what emotional beach the tidal wave of her leaving had washed me up on. All my feelings seemed tricks of light from mirrors held in the hands of malevolent strangers. One thing I did understand was what love was. Love was a trespassing wino that slept it off in the ruins of my heart; love was a lizard with a broken back, thrashing in the hot sand, waiting for the midday sun to kill it.

I checked my watch. It was six-thirty. The certified invitation on my desk said the Hill art party began at eight. Written on the invite was a short note from Marlene, asking me to leave my French accent at home.

I went to the coatrack and put on a black leather motorcycle jacket. I wanted to get there early to load up on the free food and drinks. I figured the Hill owed me a free drunk. Maybe I'd even run into some old friends.

I checked my mohawk and smiled in the mirror, then, as an afterthought, traded in my Browning 9 mm for the Myers gyrapistol. I went to the door and went down to the street.

I was tired of praying to a God I didn't understand for a salvation that would only serve to confound me. This night I would provide for my own salvation.

I never wanted anything I couldn't take.

Omega Force is caught dead center in a brutal Middle East war
in the next episode of

by PATRICK F. ROGERS

In Book 2: **ZERO HOUR**, the Omega Force is dispatched on a
search-and-destroy mission to eliminate enemies of the U.S.
seeking revenge for Iraq's defeat in the Gulf—enemies who will
use any means necessary to trigger a full-scale war.

With capabilities unmatched by any other paramilitary organization in the world, Omega Force is a special ready-reaction anti-
terrorist strike force composed of the best commandos and
equipment the military has to offer.